ONCE BITTEN, TWICE SHY

BOOKS BY JAN THOMPSON

ROMANTIC SUSPENSE/THRILLERS

Protector Sweethearts (6 Books)
JanThompson.com/protector

Defender Sweethearts (6 Books)
JanThompson.com/defender

Guardian Sweethearts (4 Books)
JanThompson.com/guardian

Binary Hackers (4 Books)
JanThompson.com/binary

CITY/COASTAL/BEACH ROMANCE

Seaside Chapel (7 Books)
JanThompson.com/seaside

Savannah Sweethearts (12 Books)
JanThompson.com/savannah

Vacation Sweethearts (8 Books)
JanThompson.com/vacation

Midtown Christmas (4 Books)
JanThompson.com/christmas

ONCE BITTEN, TWICE SHY

CHRISTIAN SUSPENSE IN BETWEEN
TELL YOU SOON AND ONCE A THIEF

GUARDIAN SWEETHEARTS
BOOK 1

JAN THOMPSON

GEORGIA
PRESS

ONCE BITTEN, TWICE SHY (GUARDIAN SWEETHEARTS BOOK 1)

Author Website: JanThompson.com
Book News: JanThompson.com/newsletter

Published by Georgia Press LLC

eBook & Paperback Cover Design: Rocking Book Covers

eBook ISBN: 978-1-944188-94-8
Paperback ISBN: 978-1-944188-95-5

To my Lord and Savior, Jesus Christ, who died on the cross to save me from my sins and rose again from the grave to give me eternal life in heaven.

~

For God so loved the world that He gave His only begotten Son, that whoever believes in Him should not perish but have everlasting life.
—John 3:16

ABOUT GUARDIAN SWEETHEARTS
CHRISTIAN ROMANTIC SUSPENSE NOVELS

Guardian Sweethearts is a collection of Christian suspense novels in between other books in Jan Thompson's story world. These sandwiched stories feature married couples who met in the books before the present ones. Therefore, the books in this series are both prequels and sequels or preludes and postludes.

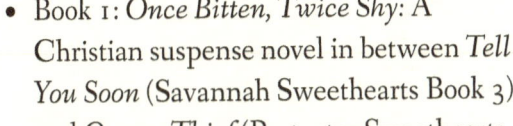

- Book 1: *Once Bitten, Twice Shy*: A Christian suspense novel in between *Tell You Soon* (Savannah Sweethearts Book 3) and *Once a Thief* (Protector Sweethearts Book 1)
- Book 2: *Check Once, Check Twice*: A Christian suspense novel in between Love You Always (Savannah Sweethearts

Book 7) and *Never a Traitor* (Defender Sweethearts Book 1)

- Book 3: *Going Once, Going Twice:* A Christian suspense novel that comes after *Reach for Me* (Vacation Sweethearts Book 2)
- Book 4: *Fool Me Once, Fool Me Twice:* A Christian suspense novel that comes after *Wait for Me* (Vacation Sweethearts Book 3)

For more information about Guardian Sweethearts: JanThompson.com/guardian

ABOUT ONCE BITTEN, TWICE SHY

GUARDIAN SWEETHEARTS BOOK 1

A cold case binds an estranged couple together.

While trying to fix their marriage, private investigator Ming Wei and his real estate agent wife, Sabine, investigate the unsolved murder of Sabine's father.

SABINE IS ON A MISSION...

Four years after their wedding, cracks appear in their marriage. Ming leaves for a multi-month project overseas, leaving his wife at home with two young kids and a business to run. To take her mind off their marital woes, Sabine helps her mother investigate her father's murder.

The undercover operation takes her through a shooting competition, which Sabine wins. Participants are invited to a mountain retreat where a banquet is to be held in their honor. Ever inching closer to danger, Sabine only has her sister, Helen, as backup.

MING RUSHES TO HER SIDE...

In spite of their personal problems, Ming can't live with himself for "abandoning" his wife and kids. He hands over the project to someone else and flies home only to find his mother-in-law babysitting their kids and dog, while his wife has gone to do something dangerous.

Ming gets involved and goes undercover to provide support for Sabine. The trail leads Sabine to people in the past, including her ex-boyfriend. Ming worries she might rekindle that old relationship. Against this backdrop, can Ming remain objective?

TROPES/THEMES:

• Alpha Hero
    • Asian Hero

- Strong Woman
- Smart Heroine
- Independent Woman
- Estranged Married Couple
- Asian American Romance
- Private Investigators
- Forced Proximity
- Cold Case
- Investigating an Old Murder

Once Bitten, Twice Shy is a married life Christian romantic suspense novel in between Tell You Soon (Savannah Sweethearts Book 3) and Once a Thief (Protector Sweethearts Book 1). The epilogue of *Once Bitten, Twice Shy* leads straight into Chapter One of Once a Thief.

In Tell You Soon, Ming and Sabine fell in love and married each other. In *Once Bitten, Twice Shy*, they now have two kids but their marriage is on the rocks. Somewhat separated, Ming works overseas while Sabine stays in Savannah to help Mom investigate Dad's death. If you recall, in Tell You Soon, Sabine mentioned that her father died in a mysterious road accident that was unsolved.

In her sister's story, Once a Thief, Helen and her mom (aka Mama Hu) commiserated about missing Dad. Well, in between those two books, we have *Once Bitten, Twice Shy*, in which we find out what happened to Edgar Hu, the founder of Hu Knows, Inc., investigative firm based in Savannah, Georgia, with worldwide clients.

ONCE BITTEN, TWICE SHY

PROLOGUE

After breaking his five-million-dollar work contract in Dubai, private investigator Ming Wei flew home to the States to apologize to his wife. In the cramped economy class, he had rehearsed everything he wanted to say to her as soon as he saw her.

At the Savannah/Hilton Head International Airport, he rented a car and drove himself home to Tybee Island. He still had the house keys.

He walked through the front door to find it all quiet. No one greeted him, not even Pickles, their senior golden retriever.

That was when he knew something was wrong.

The dog bowls—one for water and one for dry food—were gone. The dog's favorite treats were also gone.

Ming wandered around the house, hoping to hear Sabine's voice somewhere, laughing with their daughter, Hannah.

The entire house was bathed in silence.

In the master bathroom, Sabine's toothbrush and makeup were all gone. The closet still had clothes, but Sabine's favorite suitcase wasn't there.

The kids' rooms looked about the same.

He texted Sabine. No reply.

He called her. No answer.

He called his mother-in-law, Mama Hu. She picked up on the fourth ring. "Are Sabine and the kids at your house?"

"Well..."

"Tell me as it is. No need to try not to hurt my feelings. Where is Sabine?"

Mama Hu was silent.

"If she's in danger, your lack of response is going to be bad news." Ming was losing his cool.

"I don't like the way you talk to me. I'm going to hang up—"

"No, no. Please don't. I'm just worried about Sabine." Ming tried to calm down.

"I am too. But you don't have to be rude to me."

Something was up. Mama Hu sounded guilty.

"Mama Hu, don't you want Sabine and me to get back together?" Ming blurted. He felt frustrated. Defeated, even.

"That's your fault, isn't it?"

At least Mama Hu had continued talking. Ming had to keep her going until she told him what he wanted to know.

"Don't let the sun go down on your anger," Mama Hu added.

She had clearly echoed Ephesians 4:26-27.

"Be angry, and do not sin": do not let the sun go down on your wrath, nor give place to the devil.

Even though Mama Hu wasn't a Christian, she knew a Bible verse or two. Perhaps it was due to the influence of her two daughters—one of whom was supposed to be the love of Ming's life.

"I'm sorry. It's my fault for not taking better care of Sabine and our kids." Ming had no choice. At least, that had been what he'd been telling himself for months, trying to keep his company out of bankruptcy. He still believed that he could keep Savannah River Investigations, Inc., afloat.

"Sabine is raising the children alone. You weren't there at Hannah's preschool event in December. You weren't even home for Thanksgiving, Christmas, or New Year's Day. What kind of a husband and father are you? Do your kids even remember what you look like?"

"I was only gone for three months."

"That's at least ninety days. Do you want me to count the hours?"

"I had to work."

"You could've worked in Georgia. Why Dubai? You love money more than your wife and kids."

There it was, the indictment.

Ming hung his head in shame. "I missed out on a lot. Gotta put food on the table."

"Food on the table with empty seats?" Mama Hu snarled. "You know Sabine. She doesn't care if you don't earn millions of dollars. She wants you there at family dinners. You're always MIA, even when you

3

were working in the States. Now that you've started to take international clients, you're overseas a lot."

"After I get my business back on track, I'll do better."

"It might be too late, Ming. You missed all the important holidays and birthdays. You messed up, Ming."

Ming had to agree. "It's over now, and I'm home again."

"Was it worth it? Did you need the job so badly that you sacrificed your wife?"

"I'm not sacrificing Sabine." Not to mention he also lost the contract when he told his client in Dubai that he couldn't possibly have an affair with her.

Sigh.

Sabine had been right. Lorna—was that even her real name?—hadn't hired him just to investigate her fiancé's infidelity, but also to make him her lover, a little known fact Ming hadn't been aware of until just days ago, after almost three months of being in close proximity with her. He had considered it business, but apparently Lorna had a different idea.

"You left your wife alone for three months," Mama Hu repeated. "I'd be surprised if it was worth it."

"I had to take whatever job I could find to pay my bills. I'm deep in debt." Ming didn't want to talk about the albatross around his neck, but he was a hundred and sixty-seven thousand dollars in the red, due to the second mortgage he'd taken out on his office downtown plus advertising costs.

If things didn't turn around, he'd have to sell his office space and move his workspace into the toolshed in his backyard. His original home office upstairs had been converted into Hannah's playroom. Maybe he could reclaim it.

Sabine had offered to invest in SRI, but Ming had refused it. He wanted them to use her savings to pay for the children's school. He did not want Sabine to take her inheritance from her dad plus the money she'd earned from selling her shares of Hu Knows just to pay off his company debt. If things came to that, he would have to offer Sabine a share of SRI.

Now he missed Sabine so much that he was willing to do anything to get his family back. He might even sell SRI to another private investigator, if there was someone out there willing to take over his loan payments.

Money management was something that he wasn't good at. He recalled a long time ago in his bachelor days when he had to sell his beach house. Sabine had been his real estate agent. It was a good thing that his sister, Heidi, and her husband, Diego, had bought the house. At least it wasn't now a rental property for summer visitors.

"I don't care," Mama Hu snapped. "You left my daughter to parent two kids alone. Your marriage is over."

Ming felt uncomfortable hearing what Mama Hu said. "As long as we're still married, there's still a chance..."

"She's already talking to a divorce lawyer."

Ming knew that through Helen, but he still felt that it wasn't over yet. "Our marriage vows said 'until death do us part.' I'm still alive."

5

"Oh no. Don't say death. Please don't say death." Mama Hu's voice shook.

"Mama Hu?"

"Yes?"

"Where exactly is Sabine?" Ming's heart was racing a mile a minute, but he kept his voice calm.

"She's not here. Only the kids and your dog that sheds everywhere are here."

"When's Sabine coming back?"

"Uh... I don't know. It depends on whether she could find her dad's pocket watch."

"Her what?" Ming tried to process what Mama Hu was saying. Before Edgar died, he had given his entire family pocket watches. They were made of gold, but they all had homing beacons and trackers in them. This had been back in the days before GPS was ubiquitous.

As far as Ming knew, Sabine kept hers in a safe at home. She never used it because it was the last gift from her father, and she already had GPS on her own phone. She said that Helen sometimes carried her pocket watch in her purse as a reminder of Dad, but not all the time. The only person who always carried her pocket watch with her was Mama Hu. That way, Helen and Sabine could know where their mother was at all times.

"Not Sabine's. We're talking about Edgar's own missing pocket watch," Mama Hu corrected him. "Edgar bought us all pocket watches, but he himself had a special one. It's been missing for thirteen years. Old Man Leung suspected that the pocket watch might be with Gene in his mansion in Hiawassee."

As long as Ming had known Mama Hu, he knew

that she could lie at the drop of a hat. Today, she didn't even try to lie to him about where Sabine had gone. Mama Hu stated it all, as though she wanted Ming to go after Sabine.

And that's what I'll do.

"Are you watching the kids?" Ming asked.

"The babysitter's with me, but yes, the kids are going to stay here until Sabine returns."

"Okay. Good. I don't want the kids to wear you out."

"No, no. They're not. Do you want to see them? We're getting ready for lunch. I can ask the cook to make you a Cuban sandwich."

"That will be nice, Mama Hu. I'll be there in half an hour." It would take twenty minutes to get to Mama Hu's house in downtown Savannah, but Ming wanted to shower and change first.

It would give him a chance to talk to Mama Hu in person and elicit more information about what his wife was up to.

After Ming hung up, he replayed the conversation with Mama Hu. Something was off. Sabine wouldn't leave the kids with anyone—not even her mom—without specifying when she'd return.

Ming texted Helen to ask her if she knew where Sabine was. Helen didn't reply right away, and that made Ming antsy.

When she finally called him back, Ming was aghast. "My wife did what?"

Before Helen could even explain the entire story, Ming had made up his mind.

He had one day to get to Hiawassee to join the

kitchen crew of Skye's the Limit, catering dinner at The Mechanic's mansion.

Their five-minute conversation was all it'd taken for Ming to cancel lunch with Mama Hu and his kids and jump in his truck to make the six-hour-plus drive from Tybee Island to Hiawassee, Georgia.

During the drive, he called Mama Hu and made her spit out everything she knew about the situation. Ming tried not to blame Mama Hu for getting Sabine into the mess.

Edgar Hu had already been dead and buried for years. His death certificate said that the cause of death was "blunt trauma and thermal injuries with smoke inhalation." The forensic pathologists at the Georgia Bureau of Investigations had found carbon monoxide in his blood and soot in his airways. His lungs had charred in the fire and his organs basically cooked, but there were still some tissues internal enough for the coroner to examine.

It meant that Edgar was still breathing when his car was set on fire, in spite of the fact that he'd been near death from the blunt trauma to his head.

There had been no suspect. The single person of interest was Bobby Kane, one of Gene Gilroy's transient garage workers—whose minimum-wage job was to sweep the floor and clean up the tools. However, he had an alibi for that evening, a woman he'd picked up at a local bar. And he died two days later in a motorcycle accident on a rainy night.

Through the passage of time, the case grew cold due to a lack of evidence. It was the strangest thing. No witnesses, no clues, nothing.

A car on fire on a deserted road, and no one saw

or heard it. An early morning thunderstorm put out the fire before a lone motorist finally drove by it the next day and called 911.

Some of Edgar's personal effects had never been recovered. Not his pocket watch, not his satellite phone, and not his wedding ring. They seemed to be things randomly taken to show a semblance of a robbery, but Ming didn't have enough proof of his passing suspicion.

Edgar's murderer might still be on the loose, though nothing could bring Edgar back.

He was dead.

End of story.

It was Ming's unpopular opinion that Mama Hu should've let the past go.

If she wanted to do something about it, she could have asked Ming. His company could use the business. He would have done the investigation and not let Sabine get involved—or at least only be involved behind the scenes.

Not out there facing danger.

He floored the gas pedal.

CHAPTER 1

C lad in all black with a beanie cap and mask hiding most of her face, Sabine Hu-Wei limped past a thicket, being aware that there might be snakes and spiders and such lurking in the undergrowth, but fearing more for her life. The buildings she had left were at least a hundred yards away, gray in the moonlight, but she could not go back.

She had to go forward. But where was "forward?"

The midnight air was chilly and damp. It had snowed lightly one day, rained heavily another day, but today, things were back to what January usually was in Georgia. Just cold.

The full moon led her toward a cluster of oak, pine, and other trees that grew in the North Georgia Mountains at the base of the Appalachian Mountain range. Somewhere outside these woods, there was a path near a picnic area outside the villas in Gene

Gilroy's sprawling hideaway near the town of Hiawassee.

She stopped by a random tree to catch her breath and gain her bearings. It was probably a sweet gum tree, judging from the spiky balls scattered all around the base of the tree trunk. Her boots smashed a few of them, but they didn't make any noise. Perhaps last evening's rain had softened them.

As long as she made it back to the villas in the next hour, she'd be okay. Her sister, Helen Hu, was in the compound somewhere, and in contact with Leland Yang-Joule from Binary Systems in Atlanta. Leland had disabled the security system in the area between the villas and the Museum of Old Things.

Oh, don't get me started on The MOOT.

She replayed in her mind what had happened to her in the last thirty minutes until this moment and thanked God that she was still alive.

Yes, it had been harrowing as she had nearly failed to escape from The Museum of Old Things, also known as The MOOT. She hadn't been able to find her father's missing pocket watch in the maze of hallways and secret rooms. The wearable navigation on her augmented reality smart glasses was just as lost as she was.

She nearly lost her life when The Mechanic's men chased her and pushed her down toward an antique guillotine, one of the weird and bizarre collections in The MOOT.

In that split moment between life and death, Sabine had prayed that God would take care of her two children and that her estranged husband would come home and raise them.

God must have heard her prayer because the lights went out in The MOOT. The men panicked and loosened their grip on Sabine, just enough time for her to jerk her right hand away and reach for her Ruger LCP in her right pocket.

That would be faster than trying to access the *bo shuriken* spikes in her vest pockets.

She fired two shots to incapacitate two men, just when she heard the weighted guillotine mouton drop down. She glanced over to find that the angled blade had taken out a third man.

Their remaining buddies, who had survived because Sabine didn't return tit for tat, were writhing on the ground with gunshot wounds to their thighs.

She could see them through her smart glasses, but there was no time to help them. Camden la Salle's people would be there to arrest the men as soon as she opened the doors for them.

But where are the doors?

She had gotten disoriented after wandering around The MOOT.

"Cicerone, navigation," she whispered. "Show me the door I came in earlier."

Immediately, her infrared glasses projected a map of The MOOT.

Sabine was thankful that her wearable computer, on loan from Binary Systems, knew the exit—even though it had no idea where Dad's pocket watch was and had gotten her lost in The MOOT. Still, now that they had mapped the library—haha!—she should expect efficiency the next time she returned to this place.

Following Cicerone's instructions, she ran down

the corridors until she reached a familiar door. Out of breath, she dashed out into a wallop of cold January air. A couple of nights ago, there was a light dusting of snow on the mountain town but not enough to stick.

Sabine's thermal outfit kept her warm. The moon was in the sky, but Sabine didn't need its help. Her smart glasses pointed on toward the way. A cluster of tall pine and oak was the beginning of the woods behind the library.

"Forty minutes to the end of blackout," Cicerone spoke into Sabine's earpiece.

That was all the time she had to return to her villa before the security system would reactivate. If they discovered that she, the first-place winner, was missing, it would arouse suspicions and thwart a plan six months in the making.

So into the woods she ran.

"ETA to the villa?" Sabine asked her smart glasses.

"At your speed, twenty-three minutes."

Unfortunately, it would take longer than that. In the middle of the run, she tripped on a root on the ground and went tumbling down the side of an embankment—

And lost her smart glasses with its experimental Cicerone wearable augmented reality computer.

What good were the pair of fancy eyeglasses if not on her face?

Now she was lost in the woods, and it was how she'd ended up battling a thicket and hugging a tree and reflecting on her life.

Lost.

Completely lost.

She fished for her phone in her pocket. It still had battery. Good. She swiped it to call Camden.

No signal.

God, help me.

She drew a deep breath. The night was cold, and the rain had stopped. The air smelled slightly sweet from the gum tree and earthy from the decaying leaves on the ground.

The bugs were gone, so all was quiet. Winter was a good time for Sabine to come to this place because if there was one thing she had never gotten used to in Georgia, it would be the insects.

Why am I thinking about petty things right now?

Figure out how to get out of these woods already!

If not for the full moon and the cloudless sky, Sabine would be totally blind in these woods. Looking around her, all she saw were trees and tree trunks and bushes in monochromatic greyscale.

Which way to the villas?

She closed her eyes and prayed—

Snap.

A twig?

She opened one eye, as though by doing that she could have the illusion of safety. Was that a deer? Did deer walk around at night in the middle of January?

Then she heard male and female voices.

Her ears perked up.

Either help had come or The Mechanic had sent backups to finish her. After all, she had shot two men in their legs. The third died by his own hand—probably—and had nothing to do with her. If her phone was working, she'd call 911.

The voices were in the distance. Sabine was

afraid to call out for help because she had no idea who she was dealing with. Friend or foe, the voices didn't draw any closer.

That meant people were talking in one spot.

Sabine followed the voices to get a better look.

Firstly, they couldn't be Helen's people because she and Sabine had come alone. Sabine was happy to be working with her sister again after all these years of separate careers, but in a way, it was somewhat bittersweet. When Dad had been alive, he had urged his two daughters to work together so that they could eventually take over his private investigative firm. However, it wasn't until he'd been dead for years that Sabine and Helen finally had a chance to team up.

In any case, it couldn't be Helen's people.

Then who were the voices, if not The Mechanics' men?

Well, there was a third possibility. The Mechanic had stolen art. Helen had mentioned calling FBI Special Agent Camden la Salle, who worked for the Art Crime Team. Camden was an old friend whom Sabine trusted. Sabine also trusted his wife, Iris, who now managed the River Run Indoor Range, where Sabine had practiced using a flintlock for months before the invitation-only shooting competition in Hiawassee.

Sabine stood frozen at the tree, not sure what to do next. Should she go toward the voices or should she go the other way? If the latter, would she get even more lost in the forest?

Lord, help me decide.

Not expecting a pillar of fire by night as the Israelites had back in the Old Testament days, Sabine hoped that Cicerone had sent an emergency beacon to Binary Systems in Atlanta somewhere so that they could call 911 or something.

Then again, would the wearable computer be able to communicate when Sabine's own phone had no signal?

She'd have to rely on her instincts.

Her gut told her to move away from the voices.

Whether right or wrong, she didn't know. However, considering that she had caused some ruckus at The MOOT, it would be likely that The Mechanic had sent someone to come after her. She had broken into The MOOT, which apparently no one else had done before.

Helen should be looking for her by now. She could find Sabine by tracking her phone and her eyeglasses, if the signals worked. They'd find a way, or they could ask Binary Systems.

Therefore, all Sabine had to do was trust God to protect her and find a safe place to stay and wait until help came.

She was about to walk away from the voices when she heard distinct words that pierced the night.

"Who are you?" The woman's voice was sharp.

"Who are you?" The man replied. His voice carried in the wind toward her.

It was an all too familiar voice.

Ming?

No way.

Many things popped into Sabine's head, but the most urgent of which was that the man sounded like her estranged husband whom she hadn't seen in three months, but whose voice she was so used to in their almost-five years of marriage that she could pick him out in a crowd.

But...

Wasn't Ming supposed to be in Dubai, working for some socialite married to a billionaire sheikh?

The fact that he'd taken the job overseas instead of staying stateside to celebrate their daughter's third birthday still bothered Sabine. It wasn't like he couldn't find another contract job locally in Georgia. He wanted the nine hundred thousand dollars so badly that he had no problem missing a birthday, Thanksgiving, and Christmas with his family.

Therefore, who cares about him?

Sabine took another step away from the voices, but her emotions took over. What if he was really Ming? What if he was in danger? How could she just walk away?

Sigh.

Slowly, she made her way from tree to tree and thicket to thicket. Along the way, some clouds moved in, obscuring the moonlight from earth. Hiding behind a cluster of holly, she pushed away some spiky leaves with her gloved hands to take a peek.

Two people were in the clearing. The woman faced Sabine. She had never seen the woman before, not at the competition or in the compound. Then again, just because Sabine hadn't met her, it didn't mean that she wasn't a part of The Mechanic's team.

Since she had heard both male and female voices, she suspected that the person kneeling on the ground was a man. His hands were tied behind his back. He was facing away from Sabine, so she couldn't see his face to confirm his identity.

The woman raised a dagger in the air, as if to slash the man with it, but she didn't.

"Speak! Who are you?" She snarled.

Well, maybe she didn't snarl per se. Sabine didn't know how to describe her expression except to say that she looked a bit stressed.

The woman yanked something off the man's face and pushed his face to the ground. She dropped her knee onto the man's spine, causing him to yelp in pain. He tried to get up, but couldn't.

The woman pressed a dagger to his neck. "Answer me!"

"What's in it for me?" the man answered.

That voice.

Sabine's knees wobbled, and her head spun. Her heart skipped a beat.

It was Ming's voice. As clear as day, it was Ming speaking. Only he would try to talk like that even at death's door.

That made Sabine angry.

If he died, Sabine would have to raise their kids alone.

What was he doing here? Had he forgotten their agreement to never work in the same place just in case something happened to both of them, leaving their kids orphans?

Then again, they were heading for divorce, so none of that mattered, did it? Sabine's cousin, who was a divorce lawyer, represented her. She promised to take Ming to the cleaners.

Sabine didn't think they would ever reconcile.

But...

She also didn't want Ming to be dead. After all, he was the father of their kids.

Maybe she should get confirmation. At this point, she couldn't be entirely sure it was Ming.

"Speak!" The woman drove the dagger through the man's arm.

He yowled.

"Okay. Okay." His voice was pained.

"Now it's going to take you more effort to speak, but if you don't, I'll mark the other arm." She lifted her knee off the man's back. With all the strength she could muster in two arms, she yanked the man back up on his knees. He nearly toppled over, but she managed to stabilize him.

Now he was facing Sabine, and she could see his face.

It was Ming. There was no doubt.

Sigh and double sigh.

"Just taking a stroll." Ming grimaced.

That made Sabine's blood boil. How could he make a joke at a time like this? Sometimes she couldn't figure him out.

"Stroll?" the woman asked. "Through the woods in the middle of the night?"

"I like peace and quiet." Ming barely nodded.

What is he doing?

Even as she asked it, Sabine knew the answer.

Ming was buying—or borrowing—time until help came. It was a calculated move and very risky.

Then again, Sabine couldn't criticize him for it because she, too, was waiting for help to arrive.

"What were you doing in The MOOT?" the woman pressed.

"The what?"

Behind the tree, Sabine shook her head. The father of her children was about to get himself killed.

In the clearing, the woman snorted. She came around the back of Ming's head and slowly ran her dagger along Ming's jawline, breathed into his ear, and then nicked his cheek.

No!

Sabine clasped her mouth.

At this point, she wanted to forget how much she hated Ming for running away from their marital conflict instead of dealing with it. All she could think of now was how to save him.

She was twenty feet away from the duo. Her Ruger could easily fire that far. However, the woman was too close to Ming. If Sabine missed her shot, he'd also be hit. Then what?

She'd have to use her other weapons. She unzipped her vest, palmed her *bo shuriken* spikes, and stepped out of the bushes.

In one continuous move, she let half a dozen blades fly. They struck the woman point blank in the hand, dislodged her dagger from her grip, and toppled her backward to the ground as she screamed.

Sabine rushed forward, her Ruger pointing in the woman's direction. "Get out of my way, Ming."

Realizing that she had spoken his name aloud, Sabine's grip on the Ruger wobbled. She prayed that the woman wouldn't come after them in their private home, now that she knew Ming's name.

Just then, she heard drones overhead, approaching them with blinking lights.

"FBI!" Strong voices split the air.

CHAPTER 2

FBI Special Agent Camden la Salle entered the clearing with a flashlight in his hand. The other FBI agents fanned around him. They arrested the woman who had held Ming at knifepoint. Her hand and arm were bleeding from the sharp tips of Sabine's *bo shuriken* spikes.

Sabine untied the last of the ropes from Ming's wrist. She said not a word to him, and that broke his heart. All that because of his pursuit of money— money that he no longer had anyway.

"I'm not hurt, if you're wondering." Ming showed her the cut in his sleeves. "She tried to stab my arm, and I made a big noise about it, but she only slashed through my jacket."

Sabine barely nodded.

"You care, right?"

Sabine blinked.

I knew it!

Ming wanted to hug his wife, but she moved away from him rather quickly.

She was about to pick up her spikes from the forest floor, but Ming stopped her.

Camden lifted a hand. "He's right. Don't touch anything. They're all evidence now."

"To be sure, we did it in self-defense," Ming said. "That woman was trying to stab me, and Sabine saved me."

He had purposely said "we" to gauge Sabine's reaction.

She said nothing. In fact, she looked cold, like maybe she'd given up on him.

I'm sorry, Sabine. I'm so sorry.

"I threw six spikes." Sabine pointed here and there, but Ming could tell that she was primarily speaking to Camden. "I only see four."

Camden nodded. He talked to another agent, who brought a sheriff's deputy to him. Camden showed them the lethal *bo shuriken* spikes. The joint task force officers would collect the evidence.

"And your Ruger," Camden said to Sabine. "We'll return it to you soon."

"I haven't fired it," Sabine protested.

"You pointed it." Ming tried not to make eye contact with the arrested woman who was being led away by agents.

Yep. FBI agents.

Ming had questions, but this might not be the time to ask. For instance, he wanted to know how long the FBI had been involved in the investigation. Did Helen know about it?

"How do you know we were here at this spot?" Ming asked Camden.

"Helen gave us your coordinates, but she was off by a few hundred yards."

Helen Hu. Just as Ming had suspected.

Sabine's eyes widened. "That might be where my smart glasses are. I dropped them."

"Smart glasses?" Ming asked.

Sabine ignored him. It seemed that she still didn't want to talk to him.

Ming didn't push for an answer. He knew that Sabine interchangeably wore contact lenses and eyeglasses, but smart glasses? They must be something experimental that Helen was testing for Binary Systems again.

"We'll go back and get them for you, but your glasses are also evidence now," Camden said.

"Cam, Helen will explain the glasses to you," Sabine said. "They came from Binary Systems."

Binary Systems?

If the go-to security specialists were involved, then this was bigger than Ming had thought. Binary Systems didn't do small jobs. They contracted for the Department of Defense, National Security Agency, Central Intelligence Agency, and yes, the FBI as well.

Camden raised an eyebrow. "Oh? Then Helen and I need to talk."

"What time is it?" Sabine asked. "I have to get back before the security system comes online."

"Get back where?" Ming's arm went around Sabine's waist.

Sabine wriggled free and stepped away from Ming. She refused to even look at him.

"Still not talking to each other, I see." Camden shook his head. He waved to someone and asked for water.

Sabine hesitated before she took the plastic bottled water from Camden. Ming knew it was because she usually avoided plastic containers. Even at the store, she'd pay more for glass containers. She often brought her own stainless steel water bottle everywhere she went.

She finally took a sip. She was about to put the cap back on when Ming grabbed the bottle from her and drank the rest of the water.

"Why are you here, Ming?" Camden asked a question.

Ming wondered if Sabine was curious about his presence in Hiawassee. She looked disinterested. Or perhaps he was reading too much into her poker face.

"Helen called me. Said that Mama Hu sent my wife into The Mechanic's lair."

"Mom didn't send me. I volunteered." Once again, Sabine directed her words at Camden. She didn't even look at Ming.

Ming knew he had a long way to go to regain Sabine's love. However, steps had been made—all done by her. For example, when he had been tied up earlier, it was Sabine who had come out of the bushes to rescue him.

In the last few years, she had taken up a new hobby. In addition to her usual pistol practice at the gun range, Sabine had found an instructor who could teach her to throw *bo shuriken* spikes. She said that once she became proficient in them, she'd add *hira shuriken*, which were star-shaped spinners.

My ninja wife.

I better not cross her.

He chuckled. No, he was only kidding. How could she do anything to him? She loved him. And he loved her.

So why on earth was she asking for a divorce?

As soon as he had a moment, Ming would call Diego and ask for some advice. If they had to go to couple's counseling, Ming prayed that Sabine would agree. Diego's dad was a good counselor too. Both father and son were still pastors.

"You volunteered, huh?" Camden smiled. "Tell me more."

"But not tonight," Sabine said. "There's a flintlock exhibition at nine o'clock in the morning. I'm bushed, and I need to get some sleep."

"I'll have someone walk you back to your villa."

"No need. I know the way," Sabine said too casually.

"I'm not letting you walk back alone." Ming felt an alarm rising. "I'll go with you."

"I don't want him to go with me." Sabine turned to Camden.

"I don't have time to be your go-between." Camden looked a bit sad when he said that.

Ming figured it might be because Camden recalled the time when Ming had helped him to reconcile with his wife—before they were married—and he wanted to return the kindness.

However, if Camden thought that he could recip-rocate Ming's good deed by letting Ming and Sabine work together, he had another thing coming. Sabine wouldn't put up with it.

To Camden's credit, he didn't do what Ming feared would upset Sabine.

"You two—three, including Helen—stepped into an ongoing investigation," Camden said. "I hate to tell you both to leave, but you could be putting my people's lives in danger."

"I can't leave," Sabine protested. "I won first place in the flintlock competition yesterday. They're expecting me at the gala tomorrow night—or today, considering it's after midnight."

"I can't leave either." Ming stepped closer to Sabine. "I came here via Skye's the Limit, and they'd get suspicious if a server and a dishwasher are missing."

"Besides, I know your Art Crime Team wants the images I've taken in The MOOT," Sabine added.

"We do?" Camden looked amused.

"Uh-huh. Picasso's *Le pigeon aux petits pois* isn't destroyed—unless I was looking at a reproduction."

Camden had no words.

"Call Helen," Sabine suggested. "She's running the operation."

Ming watched Sabine casually push the FBI off to her sister, a well-known private investigator who had assisted the police, FBI, and even the CIA on numerous occasions.

"We can't be seen together," Sabine added. "The Mechanic knows who you are, Cam."

"So that was why we haven't seen you around in the compound itself." Ming put two and two together. "I'm guessing that's also why you're skirting the periphery, hanging out in the woods, but aren't invited to the party."

Even if Camden had undercover officers, he wouldn't tell Ming and Sabine.

"Why did Skye's the Limit let you in?" Camden asked.

That question alone made Ming suspect that undercover FBI agents were not among the catering crew.

"Because my sister was instrumental in helping Skye's sister-in-law to find her missing brother," Sabine answered. "So Skye is returning a favor to Helen."

"I assume you'll meet with Helen ASAP? Probably tonight?" Ming asked.

Camden nodded. "Soon. Like right now if I can get ahold of her."

This time, signs of their friendship returned. Ming was confident that Helen would be able to persuade Camden to let them finish their work here. For the life of him, Ming couldn't understand when people didn't want to collaborate. More hands would make light work, or whatever the saying was.

As for him, it would be the first job he'd finished in three months. After this, Ming planned to go home and regroup. His goal was to spend more time with his family—whom he'd sacrificed in a momentary lapse of judgment and the pursuit of overseas income —and to make up for his deficiency as a loving Christian husband. It could take a lot of time to prove to Sabine that he had repented of his sorry ways.

"The Mechanic might find out that you two were married," Camden added.

"Are married," Ming corrected him. "Present tense."

And then he pulled Sabine toward him—quickly enough to startle her—and kissed her on the cheek, right in front of their half-amused half-frowning old friend.

CHAPTER 3

Thanks to Camden, Ming escorted Sabine back to her villa. She didn't speak to him the entire way.

Ming wondered if it was because they were heading for a divorce and she didn't want anything she said to be used against her. Or perhaps she disliked his hyper-realistic full-head silicone mask that made him look like an older man with gray hair under an attached baseball cap.

She dipped her head as they approached the backdoor, the long bill of her baseball cap providing enough coverage to shield her face from the security cameras. Even though they were still offline, Sabine seemed extra cautious tonight.

A sudden movement in the shadows made Ming pull Sabine back. Their backs were up against the brick wall outside the villa as Ming tried to listen.

"They're working on it," a male voice said. "I'll let you know when it comes online."

There was no second voice, so it made Ming think that the man had been talking on the phone.

In the moonlight, Ming saw Sabine move, but Ming's arm instinctively stretched out in front of her chest, like a security bar.

He shook his head.

She nodded.

Ming's heart warmed up. That was their first one-to-one communication in three months.

They listened some more. Crickets.

Ming inched sideways until he was at the edge of the wall. No voices. No noises.

He reached back and grabbed Sabine's hand. She tried to pry away at first but then gave up. Ming could guess why. She knew as well as he did that this wasn't the time to play divorce court. They had to get back to Sabine's villa—to relative safety—first. Everything else could wait.

Cloud coverage blocked the moon, and Ming made his move. Hand in hand, they crossed the small courtyard and entered the villa's back porch.

They crouched down as Sabine tapped her smart-watch. Ming watched her log onto some sort of cloud server and then check the villa monitor.

It seemed to be all clear indoors.

She pressed the entry code on the keypad lock attached to the back door.

"When do the cameras come on again?" Ming asked as Sabine locked the door.

Sabine didn't reply. She was probably still upset. He could just imagine three months of seething anger percolating just below the surface. If that was really the case, then no amount of apologies from Ming was going to help.

They were alone in the small villa that had a kitchenette, a sitting area, and one bedroom.

Finally, Sabine sighed. "You can go now."

She had broken the ice by speaking first. Ming appreciated it and was at a loss for words until his smart-aleck mouth spoke without consulting his brain.

"Not a single thank you?" Ming took off his mask.

"Thank you. I could've made the walk back myself. It's literally not even fifty yards."

She'd spoken a lot of words. Maybe she was easing back to her old self, back when they had been happily married without a care in the world. Times had been tough then too, primarily due to his lack of discretion in overspending in his Savannah River Investigations, Inc.

He should've listened to Sabine when she told him that he had to cut expenses at SRI, including rethinking the expensive downtown rented office. Perhaps he should have worked from home—in his unused top-floor office—until he had paid off his company debt. He didn't want to listen to her logic that he had a money management problem, not an income problem.

"And thank you too," Ming said. "You saved my life back in the woods."

"I was passing by. I would've helped even if it wasn't you." She kept her voice even, as though raising it would arouse suspicion that she was still angry with him.

Of course she was.

Now she was equating him with a regular stranger out there.

It hurt, as though he was punched in the gut.

Perhaps that was enough conversation for the night. Ming wasn't sure if he could handle more insults from Sabine.

"I'll leave as soon as I sweep the villa." Ming tried to sound useful.

Sabine waved her phone. "No need. I already did."

"Tech from Helen?" Now he tried to sound knowledgeable.

Sabine nodded.

"Cam took your Ruger. Do you have backups?"

Sabine nodded slightly.

She was back to silence.

If Ming couldn't get her to talk again, they might not be able to rebuild their relationship.

"What kind of backups?" Ming pressed.

Sabine could have shrugged, but she chose to answer him. "Glock."

She sounded all business-like, but it was still progress, nonetheless.

"Same pink one you used at the gun range when we were first dating?" Ming gave it his best shot.

He wasn't trying to pull her guard down, but he wanted to keep talking. Bringing up the River Run Indoor Range in Savannah, where they had both gone to practice at the firing range, might trigger some happy memories for Sabine. That could be a neutral ground for them to begin their peace talks.

Sabine's face softened. Her eyes glistened.

Perhaps memories of happier days were coming back.

"Was that where you learned *bo shuriken?*" Ming kept it objective.

"Yeah. Iris introduced me to a master thrower."

Camden's older brother, Bryce, had bought the gun range and turned it into a successful business. For a while, Camden's wife, Iris, worked there. Eventually, Bryce wanted to retire and go on world cruises with his wife. He sold the business to Iris for a song.

Iris expanded the business to include not only shooting ranges, but also knife, axe, blade, and spike-throwing areas. She started workshops, seminars, and lectures to teach firearm safety to the community. Women started attending Krav Maga classes and learned to protect themselves.

"What's his name?" Ming asked casually.

"Who?"

"Your *bo shuriken* instructor."

"What made you assume it's a man?"

"No?"

"No. Women can also be *bo shuriken* champions."

Ming knew that, but he was trying to keep the words flowing in an attempt to resuscitate his marriage. "I stand corrected."

"Now leave. I need to get some sleep." Sabine stood behind an armchair, as if it was a shield between her and him.

"I miss you." Ming meant it.

Sabine's lips moved, but she ended up not saying anything.

"May I stay the night?" Ming dared himself to ask.

Sabine drew a deep breath. "It will be dawn in a couple of hours."

"As long as I'm with you..." Ming felt like he was begging for mercy.

"That wasn't important to you three months ago," Sabine snapped.

It was a loaded sentence that indicted him for leaving Sabine with two kids and no support. Well, she had support from Mama Hu and the babysitter. However, Ming knew that Sabine wanted emotional spousal support for her day-to-day activities.

"I was wrong." There, he admitted it. The humble pie tasted tart. "I made a mistake taking that contract overseas. However, I hired Cade to work with me, so I have an alibi and a proof of innocence. I was never alone with the client, not once."

Ming fancied himself clever for not working alone with the socialite. He felt he had learned a lot from Joseph in the Old Testament, who had an encounter with Potiphar's wife in Genesis 39. Having read that Bible chapter, Ming had made a decision to never be alone with a woman who wasn't his wife.

Sabine said nothing.

Ming wondered what she was thinking. At first, he had worried that Sabine would be jealous of the ultra-rich socialite woman who had hired Ming to dig up dirt on her husband's infidelity so that she could divorce him and sue for half of his fortune. The socialite must've thought that she was going to get a substantial sum because she'd paid Ming half a million dollars a month for six months of work.

Ming didn't finish the job because it turned out that the socialite was like Potiphar's wife, so to speak.

She had been the one who had committed adultery, and she was looking for a way to turn the tables on her husband before he kicked her out of his multi-million-dollar mansion in the desert.

Thankfully, Ming and Cade protected each other from the wiles of the wayward woman. However, the breach of contract carried a pecuniary penalty that Ming could barely afford, with SRI in debt. So he called Helen, his know-it-all sister-in-law, for advice.

When Helen was out of reach, he called Earl at the Hu Knows office in Savannah. In his conversation with Earl, Ming realized that something was wrong at his own house. He split the penalty cost with Cade, and then he flew home.

Thank God I came home in time.

"Cade who?" Sabine finally asked.

"A Christian man who doesn't drink or cuss."

"Good."

Ming hesitated to say more. He wondered why Sabine asked. He felt a bit jealous that Sabine had asked about Cade but not about him.

Sabine waited.

Ming relented.

"He's an expat who lives in Dubai." Ming kept it professional. "Most of the time, he works as a personal bodyguard. One of Helen's associates introduced him to me when I was looking to form a team. I'll call him again if I need any help overseas."

"Overseas..." Sabine's voice trailed off.

"I mean I'll pay him to do the work for me overseas. That way, I can stay home."

"Hmm." Sabine didn't ask any follow-up questions.

Ming realized that there was still friction between Sabine and him. It had to be addressed.

"Please forgive me," Ming said for good measure.

Still no response from Sabine.

"I've asked God to forgive me." Ming had brought up forgiveness because he knew that Sabine believed the same Christian God. Having studied the Bible a lot, she was sure to be reminded of Ephesians 4:32.

And be kind to one another, tenderhearted, forgiving one another, even as God in Christ forgave you.

Nevertheless, Ming also knew that both of them believed that forgiveness and reconciliation were not equal. He feared that Sabine would forgive him from afar but not accept him back into her heart. Then he would be finished at that point of no return.

His heart broke. He teared up. He felt stupid and ugly and sorry that he'd inflicted three months of what might have felt like abandonment to Sabine. He'd shirked his responsibility as a Christian husband and father.

"You were right, Sabine." His voice cracked. "I shouldn't have taken that job. It was a huge mistake. I lost three months chasing paper money."

"God is the one who is right," Sabine corrected him. "I'm human just as you are. I also make mistakes. I shouldn't have yelled at you and cried a river."

"It was my fault. I left you alone with a three-year-old and a baby. I missed Thanksgiving and Christmas with you."

Sabine straightened up. "Being a single mom isn't

that bad. It's hard work, but we managed—even though Hannah asked me on Christmas morning where her dad went."

"I'm sorry. I don't want a divorce. I want to come home."

He felt like maybe he should kneel on the floor or something to show that he had regretted his decision to take the Dubai job. He'd explain the details later. Right now, he didn't want Sabine to dwell on the negatives.

Both of his knees bent slightly—

"No, don't do that. Are you kidding me?" It seemed that Sabine had read his mind. "You only kneel before God and God alone."

"Let me come home, Sabine."

"Did I tell you to leave?" Sabine's voice softened. "I begged you not to go."

"I should've listened." He walked closer to her but stopped about four feet away. He didn't want her to bolt. "Will you ever forgive me?"

Sabine sighed. "If God has forgiven you, who am I to withhold forgiveness?"

One of the things that Ming appreciated about Sabine was her knowledge of Scripture. Here, she was no doubt reflecting on a verse they had both read together before. Still, he had to make sure. "Are you referring to Matthew 6:14-15?"

> For if you forgive men their trespasses, your heavenly Father will also forgive you. But if you do not forgive men their trespasses, neither will your Father forgive your trespasses.

Sabine nodded. "Have you been reading the Bible while you were overseas?"

"Every chance I could," Ming replied truthfully.

"Meaning what?"

"If I was out all night on mission, I'd be sleeping in the morning, so I couldn't read it until I got up, which could be in the afternoon. I tried to be consistent, but the days and nights sometimes ran together."

"I see. Someday you can tell me about what you did for three months."

Sabine's curiosity was tearing down the wall between them.

"Any time. Maybe over dinner?" Yes, Ming was asking for a date.

"We'll see."

"So. Back to my question. May I stay the night, or what's left of it?"

Sabine shrugged. "Suit yourself. I have to take a shower and go to bed. I have a nine o'clock flintlock exhibition."

"I don't want to leave you anymore." It was the truth. More than her safety, Ming was concerned about being separated from her—although he also knew that she could protect herself with her particular skill set.

Truly, being a real estate agent didn't bring out all that Sabine could be good at. This wasn't the time to bring it up, but Ming suspected that Sabine had become a real estate agent because being a private investigator would remind her of her father, and the remembrance would be too painful for her. It had been the sole reason that she had sold her shares of Hu Knows to her sister, Helen.

Interestingly, she hadn't spent the money that Helen had paid her. Instead, she invested it in cryptocurrencies and rental properties. Those investments alone would be enough to support their family of four and pay for their two children to go to grade school and eventually to college.

However, Ming felt bad that he hadn't been the sole breadwinner in the family. SRI was mired in six-figure debt that he had been trying to pay off. That had been the reason he took up the Dubai project, which turned out to be a big mistake. Not only did he end up paying a penalty for breaking the contract, but he also rocked his marriage.

Could it still be salvaged?

If he had to eat humble pie and beg for forgiveness, he would. However, Sabine wasn't that sort of wife to lord over him. She would want him to repent, yes, but more than that, she would want him to sit down at the table with her and sort it all out with transparency and honesty.

She was a problem solver, and this was how she solved problems.

On the other hand, Ming was too embarrassed to crawl to the meeting table.

Hence, their impasse for three months.

Sigh.

Was it all over now? He wasn't sure.

Sabine's smartwatch rang.

"Whassup?" She nodded. "Okay. One sec."

She tapped on the speakerphone. "Helen wants to talk to both of us."

Ming realized that they were both still standing in the center of the living room. He sat down on a small sofa, and patted the space next to him, but Sabine continued to stand.

"Cam found Sabine's smart glasses in the woods, and he confiscated them," Helen said.

"Do you have a spare pair?" Sabine asked.

"Not with me, but I can loan them to you later. Yours was an experimental pair from Leland. She's fuming mad, and there's nothing we can do about it. She might not get them back until after the trial. That is, if we catch The Mechanic at all."

"Huh. So Cam has confiscated my Ruger, *bo shuriken* spikes, and smart glasses."

It was a good thing that she hadn't brought her favorite pink Glock. Helen had given her the Ruger to use because it was smaller and fit better on her thigh holster. As for her *bo shuriken* spikes, she'd have to order some more or wait for Camden to return them to her.

"But you still have your smartwatch," Helen said. "Unfortunately, you can't walk into the dining hall with it tonight. It won't pass security."

On the sofa, Ming pulled a nearby chenille throw over his chest. It was warm and cozy. All he needed now was a fireplace and some soft music. He felt sleepy and stifled a yawn.

"I'm assuming you have a plan," Sabine said.

"After you go through security, stop by the women's restroom to your right and leave your purse there," Helen instructed her sister. "We'll load it up, and I'll get someone to bring the purse back to you."

Helen and Sabine talked and Ming listened. He pulled up the throw to cover his neck. He was trying to keep up with the two sisters, but his eyelids had other ideas.

When he opened his eyes again, he was lying flat on the sofa, another blanket piled up on top of him. No one was around him. He didn't recall seeing the blanket earlier, so Sabine must have brought it to him.

"Sabine?" he whispered.

There was no answer.

Her bedroom door was closed. Maybe she had gone to bed.

Slowly, Ming sat up. The curtains around the small living room were still drawn, so he couldn't look outside to see if it was still dark.

He tapped his smartwatch.

"Eight o'clock! What?" Ming leapt off the couch. He was still wearing the same boots he had on last night.

On the coffee table was a note in Sabine's handwriting.

Lock the door properly when you leave.

It was just like her to leave him a note like that. She wanted him to make sure the door actually locked before he walked away. Details like that.

He was about to knock on the bedroom door when he saw the sticky note.

I'm busy. Don't look for me.

It sounded cold, and it was confusing. Was Sabine in her room or not? Perhaps she wasn't in her room because if she was, would she have said, "Don't look for me?" Her instruction to him meant that she had left the villa.

He went to the kitchenette and washed his face in the sink. He dried it off with a paper towel.

He checked the refrigerator and found a tray of eggs, slices of cheese, and a half-gallon of milk. He decided not to eat Sabine's food. After all, he had to get back to his own hotel room, which was across the courtyard in the lodge.

It was daytime now. How could he walk around with security at full blast everywhere?

Why hadn't Sabine woken him up?

He texted Helen on his own phone which had stayed safely in his zippered cargo pocket the entire night. It was low on battery, but it worked.

MING

> I need a ten-minute blackout so that I can return to my room.

HELEN

I'll give you twenty just in case you get delayed.

MING

> Thank you. Could you give me Sabine's agenda for today?

HELEN

You'll see her tonight at the dinner.

MING

> That's not for another ten hours.

HELEN

LOL. Stand by.

While he waited for Helen to turn off the security cameras and send him Sabine's schedule for the day, he drank some water from the tap. The water from the North Georgia Mountains wasn't bad. It was cold because of winter, but it tasted almost like spring water.

Then it was time to put on his full-head mask again. In the summertime, it would make his entire head sweat, but in the winter, it kept the heat in. It made him look older by twenty years. He adjusted the mask so that the baseball cap looked aligned with his actual face underneath the silicone.

He felt like he was in a Hollywood movie, but then, masks like these could be bought off the shelf at Halloween almost all around the world. He had ordered these online, but so far they hadn't caused his face to break out in rashes.

As soon as Helen texted him, Ming was ready to go. He looked around the villa one more time and then exited through the front door into a covered hallway.

A "Do Not Disturb" sign hung on the door. Ming wondered whether that was for him—because he'd slept in—or for Sabine in general. Either way, he decided to leave the sign there.

Speaking of Sabine, he wondered if he'd see her during the day. The next ten hours might be his longest yet in recent memory as he waited to see the love of his life again.

CHAPTER 4

Standing there at the foot of an Ionic column and watching the well-dressed crowd milling about the rotunda outside the dining room, Sabine's mind rehashed the list of things that bothered her this evening.

Firstly, her stretchable velvet cheongsam was a bit tight—thanks to too many cinnamon buns the last couple of days—and she was afraid to sit down anywhere. The action might rip her seams. She regretted not having worn more loose-fitting clothes that could have allowed room for a thigh holster to conceal her small Ruger LCP handgun. However, Camden had confiscated it the night before in the woods.

After last night, Sabine had found out that since she had thrown the spikes and pointed a hand gun at Ming's assailant, those weapons would be entered into evidence. She wouldn't see them again until after the trial plus potential appeals, whenever those might occur.

Secondly, she couldn't bring her phone to the dining room. She didn't want security at the door to take it. There was no way Helen would be able to contact her this evening.

However, as per Helen, as soon as Sabine passed through security, she went to the ladies' restroom and left her clutch purse in the stall. Someone would return it to her after Helen had put her smartwatch in it.

Thirdly, she didn't have her Ruger or her *bo shuriken* spikes with her. It was too late to regret bringing her own weapons to this private retreat center, but Helen hadn't said otherwise.

Well, she still had her two special hair sticks on top of her head. She had swept up her hair into a bun on top of her head and stuck two hair sticks through it. They didn't get confiscated because they looked like a pair of cheap wooden chopsticks.

That's the point.

And she hadn't lost her cross necklace that Dad had given her many years ago. She could have worn it outside her neckline, but she had chosen to hide it inside tonight. The cross, close to her heart, reminded her of why she was here in this place tonight and why she must return to The MOOT.

Banquet security had locked the massive doors in between those columns. Why? Sabine had asked around. The only indication was that someone important was attending the banquet. Who? No one knew.

Her dress began to itch. Sabine started to scratch

her arms and elbows, wondering if she was going to break out in hives from the stress.

But what could she do?

She had to come to the private banquet in honor of the shooting competition participants. Having won the flintlock division, she had made it this far, but there was one last mile left to go on her mission before she could go home—if at all.

This last mile involved asking for help from her ex-boyfriend who had abandoned her seven years ago in the hospital while she was recovering from a serious injury. Garvey Gilroy was the key to finding Dad's murderer. Being a nephew of Gene, also known as The Mechanic, Garvey knew a lot more than he'd been telling her. He'd only given her breadcrumbs, but they were more clues than they had in thirteen years in the vehicular homicide case.

The case had grown cold, and nobody cared any longer—except Mom. She had been secretly investigating the car wreck. One thing led to another, and Mom ended up finding out about the flintlock shooting competition in the North Georgia Mountains.

Since Mom wasn't a good shooter, Sabine signed up for the competition, in the hope that she could get close to the number one suspect, The Mechanic himself.

Trust Mom to do the most bizarre things.

Sabine wished Ming were right there beside her. Two were better than one, right?

She wondered where Ming was and what he was doing. She knew that he was undercover, just like her. Thanks to Helen, Ming had shown up. He'd told her last night that he'd protect her. She doubted it.

If he really meant it, then why had he left her and the kids for three months?

After one argument too many with Ming, she packed up the kids and their senior golden retriever and moved home to Mom's house in downtown Savannah for a week until things cooled down. She could still work as a real estate agent from Mom's house since most of her listings were nearby in the same city or within driving range on Tybee Island. Plus, Mom was happy to babysit Hannah and Zachary.

One week turned into three months of non-communication between Sabine and Ming, with neither of them returning to their Tybee home they'd bought right after their honeymoon four-and-a-half years ago.

In the middle of it all, Sabine lost hope that Ming would return to the discussion table and resolve their marital conflict.

Looking to take her mind off the pain of feeling abandoned, and for something to do in between selling houses, Sabine ended up getting involved in what Mom had been up to for the last five years. Sabine still recalled their conversation.

"A flintlock competition?" Sabine asked Mom.

"Yes, from Gene Gilroy's collection."

"A name I haven't heard in a long time."

"The winner gets to have dinner with Gene."
Mom sounded terribly excited. "I can't wait to sit at his table and shoot him in between the eyes."

"Mom! If you keep talking like that, I can't possibly let my kids spend any more time with you. They're going to end up being violent and emotionally damaged."

Mom turned serious. "Gene killed your dad."

"The police already interviewed him, and he was not a suspect. Remember?"

"I don't think he did it himself. He hired someone to kill Edgar. Maybe Garvey." Mom rehashed that awful time when they saw Dad's charred body in the morgue.

"How do you know that's what really happened? And if it's really Gene or Garvey?" Sabine asked. "I know that we all want to find Dad's murderer, but even the police have no idea after all these years."

"Old Man Leung told me on his deathbed."

"Old Man Leung had dementia, Mom. You sure he didn't make it up?"

"It was during one of his rare moments of lucidity."

"Rare? Did you listen to yourself, Mom?"

"He's onto something, honey. He said that he bought a stolen painting from Gene. That was when he found out that Gene stored stuff for art thieves, and this has been going on for years, back to the time when your dad was investigating art theft. You remember that?"

Sabine nodded. "Thirteen years ago, just before Dad died."

"So I think Old Man Leung left me an assignment, but I can't do it, so you must."

Once Mom made up her mind to pursue something, there was no stopping her. The only catch with her assertiveness this time was her insistence on delegating the responsibility to Sabine.

Sabine could've said no, and if she had taken after Mom, she would have said a vehement no. However, Sabine hadn't inherited that stubborn trait, but older sister Helen had—and made it work for her as she ran the private investigative firm left behind by Dad.

In fact, Sabine had owned shares in the family business before she sold them to Helen after Dad died and before Helen renamed the company from Hu Private Investigations to Hu Knows, Inc.

Between the two sisters, Sabine was the person who'd shown interest in Dad's work first. She had only been twelve years old when Dad took her to the gun range. Fourteen when she followed Dad to work. Sixteen when she helped Dad solve a petty theft case.

However, after Dad passed away unexpectedly, Sabine couldn't bring herself to do any work there. Too many things reminded her of Dad, and she couldn't handle it. Instead, she went to college and did some modeling until the road accident scarred her legs, after which she became a real estate agent to this day.

This was the first time she'd returned to the family matter she had avoided for years. It was all because of Mom's words.

Ming is in Dubai enjoying himself. You can sit at home and mope about having to raise two kids as a single mom, or you can help me find your dad's murderer.

When Mom offered to pay Sabine's cousin, Keila,

to take care of her kids twenty-four-seven through Christmas and the first week of the new year when preschool was closed, Sabine couldn't say no. She trusted Keila over any random babysitter.

The next thing she knew, Sabine found herself at the River Run Indoor Range, refreshing her skills and getting lessons from Camden's older brother on aiming a flintlock, which she had never held before.

Meanwhile, Mom was at home, running logistics and working behind the scenes.

Two months later, Sabine entered the flintlock shooting competition and won. Second place went to Garvey Gilroy, the man she never thought she'd see again.

What would Ming say if he saw her and her ex together?

At that time, Sabine thought that Ming was still far away over there in Dubai, doing who knew what.

Sabine drew a deep breath and continued to wait, as instructed. People walked past her. No one said anything to her. It was nice not to be noticed because she wasn't one to make small talk.

The rotunda reminded her of the party at Mom's house that she and Ming had attended four years ago. They were both wallflowers who ended up dancing with each other behind the potted plants.

A smile crept up her face.

Servers came and went. One finally stopped. He wore a mask covering his nose and mouth, but Sabine could see his forehead. His eyeglasses were thick. His salt-and-pepper hair was somewhat wiry. He presented her clutch purse on a round tray.

"Ma'am, you left your purse in the ladies' room."

His voice was low and somewhat muffled by the cloth mask.

"Thank you. Did you find it?"

"No. The cleaning lady brought it to us."

"How did you know this purse was mine?"

"Isn't it yours? Luna says it is."

Luna.

Code name for Helen.

This server worked for her. Apparently.

Next to her purse on the tray, a note said "Lost & Found." Sabine was amused by it until she realized that there were probably cameras above them, watching the rotunda. This way, no one needed to question why a server walked around with a guest's clutch purse.

After the server left, Sabine opened the purse. Her pressed powder, lip gloss, lipstick, lotion, hand wipes, and a small pack of tissue were all still there.

Plus her smartwatch.

With the cameras above her, she didn't want to be seen putting on the watch. She left the watch in the purse for now.

Sabine walked down the long table filled with hors d'oeuvres, but she didn't have the appetite for any, not even mini quiches that she liked. She passed by some cucumber cups filled with smoked salmon, and almost got a plate to get a few of those.

No. She couldn't think about food right now.

"Ma'am, would you like some champagne?" The man's voice was soft.

She turned to look. The same server as before. This time, he was holding a tray of crystal flutes in front of Sabine.

"Champagne?" the man asked again.

Sabine looked up. His eyes looked strangely familiar, especially under the chandeliers, but he was wearing thick black glasses and his eyes were blue, so Sabine couldn't be sure she knew who this person was.

"Ma'am?" The server stared at her.

Sabine recognized that stare. But the blue eyes threw her off.

"Sorry. I don't drink." Sabine could barely speak. "Could you bring me some sparkling water in an unopened bottle instead?"

His eyebrows rose—the same way Ming's would when he was intrigued. "Yes, ma'am."

As he walked past Sabine, she noted that he was about Ming's height and build, and even had his gait.

"See someone you know?" Another male voice interrupted her thoughts.

Garvey Gilroy.

Sabine shrugged. "Besides you, I don't know anybody."

"You know my uncle."

"Not personally. I worked for Dad years before you did. Weren't you the one who'd introduced Dad to your uncle?"

"Yeah, when your dad needed his car fixed, he took it to my uncle's shop. They were good friends until your father passed away. I'm still sorry about that."

Sabine didn't react. She knew Garvey long enough to suspect that he was testing her. If she showed any emotions—like sniffling, for example—he might jump on that and say that Sabine still felt something about Dad's demise. It could reveal the real reason she was here.

The last thing Sabine wanted to do tonight was to arouse any suspicion of her presence, now complicated by the FBI. She knew why Mom had called Camden to tell him that Sabine would be in Hiawassee tonight, but she still thought that Mom shouldn't have mixed two projects together—although the person of interest was the same one: The Mechanic.

"We grieved for a long time," Sabine said.

"I bet."

A server passed by them with a tray of small phyllo cups with something in them that looked like shrimp salad.

"Want some?" Garvey stopped the server.

"Are you trying to fatten me up?" *When nervous, try humor.*

"No." Garvey chuckled. "I see that you're bored."

"Should I eat when I'm bored?"

"I'm just making small talk."

"I see." Sabine sensed an opportunity. "I'm bored because dinner hasn't started, and there's nothing to do because I don't have my phone."

"Even if you had it, it wouldn't work. No Wi-Fi," Garvey said. "That's because they want us to mingle and chat with one another, not look at our phones."

"That so?" Sabine thought they didn't want the guests to communicate with the outside world.

"What if I don't feel like talking to people?" Sabine asked.

"You're more of an introvert than I thought."

Garvey stepped closer. "Tell me how I can help you get un-bored."

"How about a tour of the opulence?" This was her opportunity to make a positive move toward connecting The Mechanic to Dad's death. This was the last mile she had been reminding herself about.

Somewhere in this sprawling structure, The Mechanic had a private collection of stolen items. Old Man Leung had told Mom that The Mechanic kept Dad's gold pocket watch—that was missing from Dad or the car he had died in—and had boasted about it to his inner circle of partners in crime.

Finding that pocket watch would connect The Mechanic to Dad's murder. If The Mechanic had anything to do with Dad's death, then it would prove that he'd lied to the police all those years ago.

"A tour of what opulence?" Garvey looked amused.

"What's in this giant mansion? Is there a ballroom as ornate as this space here? Or is there a super-sized garage with classic cars? Or something. You tell me." She was fishing and prayed that Garvey didn't notice.

"Hmmm. Let me think." He paused for a moment. "I know you love books. My uncle has a collection of very old books."

"Oh? Medieval?" *We're getting somewhere.*

Garvey nodded. "Quite a few rare books he's purchased at auctions all over Europe."

"How many?"

"Hundreds, I think."

"In a library?" Sabine feigned curiosity.

"Yes, a library." He leaned toward her ear, whispering, "Tell you a secret. He used to call it The

Library of Old Things, or The LOOT. However, over the years, he's added other non-book collections to the place, making it more of a museum than a library."

"What does he call it now?"

"The Museum of Old Things. The MOOT, for short."

"Oh? Interesting. I must see them. Please show me." Sabine tried to sound excited.

She had sneaked into The MOOT by herself the night before—with Helen monitoring her movements via her smartwatch. However, she had been over-whelmed at the first pass and thought she missed something in the building.

You know, like Dad's pocket watch.

A sly smile on Garvey's face made Sabine pause.

"If you promise to date me, I will," he said.

Sabine's heart dropped. "I'm still married."

"Not for long. Your husband isn't coming back."

Sabine almost said, "You don't know that."

"He's still in Dubai, isn't he?"

It seemed that Garvey's information was old, but Sabine wasn't about to let him know. "You investigated me."

"We did a background check on all the participants of the shooting competition." Garvey leaned toward her. "You should've known that."

"So you let me participate anyway."

"I was the only reason you could compete." Garvey grinned.

"Oh? And here I thought it was because I could hit the target with the flintlock."

"That too, but more than that, I thought we could rekindle something now that you're getting a divorce."

In your dreams.

Sabine held her words back, hoping to gain some trust with her ex. It had come as a shock to her two weeks prior when Helen told her that Garvey turned out to be The Mechanic's nephew. To think that the suspected murderer was the uncle of the man Sabine had dated seven years ago.

They had attended the same high school, and Dad had even given him a ride home from the football field a few times. They had lost touch after Dad passed away, but reconnected in their twenties in Savannah.

Now, he had looked for her because he'd found out that she and Ming were estranged. That was a sore point for her, and Sabine worried that her emotions might affect her decisions.

No, not that she might go back to Garvey. Not in a million years.

Once bitten, twice shy.

Garvey had abandoned her seven years ago when she was at the lowest point in her life when she was in the hospital recovering from burns on her legs and arms that destroyed her modeling career.

It had taken her three years to return to society. And then she'd fallen in love with Ming, an associate of her sister's and also a casual friend.

Fast forward four years and then some, she found herself at the crossroads of her love life. If she and Ming ended up divorced, she'd have to raise her kids alone. She had the financial independence to do so, but oh, her heart hurt something fierce.

After this weekend was over, she'd return to her day job as a real estate agent. As much as she enjoyed working with her sister, these few days had been hard for her as she thought of Dad a lot.

I miss him so badly.

That had been the main reason she'd sold her shares of Hu Knows to her sister. She didn't want to be reminded of Dad. Her modeling career had been a stop-gap, but then she veered into the real estate business just to do something different than her family members.

However, she also recalled her conversation with Ming some time ago. Ming had said that she might heal if she embraced the memory of her father by carrying on his legacy as a private investigator, whether at Hu Knows or elsewhere. By the time Ming's words of wisdom came, it had been too late because she'd already left the family business.

Now she had another set of memories to deal with. She might sell their wedding house on Tybee Island because she couldn't imagine living in the house without Ming.

Yes, Ming would have to answer to God for his choices. So much for their wedding vows four years ago.

But...

They were not that far gone yet, were they? God could do the impossible. Psalm 147:3 reminded Sabine that God could heal their marriage.

> *He heals the brokenhearted*
> *And binds up their wounds.*

A tear rolled down Sabine's cheek. Garvey almost reached up to wipe it away, when Sabine saw his hand approach her face and stepped back. She wiped the tear herself with the back of her palm.

She cleared her throat. "Do you need to ask someone permission to show me the rare books?"

"I offered a deal. You date me. I show you The Museum of Old Things."

"What do you mean by 'date,' Garvey? Going out to eat?"

"And movies."

They have food and movies in prison too.

"Show me The MOOT and we'll go." Sabine felt bad that she hadn't made it specific. "We'll go" meant nothing. Go where? As far as she was concerned, if Garvey had anything to do with Dad's death, he would be going to jail, just like his uncle.

The thing was, she had already been to The MOOT the night before. If Garvey was fishing, Sabine couldn't possibly let him know where she'd been, hence the pretense that she wanted to see The MOOT.

Sabine nodded. "Since we're going home tomorrow, I'd rather see the books now than have dinner."

"Or we could have a late candlelit dinner—just the two of us."

"I haven't had dinner by candlelight in a long time." It was true. Sabine didn't just say it to elicit an emotional response from Garvey.

"It's a date then. I'll go ask if we can do a book tour and get a separate dining room set up for our dinner." Garvey gently squeezed Sabine's arm. "Stay put. Don't go anywhere. I'll be right back."

"If you had your phone, you could have called instead of going in person."

Garvey shook his head. "Can't. This dining area is a dead zone. None of our cell phones work here."

"Oh." *Good to know.*

Sabine forgot to ask him who he would have to talk to, but she could ask him when he returned.

Now Sabine felt hungry. The banquet was starting kind of late. *What time is it?*

She lifted her wrist and then remembered she wasn't wearing her smartwatch. It was still in the purse.

The server returned with a bottle on a tray.

"Ma'am, your sparkling water in a bottle is here." His voice was still unclear. Sabine wondered if he might be Ming wearing a full-head silicone mask, but there was no way to ask without arousing suspicion.

"Do you want me to pour a glass for you?"

"No. I'll drink it from the bottle." Sabine tried to open the bottle, but the aluminum lid was on too tight. "Please can you open it for me?"

"Sure. I need to put my tray down."

"I'll hold it for you." And so she did. On the tray was a folded cloth napkin.

"You know, it's always good to be able to tell the time." The server covered the top of the bottle with the napkin and opened it easily.

"What?" Sabine wasn't sure why the server said that to her. What was he trying to tell her?

"Just a random sentence. It's good to watch the time more carefully." He handed the bottle to Sabine. "Here you go."

Tell the time.

Watch the time.

"Thank you, I guess." Sabine nodded a little, but

didn't look at him. Didn't want to be reminded that his eyes looked like Ming's. The rest of his face was hidden behind two masks: an ugly silicone mask and a cloth mask. There was no way the cameras above would be able to identify Ming at all.

As Sabine handed the tray back to the server, she noticed that he wore a band on his left ring finger. It was platinum and all scratched up.

It looked exactly the same as Ming's wedding band...

Sabine's head snapped up. Her eyes widened.

How many ugly silicone masks does he have?

The server must have noticed something. His eyes met hers as he flexed his ring finger in front of her.

"I never take it off." He smiled. "Didn't you see it last night?"

Sabine hadn't noticed at all. Well, she could say that it was dark in the woods even under the moonlight. However, she also hadn't seen the ring when they were both inside her villa with the ceiling lights on.

Perhaps she was still mad at her husband. Perhaps she was losing interest in him.

Either way, she wanted to cry.

CHAPTER 5

Ming could have stayed another minute and made sure that Sabine actually put the smartwatch on, but he hadn't. He just assumed she'd do it because they had a discussion.

Now he might not be able to listen in as Sabine and Garvey disappeared into The MOOT.

It made Ming worry, but he couldn't find the right words to pray. He walked into the kitchen with his tray and headed toward the back where the commercial dishwasher was. Undercover Helen Hu was washing dishes in a large sink.

Ming put on an apron, picked up a spatula, and made his way toward her. Standing shoulder to shoulder with her, he spoke to her. "Let me see your tablet."

It was risky for him to ask for the tablet that controlled the small drone that would follow Sabine into The MOOT.

"No." Helen ran water over a frying pan. Splashed water everywhere. Clearly, doing dishes wasn't her thing.

"Please, Luna?" Ming called her by her undercover name.

"No, Kibo." She handed the frying pan to Ming to wipe dry. Then she washed a stainless steel water jug.

"Clearly we're in a lopsided business deal. You know everything, but I know nothing."

Helen shrugged. "Feel free to quit."

Ming knew he couldn't. Seeing his wife three times in the span of half an hour made him happy.

However, as he had expected, he'd found Sabine standing by a pillar to one side of the foyer, not initiating conversations with anyone.

Ming was a bit surprised that Sabine had worn makeup at all. Usually, she disliked spending time putting foundation on her cheeks and eyeshadows on her eyelids. He didn't mind because he liked her bare face. Besides, they didn't go out much. Sabine hated parties, hated dressing up to mingle with strangers.

And there she was tonight.

Driven there, for sure.

Ming was upset that Sabine had taken her mother's place in the shooting competition—even though he knew that Sabine was a markswoman. It was no surprise that she'd won first place, but of course, Ming didn't know who else she had to compete with. Clearly, they had all been worse than she was.

Ming chuckled and corrected himself. If he had said that in front of Sabine, it would sound like he was insulting her skills. However, in the four years they'd been married, they had only returned to the gun range a couple of times.

Sabine's real estate business had taken off, and she had been the top sales agent of the year at her brokerage for four years in a row. How could she have time to do other things besides that and being a mom?

Stepping back from the sink, Ming checked the tracking app on his smartwatch that Helen had given him. It showed that Sabine was still inside The MOOT.

Probably.

Ming busied himself with a tray of drinks for the guests. When he went out, the foyer had emptied. People filled the dining room and took their seats.

Ming's watch showed that Sabine hadn't moved from The MOOT.

No, that's incorrect.

The app only showed that Sabine's watch was in The MOOT, not necessarily Sabine herself.

Just in case Ming was wrong, he checked the dining room, scanning faces to see if he could see Sabine or Garvey. He didn't see either one of them.

He went back to the foyer. Trying not to raise suspicions, he walked down the hallway, still carrying a tray of drinks. The MOOT entrance was toward the end of the hallway.

"Where are you going?" A security guard stopped him.

"Do you know where the men's room is?"

"Carrying that tray?" The guard pointed.

"I was in the foyer when I had to go. Something I ate. Please help." He tried to look desperate.

"You can go back to the kitchen. There's a bathroom there you can use."

"Okay. Bye." Ming turned around and went back to the kitchen area. As soon as he put his tray down, he went to look for Helen.

Helen was hunkered down near the high-capacity commercial dishwasher, staring at her tablet.

"Something I can help with?" Ming asked quietly.

Helen shook her head.

"Is she still in The MOOT?" Ming asked.

Before Helen could answer, Ming's watch vibrated. Ming checked the screen and found that Sabine—or her watch—had moved out of The MOOT, but not back into the building. The watch was located outdoors in the parking lot.

Oh no.

It was cold in December, and all Sabine had on was that cheongsam.

Helen looked up. "They've taken her—or at least, her watch—on the road away from the resort."

"What?" His heart dropped to the floor.

And Ming sprinted through the kitchen, ran down the hallway, and burst out of the back door into the cold January night, a frost blast of cold wind jarring him to his senses.

I should never have left Sabine alone.

CHAPTER 6

Garvey escorted Sabine to an inner chamber at The MOOT that she had never seen before. The rectangular room was filled with clocks and watches, timepieces old and new. Grandfather and grandmother clocks that had stopped. Cuckoo clocks that didn't work.

Silence filled the room.

"Why are we here?" Sabine asked.

Garvey smiled. "Isn't this why you're here in the first place?"

"What do you mean?"

Instead of Garvey answering, someone else did. An older male voice coming around the corner.

"You took your mother's place in the shooting competition because you need to find closure for your father's death." He tapped the floor with his cane as he walked toward Sabine and Garvey, surrounded by three large men. His bodyguards, perhaps.

Was the small elderly man Gene Gilroy?

Sabine had never met him in person because Dad would take his vehicles to Gene himself. However, Mom had shown her faded photos of when Dad and Gene went fishing together, back when Garvey and Sabine were still in high school.

Garvey helped the elderly man to a pair of armchairs that flanked an ornate table with a Tiffany lamp on it. Slowly, Gene sat down.

Based on her memory that Gene was seventeen years older than Dad, Sabine calculated that Gene was eighty-nine, but he moved like he was much older and more frail. Perhaps he had a medical condition that wasn't obvious.

"Since the stroke, my uncle has been using a cane," Garvey explained.

"I see," Sabine said softly.

"He worries about me too much." Gene brushed him off. "He should worry about himself, being the only one left to continue the Gilroy line."

Didn't Gene have kids of his own? Sabine recalled he might have one or two. She dared not ask how his own kids were doing.

"Sit." Gene pointed to the other armchair.

Sabine sat down as Garvey leaned against the edge of the table near Gene.

"I know you're Edgar's daughter," Gene said.

They had never met prior to this, but Sabine had heard of him from Dad, who had driven old cars that required frequent maintenance.

"And yet you let me come here to your resort," Sabine replied.

Gene nodded. "Which proves my point. If you— or your entire family—were my enemy, why would I allow you into my lair? Wouldn't that be like letting a Trojan horse into my castle?"

Sabine was processing what he said when he continued.

"Surprised me that you won first place. Edgar never taught you how to use the flintlock, did he?"

"No. I learned it for your competition." It was time to be truthful. Perhaps by being truthful, Sabine could cut through the lies.

"You put a lot of effort into it."

"You watched the competitors practice?" Sabine's eyebrows rose.

"Of course. I also know that your mom was supposed to be participating instead of you."

Garvey folded his arms. "I'm glad Sabine's here instead of her mom. I never liked—"

"Hush." Gene made a face. To Sabine, he said, "I'm not your enemy."

Sabine said nothing.

"I'm not The Mechanic," Gene added. "I might have been a mechanic in my previous job, but I'm not The Mechanic you're looking for."

Helen's research, coupled with Leland's at Binary Systems, had all pointed to Gene Gilroy as The Mechanic. But here he was, the man himself, denying it. For now, Sabine would go with the flow and call him by his real first name, Gene.

"You don't believe me." Gene shifted in his seat.

"Uh..." Sabine had nothing to say. She could try to tug at Gene's heart by begging for his mercy to let her hold the pocket watch. But if he was the murderer, then her efforts would lead nowhere.

"You put so much effort to get close to me." Gene

fished something out of his pocket. "You're looking for this?"

It was Dad's pocket watch.

Something caught in Sabine's throat. She stared at the pocket watch. Her hands instinctively reached for it, but Gene held it back.

"Please let me hold it." Sabine pleaded. "It's my only connection left with Dad."

Not really, but Sabine wanted to appeal to Gene's compassion—if he had any. Truth be told, Dad had been a Christian on earth, so he was now in heaven with Jesus. Any personal effects he had left behind would serve to remind Sabine to thank God for Dad's salvation.

Of course, the things helped the family with their grieving process, and later on, with their memories of Dad. However, they were just that: things.

Now Gene dangled the pocket watch in front of Sabine's face.

Words aside, Gene clearly had custody of Dad's pocket watch, the very one he'd taken with him on that tragic day on Interstate 95. There was something special about this pocket watch because it not only told the time, but it also told a tale.

What tale might it tell? That would depend on what Dad had recorded on it.

A puzzle enthusiast, Dad had bought the pocket watch from an old curiosity shop in Italy, back in the days when Dad and Mom had roamed Europe, two newlyweds with no kids, looking for adventures. Both of them had been collectors of small things, with Mom most interested in bejeweled eggs, including a lesser known version of Fabergé eggs that she sometimes let Sabine and Helen roll around on the living room carpet when they were kids. Petros eggs, Mom had called them.

Back to Dad, he'd been more interested in watches and timepieces. Save for the pocket watch, all of them had been stored away in a bank vault after Dad passed away, and they had thoroughly examined them for clues.

The last piece of the puzzle was the pocket watch.

"I only want to hold it, and then I'll return it to you," Sabine said. She didn't want to beg or plead, but the pocket watch brought back a lot of memories.

In fact, shortly after Dad had bought it, he'd shown it to Sabine. She didn't remember most of what he'd said, since she wasn't entirely paying attention, but if she held it, it might trigger information from the deep recesses of her memory.

"No no." Gene put the pocket watch back into his pocket. "I will return this to your mother, who should've married me instead of Edgar in the first place."

What?

To begin with, Sabine was sure that her parents had been each other's first love. Gene's love had to be unrequited at best.

Wait a second.

Sabine mentally backed up. She couldn't believe that Gene had feelings for Mom. Sabine couldn't imagine it because many people disliked Mom and found it hard to get along with her. The only four people—three now since Dad was gone—who could understand Mom and put up with her eccentricities

were Helen, Sabine, and Ming. Ming had great inter-
personal skills, so that was not a surprise.

Gene talked about Mom choosing Dad over him.
That meant they had to have known one another a
long time ago before Mom and Dad married. Some
thirty-five or more years ago now? Sabine didn't have
time to do the math in front of Gene.

She glanced at Garvey. She was mad at him now
for leading her here. Then again, she herself had
wanted to enter The MOOT a second time.

Perhaps they had restored the security cameras in
The MOOT. Highly unlikely. As far as Sabine was
concerned, when Leland said she took down the
camera, it meant precisely that. The cameras would
not rise again.

Therefore, it was most likely that Garvey and
Gene both thought that this was Sabine's first time in
The MOOT.

She could have used her smart glasses about now.
Unfortunately, they were with Camden, who was
only doing his job as an FBI special agent.

She had no spikes, no handguns, no smart
glasses...

Oh, but she still had her hair sticks. However,
there were too many people in the room for her to
deploy them. She hadn't actually practiced with them
on real people. This afternoon, Helen had shown her
how to pull apart a hair stick to reveal a long and thin
tranquilizer dart. It contained a synthetic compound
that could take down a three-hundred-pound man in
three seconds. She had two vials. But she had to do it
at close contact.

She was five feet away from both Gene and Garvey.

"All right." Gene returned to his nephew to see if the latter had anything to say.

Garvey shook his head.

Gene motioned to his men who closed in on Sabine. Sabine's chest tightened. This was the type of stress that she didn't need.

"Your father feared fire," Gene said. "You fear water."

Huh?

Sabine was trying to process what the man just said when she felt a thwacking blow to the back of her head.

CHAPTER 7

Thump. *Thump. Thump.*

Sabine woke up to find herself hanging head down from something that kept moving. Her wrists were tied, and her arms dangled. Her waist was hung over something narrow, and a tight grip was on her upper thighs preventing her from sliding off.

Her head hurt like the pits.

Maybe she had a concussion from being hit on the head. A concussion, however mild, would most certainly give her a headache.

Her face was against something flat, and she smelled leather and cigarette smoke. She lifted her head slightly to see what was around her, but it was all darkness.

Slowly, a small light shone from somewhere, and the shadow that was cast on what looked like wooden slats on the floor told her that she was being carried by a tall man over his shoulder. Yes, she assumed he was tall because her dangling hands couldn't reach the wooden floor.

Thump. Thump. Thump.

She could tell that there was nothing below the wooden floor, so the foundation wasn't solid. Was this the pier behind the retreat center?

Darkness enveloped them again.

The smell of night was damp and earthy. Hints of pine wafted by on a cold winter's breeze. Sabine could not hear water, but she guessed that they had walked some distance on the pier and were now probably over the lake.

She tried to lift her head whenever a dim light showed again. The light moved unsteadily, which made Sabine suspect that it was a flashlight.

Camping had never been her thing, but back in high school, Dad would teach her and Helen how to survive in the North Georgia Mountains.

Just in case, he'd say.

To this day, Sabine hadn't had to use any of the outdoor survival skills that she'd learned. However, tonight's flashlight—with its light appearing and disappearing randomly, and pointing at all angles—reminded her of Dad. Once, when they were each standing on the opposite sides of a stream at a campground at night, they had used their flashlights to send Morse codes to each other.

If Dad were here, he'd know what to do.

But she was fatherless now...

No.

Psalm 68:5 reminded her that God was her Heavenly Father now.

A father of the fatherless, a defender of widows,
  Is God in His holy habitation.

Sabine began to pray.

Lord God, Heavenly Father, please show me what to do.

As she prayed, she knew she had to get to her hair sticks.

She tried to lift her hands, but her arms felt weak. Why?

She prayed that God would heal her arms quickly so that she could move her hands. Her fingers were still free, and she needed to reach for her hair sticks and unleash the Kraken tranquilizer darts.

Give me strength like Samson's to defeat this Goliath like David did.

Oddly enough, she didn't feel fear. Her old fearlessness from her teenage years hanging out with Dad —"catching criminals" as he'd like to put it—was coming back to her. She was meant for this.

No, not death.

Solving problems.

Maybe Dad's cold case was her reentry and practice round to dust off her rusty self.

Well, what a time to have an epiphany. Dangling upside down and on the way to who-knew-where.

Thump. Thump. Thump.

What was that, anyway? She'd heard it since she'd woken up. She couldn't place it.

Slowly, they entered an area where dim lights shone from above. Looking down, Sabine confirmed that they were indeed walking on a weather-worn wooden pier.

She hadn't been here before, but she had seen it from the second floor of the retreat center. The pier led to a covered dock, but she didn't recall ever seeing any boat.

The person carrying her wore boots and a large pair of jeans that covered his very large thighs and calves.

Sabine wondered if the tranquilizer dart could penetrate those thick jeans.

She had to make a decision. She didn't know where they were taking her, but Gene had hinted at it.

Your father feared fire. You fear water.

Yes, Dad's car had been set on fire with him inside. Then again, the GBI had said that had died before the vehicle fire. How could Gene not know that?

Perhaps someone had been feeding him lies in these thirteen years. Somehow Gene had gone along and believed them. That meant he had considered his source to be credible. Who might be that source?

Gene might have erroneously thought that Dad deserved to burn in the vehicle fire because he had feared fire. That thought process might have caused Gene to plan for Sabine's death by drowning.

Yes, Sabine was afraid of water because she nearly drowned as a child and never went in a pool or the ocean ever again since then. Gene might have known that on his own, or Garvey might have told him.

"How does the boss want it done?" a husky male voice asked.

"Dunno." The man carrying Sabine coughed. "I think we just drop them into the water."

Them?

Who else was captured along with her?

The lights went out again.

From the size of the man carrying Sabine, she could tell that he was overweight. She could hear him huff. Every time he spoke with the other man, he'd cough in spurts.

In the dark night, she had to act swiftly before the two abductors noticed.

She tried to lift her hands again, and this time she was able to reach her ballet bun on top of her head. She prayed that her hair sticks were still there. Yes, they were, but they were about to fall out as her hair bun felt messy. It was about to unravel.

She couldn't see what she was doing, but she also didn't want to drop the hair sticks. She closed her eyes —as if it mattered—and prayed—yes, that mattered— and put both hands on one hair stick. She couldn't take both out and use them effectively with her wrists still tied together.

She pressed one end of the hair stick and felt a dart coming out of its sheath.

As she was doing that, she heard a third pair of boots running toward them. It was faint and in the distance, but she heard the pounding on the pier.

She lifted her head and tilted her neck back as far as she could so she could look into the distance. All she saw was a shadowy figure.

Friend or foe?

The next moment felt like slow motion because she started to feel lightheaded, hanging upside down with blood pooling and putting pressure on her brain —thanks to gravity and her likely concussion.

Sabine held the safe end of the dart tightly in both hands, and with a quick move, she jabbed the needle into the tree-trunk thigh in front of her.

She pressed the needle deep into the thigh and prayed that the needle would survive the thick layer of jeans, fat, and muscles. The last thing she needed was for the needle to break or jam before doing its job.

She had only practiced it twice with an empty needle in Helen's office in Savannah, so this had better work.

Sure enough, his knees buckled, and he collapsed onto the wooden pier. Sabine dislodged from his large arms and fell away just as his head hit the floor.

"Hey hey!" The other man sounded like he was panicking. "Ernie! What's happening, man?"

A flashlight shone into Sabine's face as the man drew closer to her, his other arm raised. He pointed a gun at her face. "What did you do to him? What did you do?"

He didn't get the answer he sought because a shot rang out. He dropped to the floor and didn't move afterwards.

In the dim light, Sabine saw another person on the other side of the man who had just gotten shot. This third man was out cold, but his face was turned the other way, so Sabine couldn't tell who it was.

He wore a different kind of boots than the other two. His boots were chunky. Maybe those had made the thumping sound she had heard. It could certainly happen if he'd been dragged across the wooden pier instead of being carried like Sabine was.

"Sabine!"

It was Ming. His voice came from maybe five or six yards away, but Sabine couldn't be sure.

She tried to get up, but her legs felt weak. She felt pins and needles all over them. All she could do was sit down and wait.

Above her, the sound of helicopter blades drew near. The choppers projected powerful searchlights onto the pier.

Nursing a headache, Sabine squinted toward the sound of pounding boots. In the middle of the crowd was Camden, his weapons drawn. Maybe he had done the shooting earlier.

"Sabine!" Ming's voice drew closer.

Sabine didn't see Ming anywhere, but suddenly, he was kneeling in front of her, wrapping his arms around her.

He was asking her something, but she couldn't hear it on account of the loud helicopter. It continued to hover above their heads since there was no place for it to land on the narrow pier.

Instead of repeating his questions loudly into her ear, Ming clammed up and kissed her on the forehead. Then he tightened his arms around her, his bulky Kevlar vest sandwiched between them.

Sabine felt comfort and love.

Just like old times.

CHAPTER 8

Well, first, they had to go to the Hiawassee Hospital and then give a statement to the FBI before they could go home.

The hospital was small, but it had a helipad on top of the building. Its proximity to the mountains meant that its Emergency Room was often the first stop for injured hikers in the area. If their injuries were serious, they would be flown to the Level 1 trauma center at the Northeast Georgia Medical Center in Gainesville.

Fortunately for Sabine, her injuries were not life-threatening.

In an examination room, under Ming's watchful eyes, a nurse treated Sabine's injuries, which were mostly abrasions. She had a knot on her head where they had hit her with some blunt object. A CT scan revealed that there was no swelling or bleeding in her brain. So all she had was the concussion.

The doctor told Ming that she had to rest for one to three days before she could handle the six-hour drive home to Savannah. Or they could drive to Atlanta and fly home from there.

Outside the room, Ming sat with Camden in the waiting area.

"By the mercy of God, you found me before I got on the pier," Ming said to Camden. "You might be arresting me now."

"Knowing you, it's better for me to shoot than you, is all I can say."

Ming thanked God that they had reached Sabine in time and that they had made it off the pier alive. If Helen hadn't asked Leland to point their satellite at the compound to see if there were any outdoor movements, they would still be chasing the smartwatch all the way down to Dahlonega.

Sabine could very well be dead by now.

"With her concussion, she probably can't sit in the car for six hours," Camden said.

"I agree. So we're going to stay somewhere for a few days, then we might drive to Atlanta and fly home —or just drive home." Ming didn't want to spell out where "somewhere" was because they were in a public place.

Thanks to Helen's connections, a cabin at the Still Waters Community was available for Ming and Sabine to stay off the grid for a few days. Helen had sent her two kids and the family dog, plus Mama Hu, to a safe house outside Savannah—just in case.

All Ming had to do was drive his wife forty-five minutes from Hiawassee to a piece of private land outside Dahlonega. After a few days, they'd have to go to Savannah to get their kids and go home to their house on Tybee Island.

Ming had thought about all the possible options of getting from here to Savannah. On the one hand, he felt that if he drove Sabine, they'd have more one-on-one time on the six-hour road trip. On the other hand, if they flew from Atlanta to Savannah, it would only be an hour-long flight.

Yeah, they'd have to drive a little more than one hour south from Still Waters to Hartsfield-Jackson Atlanta International Airport because neither Hiawassee nor Dahlonega—an hour away—had a commercial airport.

Ming decided that he'd discuss it with Sabine in a day or so, after she felt better. He prayed that her concussion was mild enough that she'd bounce right back. That the three days at Still Waters would be enough. That as soon as she felt better or stopped having headaches, that they could have a family meeting to deal with their marriage and figure out a way to stay together.

He didn't want them to give up on each other, but he also didn't want them to simply put up with each other. They had loved each other so much, so could they repair the rift?

He wanted to take Sabine home as soon as possible. And he wanted to stay home with her and the kids. He had no idea what had overcome him to accept the project in Dubai. So far away from the love of his life and his kids. What was he thinking!

From now on, Ming didn't want to be more than a few days away from home. If at all possible, he wanted to work in town in Savannah or nearby. That way, he could see his family for dinner every night. If he could help put his kids to bed, that would give Sabine more time to herself. She liked to read, but lately, she hadn't had much time to read more than children's books.

Sharing some of the parental chores was something that Ming had shirked lately. His company was in debt, so he'd been overwhelmed.

Camden's phone rang. "I have to take this call. I'll see you at your cabin in the morning. We need to get some statements from both of you."

Ming watched his friend go, and then came Helen, walking toward him, holding a phone to her ear.

She hung up before she reached Ming. She didn't have her five-inch boots on today, so the top of her head only came up to his shoulders. However, she was the big sister and called all the shots at Hu Knows, Inc.

Just then, Sabine came out of the examination room. Ming immediately offered a hand to steady her. Sabine smiled a little.

"If Ming hadn't run fast enough, we'd be fishing you out of the lake," Helen said.

Sabine's eyes went to Ming.

Ming pointed at Helen. "If you hadn't called Leland, we'd also be fishing her out of the lake."

"And if Camden hadn't shown up, you'd have ended up shooting the guy, and they could have arrested you." Sabine's voice cracked.

She sounded like she cared for Ming.

Ming's heart warmed. "You still love me, don't you?"

She didn't reply.

Ming rubbed the back of her hand. "At the end of the day, God saved us."

"So that you can work on your marriage," Helen quipped.

When did Helen have such a sharp tongue? More and more, she was behaving like Mama Hu, the witty one. She could slice and dice people with just her words.

"How's your headache?" Ming asked Sabine.

"Better. I need to rest."

"The cabin's ready." Helen handed Ming a key fob. "Don't scratch my rental SUV."

Ming pocketed it. "Where is it parked?"

"I'll text you the location. I took a photo of the lamp post." Helen sent the photo.

"Hmmm. Okay. How are you going to get around?"

"I'm working with Cam on The MOOT, and his people are driving me around and even feeding me." Helen smiled. "Don't worry about me."

"What about my stuff in the villa?" Sabine asked. "I need my toothbrush and change of clothes."

"Already packed in the SUV," Helen said.

"Thank you." Sabine gave Helen a hug.

"What are sisters for?" Helen asked.

"What about my stuff?" Ming asked.

"One of Cam's men packed it all for you. Your duffel bag is also in the SUV."

"You rock, Helen."

Helen smiled. "My sister's the brave one. She married you."

Ming wasn't sure if he should be angry or

amused. He glanced at Sabine to see how she reacted. Sabine didn't say anything.

"All right. Let's get out of here." Helen changed the subject. "I've already given them my insurance information."

"Is Hu Knows paying for my hospital visit?" Sabine asked.

"And your cabin for a few days. After all, whenever you do any work for Mom, it becomes a Hu Knows operation."

"Oh? That's nice of you, Sis."

Ming watched the two sisters talk, wondering why they hadn't sorted out an agreement before this. He recalled that Sabine had often done work for Helen without charging any fee. In many ways, Sabine was an occasional volunteer when it came to the company that her father had started many years ago.

"Maybe I'm trying to entice you to buy back your shares of Hu Knows and help me run the company. Do it in memory of Dad, if not for anything else. After all, he meant to pass on the company to both of us, not just to me. You and I had the majority shares before you sold yours to me."

Sabine didn't say anything.

"Fine. If you want to be my silent partner, that's okay too." Helen chuckled.

"Are you forgetting something?" Ming asked.

"What?" the two sisters said in unison.

"My wife just had a traumatic experience, and she has a concussion. We need to get out of here so that I can take her to get some rest."

"Speaking of which, is Garvey okay?" Sabine asked.

Ming frowned. He had just called her "my wife" to remind her that he still cared, and here was Sabine mentioning another man's name. He didn't like her asking about other men, especially her ex-boyfriend from way back when.

As if sensing his jealousy, Sabine reached for his hand and held it.

"He's down the hallway somewhere," Helen said.

"Something doesn't add up," Sabine said. "Garvey was given freedom to invite me to The MOOT, but then they knocked both of us out and dragged us down the pier. How could his uncle be so cruel?"

"Maybe that was the intention." Ming's voice was stoic. "Your emotions make you feel sorry for Garvey."

Sabine didn't reply. She also didn't let go of Ming's hand.

"I'll find out more and let you know." Helen swiped her phone.

"How about you come with us to the exit?" Ming asked Helen. "You can wait with Sabine while I go get the SUV. After I pick her up, you can go your merry way."

"Normally, I don't like people talking to me like that," Helen said. "But since you're my brother-in-law, I'll make an exception."

"I'm sorry. I wasn't..." Ming cleared his throat. He realized that Helen didn't like his tone of voice. He wondered if Sabine felt the same way sometimes when he ordered her around. "Helen, could you do us a favor? Would you be willing to come with us to the exit and wait with Sabine while I get the car? I don't want her to be alone."

"No need to rephrase," Helen said. "I got it."

"Thank you."

"Before we split up, how about we pray?" Helen asked. "Let's thank God for saving us and pray that He will heal Sabine's concussion."

They closed their eyes, but nobody prayed, so Ming did. "Father God, thank You for rescuing Sabine tonight and bringing us safely here. Thank You that her concussion is mild. I pray for a quick recovery. In the name of Jesus, I pray. Amen."

Sabine echoed with her own "amen."

She looked up, first at her husband and then at her sister. "It doesn't make sense. It seemed to me that Gene thought that Garvey killed Dad by setting his car on fire. However, you'd think that if that were so, the SPD would've arrested and tried him for murder, you know, thirteen years ago."

"Maybe in Gene's mind, Garvey got away," Ming suggested.

"Because they were smarter than the SPD detectives and GBI forensic pathologists?" Helen asked.

"No, maybe because they know someone inside the SPD," Sabine said quietly. "That person might have been feeding lies to the Gilroys."

"And he'd do that because..." Ming raised an eyebrow.

Sabine had no answer.

"I think that until Cam arrests Gene Gilroy for the attempted murder, Sabine is still in danger." Helen's words were grave. "I could hire a bodyguard."

"I'll protect Sabine," Ming said immediately.

"I can pay you." Helen looked serious. "Even though we're investigating Dad's murder, technically Sabine was working with Mom. Mom is still on the Hu Knows payroll."

"No need, Helen. This is what I should do as her husband." Ming could use a good paycheck, but he didn't want Sabine to think that he only protected her for money. He wanted her to know that he genuinely loved her.

He turned toward his wife. "Are you okay? Still have a headache?"

"A little, but I'll be all right." Sabine looked exhausted.

"We'll pick up Tylenol at the pharmacy on the way out to the cabin," Ming said.

"It will need to be a twenty-four-hour pharmacy since it's so late at night," Helen suggested. "Or a gas station. When you get there, fill up the gas tank. Save the receipt to get reimbursed."

"Will do." Ming rubbed Sabine's arm. "Shall I carry you so you don't have to walk? Save your energy?"

"What?" There was merriment in Sabine's eyes. "You mean you don't want to look weaker than Mr. Big Jeans on the pier?"

"Say that again." Ming's eyes widened. He wrinkled his nose at her and pretended to snarl.

Sabine laughed.

Whether he looked funny or downright stupid, it didn't matter because his reaction had made Sabine laugh.

Music to my ears. My wife is laughing again.

He smiled back and laughed with her.

CHAPTER 9

On the middle-of-the-night drive to their cabin in the Still Waters Community, Sabine received a text from Helen to tell her that Gene Gilroy had been arrested outside of his retreat in Hiawassee. It was as though he hadn't put in any effort to escape.

"Can you believe that?" Sabine asked after she had read the text aloud to Ming at the wheel.

A second text arrived from Helen. Sabine read it aloud as well.

"Garvey snitched on his uncle?" Ming chuckled.

"Maybe it's because his uncle had him dragged out to the pier."

"Why though?"

"That's the million-dollar question."

"How are you doing?" Ming asked.

"I'll feel much better when I can lie down."

"Fifteen more minutes." Ming drove as smoothly as he could on the country road. There were no street lamps to guide them forward, but only the SUV headlights.

"Just keep the speed limit, okay? I'm fine. Don't worry."

Ming nodded. "At the next red light, I'll text the resident RN to let her know we're arriving."

"What for?"

"So she can drop in and check you."

"Why?"

"Your concussion."

"Truly, I'm fine. I have a little headache, but that's all. I'm still functional."

While Ming debated with himself on whether to disagree with Sabine, she kept talking.

"I just need to get to a bed and go to sleep. I'll see the RN after I wake up, okay?"

Ming sighed. "Okay. I'm sorry."

"About what?"

"Everything. I shouldn't have gone to Dubai when you raised all those concerns three months ago. If I had just stayed at home, we wouldn't be separated, and you wouldn't have called a divorce lawyer."

"Let's talk later. How about we have some peace and quiet right now? The doctor said I shouldn't be discussing anything heavy because I need to mentally rest."

"Okay." Ming drove silently the rest of the way.

Having known her for years, Ming had never seen her this exhausted.

Tyrone Hall met them at the gate of Still Waters and drove his pickup truck ahead of them so that Ming could follow.

The night was dark, and stars were out. The clear

night sky was brilliant, and Ming wished that he had his telescope. Unlike Savannah or Atlanta, the countryside had no city lights for miles and miles.

The small cabin was near a pond. That made Ming worry that the sight of the pond might trigger something in Sabine. It was too late to request a cabin change, but he decided to wait and see. If Sabine reacted to the pond being within visual range of the cabin's porch, then he'd ask Tyrone to move them.

Sabine said nothing as Ming led her into the cabin in the nippy cold. As soon as Ming opened the door, he could feel the warmth inside. Tyrone had turned on the heater for them.

The sitting area had a sofa and two armchairs. No television. Across a small hallway—if it could even be called a hallway—a small dining table separated the living room from a galley kitchen.

"Would you like to sit down here while I bring in our bags?" Ming pointed to the sofa facing a fireplace.

"No, I want to lie down in bed. Where's my bedroom?"

My bedroom.

Ming's heart sank. "Wait here. Let me see where the bedrooms are."

Sabine sat down on the sofa.

Ming dashed here and there but only found one bedroom.

Helen, what did you do?

He nearly smiled. He opened another door, but it led to an enclosed porch with a sauna. He returned to the living room.

"There's only one bedroom," he declared solemnly.

Sabine shook her head. "Helen."

"I should've thought to remind her before she made the arrangement," Ming said. "I'll sleep on the sofa."

Sabine pointed to the sofa she was sitting on, the only one in the room. "This one? It's too short for you. If you get deep vein thrombosis, you're going to sue me."

"I won't."

Sabine got up slowly. "Lead the way."

Moments later, they were standing in the only bedroom of the cabin. There was a king-sized bed in the middle of the room with a rustic headboard and a pretty double-ring quilt. There were extra blankets on a nearby armchair.

"I could use those blankets in the living room." Ming still thought that he should sleep on the sofa until they ironed out their disputes.

"Did you forget something?" Sabine asked.

"What?"

"We're married."

Ming lifted his left hand to show her his wedding band on his ring finger. "Haven't forgotten."

"But you did forget something." Sabine sat down on the bed.

"Tell me."

"Ephesians 4:25-27." Sabine recited the verses, in which Paul quoted reminders.

Therefore, putting away lying, "Let each one of you speak truth with his neighbor," for we are members of one another. "Be angry, and do not sin": do not

*let the sun go down on your wrath, nor give place
to the devil.*

"That is to say, in a marriage, we shouldn't let the
sun go down on our anger with each other," Sabine
said. "However, you and I have let it fester unresolved
for three months."

Ming nodded. "I'm sorry. The fact that you had to
call a divorce lawyer meant that I have failed as a
husband."

"Well, she's one of my former clients—I sold her
house on Tybee—and we were having lunch while
you were gone when the topic of marriage came up."

"Oh, I see. I was worried that it was a deliberate
action."

"Plan A was to get us both to Diego or his father
for marital counseling and conflict resolution."

"Let's do it." Ming had no problem with his
friend, Pastor Diego Flores, or his father, a semi-
retired pastor who was now the part-time counselor at
Riverside Chapel where they all attended church.

"The other day, you asked me to forgive you,"
Sabine said. "I told you that if God has forgiven you,
who am I to withhold forgiveness from you?"

Ming's heart was touched that she still remembered their conversation at the villa.

"I can forgive you and never cross paths with you
again," Sabine said. "That's an option, you know?"

Ming feared that she had considered that.

"You and I know that forgiveness is not synony-
mous with reconciliation," Sabine reminded him.

"Yes. You might forgive your dad's murderer—
whom we suspect was a family friend—but you might

not be friends with him any longer. Forgiveness, yes. Reconciliation, no."

"Right." Sabine smiled. "Fortunately for you and me, that's not the case. If you were unfaithful to me, then I might still forgive you, but we would never be reconciled. I'd take the kids, and you would probably die a lonely man."

"I never cheated on you."

"I know. Otherwise, we wouldn't be having this conversation right now."

She knew.

Ming wondered what else Sabine hadn't been saying.

"Our villa conversation alluded to Ephesians 4:32 that tells us to be kind to each other," Sabine said.

"Your memory is pretty good, considering your concussion and all." Ming wanted to remind Sabine that she wasn't supposed to do mental calisthenics, but talking about the Bible was natural to both of them and wasn't mentally taxing at all.

"It was only yesterday morning, Ming."

"Oh?" All the days and nights were running together for him.

"I would include two more verses, the ones before verse 32." Sabine didn't say what they were.

Ming tapped his smartwatch. "Open Bible. Read Ephesians 4:30-32."

And do not grieve the Holy Spirit of God, by whom you were sealed for the day of redemption. Let all bitterness, wrath, anger, clamor, and evil speaking be put away from you, with all malice. And be kind to one another, tenderhearted,

*forgiving one another, even as God in Christ
forgave you.*

"I'm sorry that I haven't been kind to you." Ming
sat down beside Sabine on the bed. "From now on,
with God's help, I will do my best to be the husband
that God wants me to be for you."

"I know what you did, and I forgive you, Ming,"
Sabine said. "From now on, with God's help, I will do
my best to be the wife that God wants me to be for
you."

Wait a minute. She said, "I know what you did."

Was Sabine saying that she had investigated him?
Why wouldn't she, being an erstwhile private investigator and all? If she hadn't, her sister surely had.
Helen wasn't going to let Ming get away with making
her sister unhappy.

It was clear to Ming that Sabine had concluded
that he hadn't committed a sin she couldn't let go.

"I want to repeat myself," Ming said. "It never
occurred to me to cheat on you—ever."

"I know. Your weakness is the love of money."
Sabine pointed to Ming's smartwatch.

Ming understood. "Open Bible. Find the verse
that talks about the love of money being the root of
evil."

Ming's smartwatch read 1 Timothy 6:10.

*For the love of money is a root of all kinds of evil,
for which some have strayed from the faith in their
greediness, and pierced themselves through with
many sorrows.*

"Many sorrows indeed." Ming bowed his head. "I'm perpetually short of money. That's my problem."

"Our problem." Sabine put her hand on his thigh. "We're married. We're a team. We sink or swim together."

Ming nodded.

"While you were gone, a friend told me about a financial course by Dave Ramsey. There are seven baby steps, with guides to pay off our debts. If we do this right, we will be debt free, with no house or car payments, and have money to pay for our kids to go to college."

"Sounds like a plan."

"I think we could do it together, if you want. We can take the online course as a couple in the privacy of our own home."

"Let's do it." Ming squeezed Sabine's hand. "I've decided that I'd rather earn less money and hang out with you and the kids than to earn more elsewhere without you."

Sabine nodded. "Therefore, in light of all that, why did you say you wanted to sleep on the sofa tonight? You've left me alone for three months. Isn't that enough? Besides, who's going to warm the bed for me? It's winter, remember?"

Ming couldn't stop smiling. "I love you, Sabine."

CHAPTER 10

For the next three mornings, Ming and Sabine made breakfast together and studied the Bible as a couple in the cabin. It was cold and quiet, and they spent most of their time indoors in front of the fireplace.

Sabine's headache dissipated, and she wasn't affected by the sight of the pond in front of the cabin, but she also refused to step on the small dock where some of the Still Waters residents set up their fishing poles.

For lunch and dinner, they ate with the residents at the community center. Off the grid, there was not a single cell phone in sight. They got to know the residents and vice versa.

When she found out that many of the people who lived in Still Waters were Christians and attended the little log cabin chapel they had built onsite, Sabine felt emboldened to wear her cross outside her blouse.

She had hidden it a lot because she didn't want to lose the precious gift from Dad.

Remember the cross.

Dad's words made Sabine reach up to put her palm over the cross dangling outside her turtleneck as she walked back to the cabin after lunch on their third day at Still Waters.

Ming held her hand and watched her.

"What?" Sabine asked.

"Nothing. I just like looking at you." Ming squeezed her hand. "I've enjoyed our mini retreat—even though the weather is cold—and we need to do more of this sort of getaway."

"Not only getaways, but since we've become parents, we've had very few date nights in town."

Ming nodded. "I know."

"Most of the time, we took the kids with us when we went out," Sabine reminded him. "Occasionally, Mom watched Hannah, but that was when Zachary was an infant, and I was too tired to chase after Hannah."

"And I wasn't around enough."

"So what do you think we should do about it, Husband?" Sabine had some ideas and suggestions, but she didn't want to do all the thinking.

"Hmm. Maybe we should have a date night every week, Wife." Ming put his arm over Sabine's shoulders. "How does Friday night sound to you?"

"I'd like that."

"I know you're wary of your mom babysitting both kids because they might be too much for her."

"Not only that, but she's not a Christian, so I often wonder what she'll teach Hannah. Don't get me started on what she wanted to teach Helen and me. By the mercy of God, Dad was saved, so he took us to church. Our daughter is like a sponge."

Ming nodded. "So let's pay a babysitter."

"I'm not sure about our current babysitter either," Sabine said. "I do need her to watch the kids when I show houses, but that's not much these days since I became a broker and spend more time dealing with contracts, trust funds, managing the brokerage, and such things."

"If I work from home, I'll watch the kids when you have a closing or somewhere you need to go." Ming meant it.

"You, working from home?"

Ming nodded. "I may have to give up my office space in downtown Savannah because I can't afford it anymore. I can work from home."

"Your home office is now Hannah's playroom."

"I can share the space with her and keep an eye on her during the day."

"If we're both away, how about I still call Mom? I trust her more than our current babysitter, even though the latter says she's a Christian."

"If your mom comes to our home and watches the kids, we could be a Christian influence to her," Ming suggested. "Your mom needs Jesus too."

"For sure. Okay. Let's see how we can work it out."

"Alternatively, we could also ask my sister," Ming suggested. "We know how much she adores the kids. She probably wouldn't mind having them at her house for a couple of hours."

Heidi had no children of her own, but she was a doting aunt to Hannah and Zachary.

"I hate to bother her because she's busy teaching in college, and her husband is busy pastoring." Sabine had a good relationship with her sister-in-law, Heidi, and her husband, Pastor Flores. Heidi, Ming, and Pastor Flores were some of the core members of Riverside Chapel.

"Or friends at church with kids Hannah's age," Ming said. "I'm sure we could work out a reciprocity plan. We could watch their kids on their date nights, and they could watch our kids on our date nights."

"Sure."

They reached their cabin and stopped at the front door. While waiting for Ming to punch the code on the keypad, Sabine realized something.

"You know, we just had a conversation without arguing," she said.

"Oh yeah, we did." Ming chuckled. "Did we start arguing once we had kids or what?"

"Now we're on a three-day retreat in the middle of nowhere, and maybe we're rebooting our relationship."

"Rebooting?" Ming opened the door. "Did you spend too much time at the community center with those IT people?"

"Ooh, a hint of jealousy, Husband?"

"Just thinking aloud, Wife." Ming drew Sabine close to him and wrapped his arms around her waist.

Sabine looked up, her lips smiling and ready for him to plant a kiss—

"Ahem!"

A woman's voice.

Startled, Sabine turned her head toward the voice. "Helen!"

Helen was sitting on the sofa, legs crossed. She was wearing a pair of long chunky boots with five-inch heels. Sometimes, Sabine wondered how she could run in those heels.

"Hello, lovebirds." Helen waved.

Sabine tried to peel Ming off, but he wouldn't let her.

"How did you get in here?" Ming asked.

"I rented this cabin. It's under my name." Helen smiled. "Actually, I didn't mean to come indoors, but you took forever to eat lunch, and I was getting cold standing outside. I didn't feel like walking all the way back to my car in these heels. Since I knew the code to the door, I decided to wait inside."

"No worries." Sabine pushed Ming away and sat down next to Helen. "What brings you here?"

"I wanted to text you, but lo and behold, this community is off the grid. I had to personally drive here to talk to you." Helen leaned back on the sofa. "Tyrone told me they might not always be off the grid, but for now, most of the residents insist on it. I think it's a matter of time before they adopt the way Mendenhall Retreat does things. That retreat is safe even while being connected to the internet."

"Mendenhall Retreat?" Sabine asked.

"Yeah. The one outside Gatlinburg, Tennessee, that also houses people who don't want to be found —except that Mendenhall mostly accepts former military and people with special clearances. Still Waters deals more with civilians who need a hideaway."

"Like us." Ming sat down on one of the armchairs across from the sofa.

"Would you like something to drink?" Sabine asked.

"Water is fine, but I'll get it myself. Just tell me where," Helen said.

"I'll get it." Ming got up and left for the kitchen.

"You look good," Helen said.

"I've slept for at least eight or nine hours each night. I was so tired."

"How's your head?"

"Actually, the bump has gone down, and I don't have a headache anymore. Thank God."

"Yes, thank God, indeed." Helen took the cup of water from Ming and thanked him.

"What updates do you have for us?" Ming sat down again.

"Gene Gilroy still denies that he's The Mechanic," Helen said. "However, he confessed to the crime and took all the blame for Dad's death—even though the police ruled him out thirteen years ago."

"So he's not The Mechanic, but he is The Murderer." Ming chuckled.

Neither one of the Hu sisters thought it was funny.

"Your intel said he is The Mechanic," Sabine said to Helen. "I read the full report myself. I'm convinced he is. Dad said he was going to meet someone at the garage. Gene owned a garage and had done work on vehicles for Hu Knows when it was under the old name."

"I'm convinced too," Helen said. "But does it matter? He's confessed."

"Maybe it's a ploy," Ming suggested. "If he says he's not The Mechanic, then they can't pin the other five or six murders on him. He might've figured that he could handle one murder and no more."

"Or he's taking the blame for somebody," Sabine said.

All eyes were on her.

"Think about it. If he was protecting someone, then he would want to be caught. He confesses to everything right away and goes to jail. The real murderer goes free."

They waited for Sabine to say more.

"After all, Gene Gilroy is eighty-nine years old. If they give him a life sentence, how long will that be? Perhaps they might put him on house arrest to live out the rest of his life. Either way, he might think that whoever he is protecting should be free."

After she finished, Helen asked, "What kind of a conjecture is that?"

"I don't know." Sabine shrugged. "It just popped into my head."

"On which side of the concussion?" Helen laughed.

"Actually, I'm feeling a lot better. Praise the Lord. No more headaches. Sorry to get y'all worked up."

Ming blew his wife a kiss. "I'm happy to be with you, my love—in sickness and in health."

"That's too sweet for me." Helen pretended to gag. Then she turned to Sabine. "Go on."

"I didn't grab it out of thin air. On the day I met Gene in The MOOT, Garvey stood by his side and didn't say a word. That made me think of what might've been unsaid. Shortly after that, Garvey and I ended up on the pier. Color me shocked when I found out that Garvey was the other victim. What was the meaning of that?"

"Another coverup?" Ming folded her arms. "They tried to make it look like Gene disliked his nephew."

"We don't know for sure. Garvey wasn't on the radar," Helen said.

"If Garvey wasn't on the radar, then he could technically have gone free." Ming made a gesture with his hands. "Why this setup?"

"Maybe because they knew that the Feds were closing in, and this was the end of the line," Sabine said. "I'm guessing we need to find out more about this uncle-nephew relationship."

"I'll get on it as soon as I leave this place and reconnect to the internet." Helen sipped more water. "There's one other thing I need to tell you. They found hundreds of millions of dollars worth of paintings and art pieces—some going as far back as the baroque era. The rest of them have been sold on the black market. However, they couldn't find Dad's pocket watch."

"No?" Sabine wondered how that could be possible. "I distinctly saw Gene holding the pocket watch in his hand. I told Cam so."

"Maybe he never had your dad's real pocket watch," Ming said to Sabine. "A fake watch might explain why he didn't let you hold the watch in your hand."

"Looking back, I'm glad he didn't because I wouldn't have wanted to get my fingerprints on it in the middle of the FBI's investigation."

"What's so special about the pocket watch besides its sentimental value?" Ming asked.

Helen waved to Sabine. "You explain."

Sabine nodded. "Dad's a puzzle enthusiast. He often took puzzles with him to work, especially when he was doing surveillance work—which he considered boring. To while away the time or to wait for an action moment, he would mull over the puzzles he brought with him."

"On the day he died, he told Mom that he had bought a puzzle pocket watch that could record encrypted audio, but he didn't say more because Mom was heading out to the hair salon and lunch with friends, and Dad was driving out of town." Helen steeled her voice. "Only, he never came home."

The Savannah Police Department—back in the old days when it had been the Savannah-Chatham Metropolitan Police Department—had determined that Dad had burned to death when he was trapped in his overturned burning car.

"The pocket watch wasn't with him when they found his charred body," Ming stated what they all knew. "Considering it was a recording device, it might provide clues about the last moments before your dad lost the pocket watch."

"Exactly," Sabine said. "Now it's missing again."

"So what do we do?" Helen asked.

Normally, Helen knew what to do. If she had to ask, it could mean that she wasn't sure about the direction she was going and she needed confirmation. It could also mean that she really had no idea how to proceed.

"So to borrow a term from the IT world, we set up

a honey trap to lure the current keeper of the pocket watch," Sabine said.

Ming drew a deep breath. "Told you that you're spending too much time with the IT people here. Now you're even speaking like them."

"What are you talking about?" Helen laughed. "This community is off the grid. What IT people?"

"They do have IT people at Still Salvage, Inc., where they recycle old computer parts," Ming explained. "Sometimes they work for Binary Systems."

"Oh? Interesting." Apparently, Helen hadn't known that.

"The security team, led by Tyrone Hall, also has access to the internet." Sabine turned to Ming. "Are you jealous?"

Ming didn't answer. His shoulders tensed up.

Sabine got up from her seat next to Helen and walked toward Ming's armchair. Behind the chair, she massaged his shoulders. "Relax, Husband."

He didn't push her away. "You're exclusive to me, Wife."

"Of course. Next time I talk to those IT people, I will bring you along. You can tell them what's what."

"I don't think there's a next time." Ming's voice was firm. "We just need to go home, now that Gene is caught. They'd have to build a case against him, but all that stolen art might put him away for a while. As for Garvey, how about we let Cam and the Feds deal with him? He's probably already on their radar. Is he still in the hospital?"

"He stayed overnight at the hospital and then was discharged," Helen said. "He was very helpful to the police. His testimony might put his uncle away for good. However, they couldn't find him this morning. He has disappeared."

"Disappeared?"

Helen nodded. "Just like that."

"Did his uncle make arrangements for that to happen?" Ming asked.

Helen shrugged. "Cam is investigating now. It's out of our hands, but we need to be on the alert."

"Gotcha. I don't know if we can do anything about it, though." Ming's face turned from happy-to-see-you to an icy frown.

"I gather we're safe for now because Still Waters is heavily guarded," Sabine said for Ming's assurance. "After all, people in danger come here to stay alive until their storms pass by. Psalm 57:1."

> Be merciful to me, O God, be merciful to me!
> > For my soul trusts in You;
> > And in the shadow of Your wings I will make
> my refuge,
> > Until these calamities have passed by.

"Today is our last day here," Ming reminded Sabine. "We go home in the morning."

"Where are you staying tonight?" Sabine asked her sister.

"I'm flying home," Helen said. "We can work on the honey trap from Savannah. That's a good idea, actually. You sure you don't want to come back to Hu Knows? I mean, if you can come up with this idea when you have a concussion, imagine what other great ideas you can come up with when you don't have a concussion."

Ming put his hands on top of Sabine's, which were still on his shoulders. "I get first dibs on working with Sabine."

"Oh?" Helen's eyebrows rose.

"I can offer her a partnership in SRI." Ming turned up his face, perhaps to gauge Sabine's reaction.

It sounded like Ming was still adamant about keeping his struggling investigative firm going. Sabine knew that Helen had previously offered to merge his company with Hu Knows, but he had refused on the grounds of wanting his own independence.

If it made Ming happy, Sabine could join SRI. Then they could discuss cases together. They would see each other more than just at home. They could travel for work together.

But then who would take care of their two young children?

"Let me pray about it," Sabine answered.

It was the best response she could think of at that moment.

CHAPTER 11

February

Helen's network yielded results five weeks later in February when she tracked down Garvey Gilroy in Nuevo Laredo, a lawless city across the border in the Mexican state of Tamaulipas. The US Department of State had marked a "Do Not Travel" advisory for the area.

Nevertheless, Ming had been to Mexico on assignment multiple times. Notably, four years ago, when Sabine and Mama Hu had been abducted by a notorious criminal, Ming flew to San José del Cabo to confront him and beat their location out of him. Helen and Binary Systems had provided cover for him all the way.

As much as Ming wanted to go to Mexico and not miss out on the action, he knew that there were times he had to take a backseat and let others play in the field.

As a family man, he couldn't be reckless anymore. It wasn't like he was a soldier without a choice. He ran his own investigative firm, and he could do whatever he wanted. Staying or going was all up to him. However, his decisions would have to include his family.

Sabine was now five weeks pregnant with their third child. Thanks to the three nights in the cabin at Still Waters, they were going to be parents for the third time.

This child was another gift from God. Psalm 127:3 spoke of it.

Behold, children are a heritage from the Lord,
 The fruit of the womb is a reward.

With this new baby, Ming's responsibility as husband and father had just risen another notch. Thankfully, SRI was also rising from the ashes of debt so that they could afford to support a family of five.

For that, he had to thank God for Sabine, his new business partner at SRI. With her on board, their management style changed slightly. Instead of competing with Hu Knows and other larger investigative firms, SRI would focus on smaller projects. Sabine worked a deal with Hu Knows to get first dibs on projects that they deemed too small for them or outside their purview.

As far as Helen was concerned, she only wanted to look for lost treasures and find lost people. She would send everything else to SRI or to Pilar Santiago.

To buy forty-nine percent of Ming's company,

Sabine sold two investment properties and cashed out a part of her inheritance. That reduced his debt substantially because Sabine's trust fund paid in cash.

In many ways, they owed Sabine's dad, who had created and filled Sabine's trust fund in the first place. He had also done the same for Helen and Mama Hu.

To cut expenses and work toward being debt free, Ming sold his downtown office. He had to adjust to working in his home office with Hannah cycling around his desk on her tricycle, but after a while, he enjoyed being home with the kids because of his flexible schedule. He even helped to change Zachary's diapers when Sabine attended meetings at her brokerage.

And then one Friday, Helen called them both to notify them that Garvey had been spotted in Nuevo Laredo. On the video call from Atlanta, Helen told them how Cayson Yang from Binary Systems had tracked him down. Camden la Salle's Art Crime Team led the charge to extricate a fleeing Garvey from Mexico.

Tipped off that his hiding place was about to be raided, Garvey had escaped before the FBI arrived. However, he had left behind his messenger bag. Inside it was Edgar Hu's pocket watch.

Camden returned home to the States with only the pocket watch and no arrest.

"Wait a sec," Sabine said. "Could someone have planted the pocket watch in Garvey's messenger bag?"

Ming stared at his wife, wondering what to think about her question. He disliked Garvey for having been Sabine's former boyfriend, but at the same time, her question made sense.

"The FBI is investigating that angle also," Helen replied.

Sabine nodded and said no more.

"About the watch..." Ming prompted Helen to continue her story.

Because of the background that Helen had provided to Camden, the FBI knew not to mess with the pocket watch. Camden sent it to Binary Systems for processing. Helen had arrived in Atlanta, but she had never seen the pocket watch before. Mama Hu had seen it when she last talked to her husband.

Only Sabine had seen the inside of the watch.

"Did you go to Atlanta just for that?" Sabine asked Helen.

"No, actually. I was in Huntsville with Earl on another project when Cam called me and asked for my help with the pocket watch. So I left Earl in Huntsville and drove here," Helen explained. "Cam got the wrong person, right? The person he wants is you, Sabine."

Now at Binary Systems—the security company that often did work for Helen as well as for defense contractors and the government—the pocket watch was being poked and x-rayed by Cayson Yang, the CEO of Binary Systems, under the watchful eye of Camden, who had taken custody of the evidence.

"Cayson here is trying to pry open the bottom of the pocket watch without breaking it," Helen said. "They were unable to do much with the pocket watch."

Sabine turned to Ming. "Shall we go?"

"If Hu Knows pays for our travel expenses, then yes," came Ming's reply.

"We'll pay," Helen said on video. "Call Mom to see if she wants to come. Might as well."

After they hung up, Sabine called her mom, and the latter said no. She didn't want to go to Atlanta to hear her husband's last words before he was murdered.

Actually, Mama Hu had a point. They had no idea what was in Edgar's pocket watch. It could've been nothing at all.

"Mom said to get a transcript for her and save the recording for when she is ready to hear it," Sabine told Ming after she'd hung up the phone.

"Do you think she's still grieving after all these years?" Ming studied Sabine carefully because she too might still be grieving her dad.

"I don't think the sadness can ever fully evaporate, you know? To this day, I still miss Dad. I will always miss him until I see him again in heaven."

"When my parents died, Heidi and I were very young. I still remember my parents, but I don't have enough memories to make me grieve."

"I hear you. I thought that as time went by, I would think of Dad less and less, but this pocket watch is a closure for me," Sabine said. "I'm very glad that we did this. It's all because Mom didn't give up on looking for Dad's killer."

"It won't be over until Gene goes to court—assuming he wasn't lying about being your dad's murderer."

"And you can be sure that Mom will be in court

to watch justice get served. Helen is working hard to get the best prosecutors. The murderer is going away for a very long time."

They packed very quickly, and that very afternoon, Ming and Sabine dropped off Hannah, Zachary, and Pickles—the senior dog—with Heidi, who still lived in Ming's old oceanfront house.

Heidi and Diego would take the kids to church on Sunday morning and return them to Ming and Sabine in the afternoon.

Diego was happy to see Heidi so delighted to have those two kids with them for the weekend, and Ming suspected they might consider adopting instead of remaining childless.

The kids taken care of, Ming drove Sabine to the Savannah/Hilton Head International Airport for their hour-long flight to Atlanta. They arrived early enough to give them time to go upstairs to eat a quick dinner at the fast food joints after they checked in their suitcases at the airline counter.

"Might have been cheaper to have eaten in Savannah and cheaper still at home." Ming tried not to sound like he was complaining, even though he literally was.

"I think it's okay once in a while. We don't fly every week, do we?" Sabine pointed to burgers here and pizza there. "I'll have some chicken tenders or salad, nothing greasy. Don't want to throw up mid-flight."

Ming wondered when Sabine might start to have her morning sickness and if that would affect her flying this afternoon. Truth be told, Sabine had hardly been sick in her last two pregnancies. She felt queasy every now and then, but nibbling on saltine crackers helped her weather the phases.

In any case, he had come prepared. He had stuffed saltine crackers and ginger candy into his laptop bag, as well as some empty brown bags and plastic bags in his duffel—just in case Sabine threw up on the flight—plus hand wipes. Sabine liked ginger ale, and she could get it on board the plane from the flight attendants.

The flight from Savannah to Atlanta would only be about seventy minutes long, and then they'd be on the ground again. If they had to stop at the women's restroom multiple times, then they'd do that.

Ming had calculated enough time for them to drive from the Atlanta airport all the way to Alpharetta, where the Binary Systems offices were—where Helen was waiting for them.

"Oh, and Auntie Anne's pretzels, my favorite." Sabine made a beeline for the soft pretzels.

Ming followed, carrying their laptops, one on each shoulder, plus his carry-on duffel bag. He looked like a pack mule, but he didn't want Sabine to carry anything heavier than her small crossbody purse.

Two pretzels, a hamburger, and a tray of chicken tenders later, Ming and Sabine sat down at an empty table. Ming said grace and asked God to bless the food and their flight before they dug in.

"I'm happy just to be with you," Sabine said.

Her love language was quality time, and it showed. Ming felt bad that he had left her for three months. Affairs were never in the picture because they loved each other exclusively, but there were other ways to break a marriage, such as not understanding how to love his spouse the way she understood love.

While his love language was acts of service, he had to be careful about the quality of his *doing* for her when all Sabine wanted was his *being* with her.

He knew that he had dropped the ball when he left Sabine alone for three months. It had been an unnecessary pain for her. Truth be told, he could have earned the same amount of money working in the States—although he would have to work more hours stateside to match his income overseas.

Not adverse to hard work, Ming should have taken the longer road because it would have meant more family time and...

Well, that was how Sabine got pregnant again.

He smiled.

"What?" Sabine asked, sipping water from her own water bottle.

All around them, a steady crowd of people walked back and forth. It wasn't too busy today, even for a Friday, because it was still winter. Come spring break and summer, this airport would be crowded, and they might not be able to find an empty table.

"I was just thinking about us." Ming reached across the table to put his hand on Sabine's. His jacket sleeve was a bit bulky and nearly knocked over Sabine's water bottle.

They had both worn winter jackets because it would be cold this weekend. February was still wintery in Georgia. Even though it was currently in the upper fifties in Atlanta, the sun would be setting and the weather would be cooler by the time they landed, picked up their luggage, and drove out of the airport.

"We've come a long way in four years." Sabine dabbed her lips with a napkin.

Her pink lips that he enjoyed kissing day and night, a privilege that he had as her husband.

Their bistro table was small, and Ming was only four feet away from Sabine, even as they sat on opposite sides of the table. As he watched his wife, Ming wondered how he was going to make it to Atlanta without his mind going to all sorts of romantic thoughts. Already, he was nearly knocking knees with her.

"I'm assuming you already have a rental car waiting for us in Atlanta," Sabine said.

There you go.

Ming's mind snapped back to work mode. "Yes, my love. All arranged."

This was a work trip, after all. Helen was paying for all expenses for this weekend for both of them because Sabine was now also working for her company—although she was only doing it part time on account of her day job as a real estate broker.

"If this weekend works out, I might do less in real estate and do more at SRI," Sabine said. "I'll only do work for Hu Knows as needed."

"I'd love that. It's lonely working alone at SRI, so I'm glad to have a partner who knows the business."

"Well, as you know, I'm a bit rusty because I left Hu Knows after Dad died."

Sabine didn't have to tell Ming that Hu Knows

was getting very big and had offices in Europe. Ambitious Helen might even open an office in Asia if the need arose.

Ming knew that Sabine was like him. They both preferred smaller establishments. SRI was most suitable for them. While it brought in less income than Hu Knows, it also had low overhead and low legal drama. On the other hand, Hu Knows had to hire law firms to handle their large international work contracts.

"I think your dad would be proud to have you continue as an investigator in some capacity," Ming added. "You don't have to be at Hu Knows to make that work. In fact, our friend Pilar is working on her own in Miami also. Helen has invited her to join Hu Knows, but she also said no. She'd rather do her own thing."

"Understandably. There's more control if you run your own business." Sabine nodded. "In this day and age, there are many ways we can do our PI work without having to be physically present in person."

"Right. We have technology," Ming said. "That's why I think it will be useful for us to visit Binary Systems for the first time, to establish some connections with Cayson Yang and his cousin, Leland—in case we need their help in the future."

Sabine broke off a piece of pretzel. "I see you finished your pretzel. You want some of mine?"

"No, I'm full from the hamburger and fries—food that I should probably avoid if I don't want to put on extra pounds."

"I haven't noticed. You work out a lot anyway."

As if on cue, Ming flexed his arm muscles, although no one could see it under his winter jacket.

Sabine laughed.

Ming loved to hear her laugh. She laughed happily and without any reservation.

"I love you so much, Sabine."

"Because we get along?" Sabine asked.

"You know, even when we don't get along, I still love you." Ming meant it.

"Same here, Ming. Same."

They had half an hour to kill before they had to go downstairs to catch their flight. Ming didn't have any plans, but Sabine wanted to walk around and get a couple of Savannah T-shirts for their kids. So Ming followed her around.

The Savannah airport wasn't enormous like the Atlanta airport, so it didn't take long before they ran out of bookstands and souvenir shops to browse through.

Eventually, they made their way to the gate downstairs.

Sabine texted Helen to tell her that they were at the gate. Helen called back.

"No need to come," she said.

"What?" Sabine motioned for Ming to get close to the phone so he could listen in.

There was a small crowd at the gate, so she couldn't put it on the speakerphone.

Ming leaned over until his ear was right next to Sabine's phone. He had great hearing, so he could hear Helen on the phone.

"It's not Dad's pocket watch," Helen said.

"Oh." Sabine sighed.

"It's a very good replica, but it's merely a regular pocket watch." Helen went on to suggest that if it was the same watch that Gene held in his hand in The MOOT, then it might explain why he wouldn't let Sabine hold it.

"Makes sense." Sabine didn't say more because she was in a public place.

Ming also didn't say a word. He merely listened.

"Then again, as far as we know, Gene didn't have counterfeit goods or fake timepieces in The MOOT," Helen added. "Which means that the real pocket watch is still somewhere."

"How do we find it?" Sabine asked.

"Operation Honey Trap, I guess. We'll figure out how much money we can dangle."

Essentially, they'd have to smoke out the person who was now in possession of the pocket watch. Neither Ming nor Sabine believed that Gene was telling the truth. He had made himself the sacrificial lamb at eighty-nine years old, not realizing that the real murderer could continue to commit more killings after Gene was gone.

Then again, a gut feeling or a hunch did not a sentencing make. They had to find real evidence and proof.

Perhaps by finding the pocket watch—assuming that it wasn't already lost or irrecoverably damaged—they could get to the truth of it. That was, if Edgar actually left a useful recording of some kind.

If not, they had tried for thirteen years. Some murder cases would never be solved.

Helen went on to say more, but Ming tuned out shortly after she mentioned the phrase "honey trap."

He didn't know why he'd reacted that way. She could have called it a bait or lure, but no.

Well, okay. Maybe he knew. He didn't like the name just because Sabine had picked up the phrase from the IT dudes at Still Waters.

After Sabine hung up, she stared at Ming's sullen face and then broke into a smile. She leaned over and whispered in his ear. "There's no one else, so don't worry."

He whispered back, "Call it Operation Fly Paper."

"Yes, dear." Sabine chuckled.

"Is she canceling our trip?"

"No. She said to go to Atlanta anyway and take it easy. It's too late to cancel the flight and hotel room," Sabine said. "Maybe we can visit Midtown Chapel on Sunday. I've been wanting to hear Pastor Kim preach. I watch his sermons on YouTube sometimes."

"So it's a paid vacation weekend for us then?" Ming asked.

Sabine nodded.

"She's not asking us to make even a partial payment?"

"No, but we're on standby in case they need us."

Ming doubted that they'd find the pocket watch by this weekend. It would be nothing short of miraculous or even incredulous. He suspected this could drag on for weeks, if not months. Then again, it had been many years. If they didn't find any new evidence, Gene could be tried for Edgar's murder, and that would be the end of it.

Was that enough closure for Sabine?

Ming reached over to clasp her hand in his. He

understood that getting the pocket watch back would be icing on the cake.

"I guess we'll go," Sabine said. "We've been so busy since we came home in January, so this is our first opportunity to get out of town for the weekend."

"But for the most part we're on our own."

"Sounds like it. I guess we can consider this our romantic getaway."

Romantic?

"Hmm... The last time we spent three days in a cabin..." Ming whispered in his wife's ear.

She whispered back, "No worries, Husband. I'm already pregnant."

Ming feigned shock. "What are you talking about? What were you thinking?"

"Shhh." Sabine laughed.

There it was again, the genuine laughter that brought joy to Ming's heart. It reminded him of Proverbs 17:22.

> *A merry heart does good, like medicine,*
> *But a broken spirit dries the bones.*

Ming thanked the Lord for bringing Sabine into his life. He was determined to devote himself to loving and caring for this beautiful wife of his, as well as his children, including his unborn third child.

He reached over to touch Sabine's tummy. She let him put his warm hand on top of her winter jacket. The baby in her womb was still small, but Ming silently prayed for him or her to be healthy all the way.

There, at the airport, Ming dedicated his entire

family to the Lord. He prayed for their provision and protection, knowing that God was sovereign over all the days of their lives.

He prayed that he would be the best Christian husband he could be to Sabine.

So help me, God.

CHAPTER 12

April

Sabine was surprised at the number of fake pocket watches that appeared on the scene after her paternal Hu and maternal Wu families offered reward money on the dark web.

She was even more surprised that the Wu side of the family tree contributed any money at all, considering they had all stopped being close to Mom since she married Dad. Not having enough time to travel to Georgia was their cover story, but Sabine knew better. The Wu family had disliked Dad for whatever reason that was now lost to time.

In any case, none of the timepieces belonged to Dad.

It was like looking for a needle in a haystack without using a magnet or a metal detector.

Well, the magnet was the one hundred thousand dollars that they had collected.

"Maybe it's not enough," Mom said when she came over to pick up Hannah for their grandma-granddaughter sleepover at Mom's house in downtown Savannah.

Hannah was still napping, but Sabine had packed her bag of clothes and toys. Mom had some toys at her house, but these were Hannah's favorite blocks.

Zachary was also napping upstairs, but he wasn't going with Hannah to Grandma's house for the weekend.

Sabine started a kettle on the stove to boil water for tea.

"How much do they think an old pocket watch is worth?" Sabine ushered Mom to the living room where the afternoon April sun shone in through tall windows.

Mom was the reason those windows were clean and clear. She had asked Sabine if she could pay for a housekeeper or a cook. Sabine opted for a window cleaning service. Their house on Tybee Island had many windows. After the cleaners finished, the windows were cleaner, and more sunshine streamed into the house.

"It's already April, and the needle hasn't moved." Mom sat down in a recliner that she'd given to Sabine when she upgraded her own furniture.

It was funny that Mom also used a needle metaphor, albeit in another sense.

"I think I like this one better than my new, more expensive recliner." Mom propped her feet on the raised footrest.

She was wearing stockings under her Vera Wang pants. She had been wearing stockings for decades.

It went well with the high heels she still wore. Some of her shoes were birthday gifts from Dad. It was kind of sad that the shoes had outlasted their marriage—if death was considered the end of a marriage.

As for Sabine, she couldn't remember the last time she'd worn stockings or even knee-highs. She opted for more casual footwear, like sandals, instead of pumps.

She kicked off her house slippers and lay down on the sofa across from Mom with a glass water bottle.

"Glad to see you stay hydrated," Mom said. "Stay off salt. When I was pregnant with you, my feet were swollen almost all the time."

Sabine lifted a foot in the air. It didn't look too bad. "My feet were swollen a bit when I was pregnant with Hannah, but not so much with Zachary."

"Each pregnancy is different, for sure. How's your morning sickness?" Mom asked.

"I'm past that. In my second trimester now."

"When I was carrying you, I was sick for half my pregnancy."

"Must be hard."

"Yeah." Mom smiled as a memory surfaced. "Your dad massaged my legs and cooked for me. He was a sweetie."

"Did he cook a lot for you?"

"And for Helen. She was only two at that time but, oh, what a picky eater she was. She had your dad wrapped around her little finger. He'd cook anything for his firstborn."

"I miss Dad." Sabine wiped a tear from her face.

Mom nodded.

A knowing silence passed between mother and daughter.

"But I can't be sad. Dad's in heaven with God now," Sabine said.

"You know I don't believe any of that." Mom made a circle in the air with her fingers.

Sabine couldn't read the gesture, but she didn't feel like asking Mom what she meant with all that finger movement. She let it go.

Then Mom dropped the bombshell. "I went to see Gene Gilroy."

Sabine sat straight up. "You what?"

"He's at the Richmond prison, where Iris's dad is serving life for killing his wife."

She had to bring it up. Sabine didn't know why Mom mentioned Iris's dad.

"Why did you visit Gene?" Sabine asked, trying to stay on topic.

"I wanted to know why he killed Edgar. There had to be a logical reason. I mean, Edgar was the kindest and most generous man I knew."

"What did Gene say?" Sabine was curious now.

"He said that Dad's death was accidental, and he didn't mean for it to happen." Mom sighed. "I thought he said that in an attempt to reduce his own sentence."

"Same thing he told his lawyer—as conveyed to us. Is there anything that he told you that we don't already know?"

"He told me to have pity on Garvey because he is the last Gilroy."

"We don't even know where Garvey is," Sabine

said. "He might have left the country, hiding somewhere safe."

"What's funny is that Gene has no memory of that day when Dad died," Mom said. "Gene said he killed Dad, but he couldn't recall what happened."

Bingo.

Sabine was convinced more than ever that Gene was protecting someone. "But he could be lying."

"I know." Mom drew a deep breath. "I wish life was easy and people didn't lie—including myself—and that we all lived happily without killing one another."

"You're describing heaven, Mom."

"Oh, don't get me started."

Sabine didn't want to ruffle her feathers again, but every time she mentioned God and Jesus and heaven, Mom would react like that.

To think a calm and steady Christian man like Dad had married a volatile and explosive woman like Mom.

Unfathomable.

The kettle in the kitchen whistled.

Sabine got up slowly. Her three-month-old belly wasn't heavy yet, but she didn't want to fall or anything.

"What kind of tea do you want, Mom?" Sabine put on her slippers.

"Long Island iced tea, please."

Sabine chuckled. "Mom, you know that we don't drink. How about some peppermint herbal tea?"

"Fine. Next time I'll bring my own flask."

Sabine suspected Mom really meant it.

Whenever Mom was stressed, she thought of two

things: alcohol and ice cream. Sabine believed it was because Mom was unsaved. However, Sabine also knew of Christians who used alcohol to relax. So who was Sabine to judge Mom?

Mom also got up and followed Sabine to the kitchen.

"I think I'll add two bitcoins to sweeten the deal and speed up the process."

"Mom, that's a lot of money. Do you think the pocket watch is worth that much?"

"Yeah, but the goal is to get the message out about the pocket watch. Is it not?"

Sabine nodded. "We've also established that Dad's pocket watch was different from the ones he'd given us. Ours only have GPS—even though it's using technology from thirteen years ago—but his has a recording device in it.

"Probably solid state."

"Huh?" Sabine didn't understand Mom, and she wondered if Mom understood what she herself was talking about.

Then again, every now and then, Mom's actions were a mystery to both Sabine and her sister.

Just then, Hannah came downstairs with her straight black hair all askew. She carried a teddy bear in one arm.

"Gamma, let's go," she said as soon as she reached the bottom of the stairs.

"All right, princess. Let's go." Mom turned to Sabine. "No need to make me tea, dear. We're leaving now."

Sabine left the cups on the counter and went to

get Hannah's pink Hello Kitty rolling suitcase that she had placed near the coat closet.

"I'll see you tomorrow at noon then." Sabine opened the kitchen door to the garage and then opened the garage door.

"No hurry. We're not going anywhere. Just come after lunch."

Sabine followed Mom and Hannah out to Mom's Jaguar. Mom had installed her own two car seats so that they would always be there whenever she had to transport Hannah or Zachary. However, she preferred Hannah because they could talk to each other. Zachary only burped and spat.

Sabine waved and watched Mom back her car out of the driveway and drive off before she closed the garage door.

Then she went inside the house through the kitchen and made tea for herself. She looked down, and there was old Pickles, barely able to shuffle across the kitchen floor toward her. She patted the old golden's head.

"Were you napping too?" As she said it, she strained her ears to see if she could hear Zachary upstairs. Not a sound.

Letting the loose leaf tea steep in the teapot, Sabine swiped her phone to check the baby monitor app. It showed that Zachary was still sound asleep.

She decided to wait a few minutes before she checked on her nine-month-old baby.

She needed some mommy time. She carried a tray with the teapot and a cup and padded back to the living room to sit down on the sofa she had left earlier.

Sabine checked her phone to see if Ming had texted her. He was meeting a client in Savannah and wouldn't be back until five or six o'clock. She didn't want to send him a message because he might be distracted.

She sipped tea and thought about her conversation with Mom. One thing that Mom had said earlier bothered her. Well, two things.

He told me to have pity on Garvey because he is the last Gilroy.

Gene has no memory of that day when Dad died.

Apart, the two statements seemed benign. But plied together, they spoke volumes to Sabine.

Firstly, Gene was protective of his nephew, Garvey. If something happened to Garvey, their family line would end.

Secondly, Gene was showing his hand. He was probably not there when Dad died. This would support the notion that he was protecting Garvey.

Did that mean that Garvey might be the one they were looking for?

After sipping tea, Sabine made herself comfortable on the couch, propping her feet on a throw pillow. It didn't last for long, as she soon heard Zachary crying upstairs.

My baby is awake.

An hour later, Sabine was cuddling Zachary in the living room when Mom posted in their online family chat room.

Somehow, Mom had called her side of the family and managed to get her siblings and cousins to increase their contribution to match her new addition to the reward fund. Dad's side chipped in too. The reward money ballooned to half a million dollars, most of which was in bitcoin.

Sabine tried to remain calm, like Dad would have done in this sort of crowdfunding event. She had no confidence that the criminal would show himself—or herself—at the exchange. To prevent themselves from being arrested, they'd probably hire proxies to do the trade.

Prepare for more fake pocket watches!

Sabine sighed.

CHAPTER 13

The fountain in the center of the century-old courtyard made gurgling noises that had always bothered Ming. He understood that the working fountain was meant to cancel out the traffic noise beyond the brick fence all around this Savannah square, but it also prevented Ming from hearing any unusual sounds of danger. All he could hear were the screams and laughter of four kids on the small inflatable on the other side of the fountain, and Camden's wife, Iris, telling them to be careful.

Camden himself would've been here if he wasn't at work, even though this was a Saturday afternoon. Whenever he was out of town, sometimes Sabine and Iris would get together on Saturdays. Sunday was for church, and weekdays were for school, so Saturday was the only day for the kids to play with one another.

As Ming flipped the steak and hot dogs on the grill, he felt confident that his FBI friend would get to the bottom of the case, now that he was interrogating

Gene Gilroy. Sure, Garvey had disappeared, and the pocket watch was nowhere to be found, but Ming had to trust God and be patient.

He kept telling himself to pray and wait, but something inside him wouldn't calm down. Perhaps it was his prejudice against Garvey, the ex-boyfriend of his wife. While Sabine had made it clear that she wasn't going back to Garvey, Ming wasn't sure if the feeling was mutual.

Ming had profiled Garvey. After he dated Sabine for something like a few weeks, he dumped her when she and Helen got into that wreck on the highway. It had turned out that the wreck had been caused by the reckless driving of a drunk driver and had nothing to do with Garvey. Still, seeing Sabine all broken and bleeding in the emergency room put him over the edge, and he left her to recover on her own.

In the following three years after the wreck, they had zero contact with each other. Their lives had bifurcated. Sabine received and changed careers from modeling to real estate, and that was when she met Ming, who was working with Helen on some projects.

In the four years that Sabine and Ming had been married, Sabine hadn't crossed paths with Garvey until Mama Hu started looking into her husband's death.

It was all clear now that Garvey had fast-tracked Sabine into the flintlock competition. Even though Sabine had won it on her own accord, Garvey and his uncle had known all along that Sabine and Mama Hu were looking for Edgar's murderer.

And they had let Sabine enter their lair.

It all smelled like a trap.

The one thing Garvey and Gene hadn't antici-
pated was Camden la Salle and his arsenal of FBI
agents. Not undercover, but covertly working behind
the scenes, Camden and his team had watched Helen
and Sabine go undercover at the Hiawassee estate.

And now Gene was behind bars, awaiting trial.

If Gene was really The Mechanic—contrary to
his vehement denial—then it would follow that he'd
have people outside the jail doing his bidding. They
would continue to protect that no-good nephew
of his.

Ming closed the grill cover. The only reason he
had been assigned to grilling was that he was very
good at it. Sabine sometimes called him the grill king.
However, this time, he didn't feel like being the cook
because he was moping.

Yeah, that was the word.

Sometimes, Ming was hardest on himself, more
than anyone else. He still felt bad about not being
around at the beginning of Sabine's mission to smoke
out The Mechanic and retrieve the pocket watch. He
still felt guilty for not taking care of his family. Going
overseas alone without Sabine had been a mistake,
and he vowed never to repeat it.

I'm here now, making up for lost time.

His Sig Sauer was in the zippered pocket of his
cargo shorts because he thought he might need it.
However, he had spent the last two hours playing
with the kids and setting up the grill on a pretty April
day that looked like nothing bad was going to happen.

"You doing okay over there?" Sabine's voice came
closer. She carried a bowl of cut watermelon as she
walked toward him. She was wearing a pretty floral

blouse over a pair of stretchy maternity shorts. She wasn't showing much yet, but she was three months along now.

"Want some?" Sabine lifted a cubed piece of watermelon on a fork and fed her husband.

"Mmm... Sweet and cold. Gimme another one."

Sabine fed him one more piece and another. "Why don't I just give you the entire bowl?"

Ming laughed as he chewed on the watermelon. For some reason he looked up, and there on the second floor window of the historic mansion the curtain closed just after he saw what looked like the bill of a black baseball cap.

He couldn't ignore it. "Is someone inside the house?"

"Mom went inside to take a phone call. Why?"

Paranoia will be the death of me.

"Probably nothing. Isn't that the study?" He pointed up.

"Yep. The study where Mom pays the bills and surfs the web on her laptop. She sometimes sits there on her couch to chat with her friends." Sabine curled her lips. "Hmm. She never closes the curtains. She likes to look outside at the street and beyond."

"Your mom didn't wear a baseball cap earlier, when we first came in." Ming tried to keep his voice low.

"No. She hates those things. She prefers what she calls 'real hats,' like those she wears to the Kentucky Derby. Why do you ask?"

"I thought I saw someone upstairs with a baseball cap on."

"Hmm. You want me to text her?" Sabine put the

bowl down on the side table attached to the grill. She swiped her phone, tapped, and waited. "She's not replying."

All sorts of lights appeared around Ming's head. "I think I'll go check."

He was about to leave the grill to Sabine when something pricked his conscience. He shut off the grill.

He placed his hands on Sabine's shoulders. "I need you and Iris to take the kids and leave. Go to the nearest police station and wait."

Sabine opened her mouth to say something but didn't. She only nodded.

Ming was glad that Sabine knew him well. He was serious about their safety and never joked about such things.

Ming escorted Sabine over to Iris to get the kids off the inflatable. Sabine wore sandals because her swollen feet didn't fit in her walking shoes. In sandals, she couldn't walk as fast as she could if she were wearing boots. In boots, she could run.

"No, no!" One of Iris's kids fussed, not wanting to get off the inflatable.

Ming let Iris deal with her adopted kids while he looked for his own. Next to the inflatable, Zachary was asleep in a stroller. Sabine motioned for Hannah to get off the inflatable.

"Why, Mommy?" Hannah's eyes were all innocent.

Ming knew he would give his life to save his daughter but prayed that it wouldn't come to that.

"Because we're going to get ice cream," Sabine said, loudly enough for Iris's kids to hear.

Immediately, all four kids—Iris's three and Sabine's one—bounced right off the inflatable.

Clever wife.

Ming managed a smile. He ushered the women and kids around the building to the narrow driveway. Iris's van was in the driveway. Ming and Sabine had parked in the parking garage on Bull Street.

"Let's take my van," Iris said. "I have an extra car seat in the back for your Zach. Peggy is tall enough and can sit without a booster seat, so Hannah can have hers."

As the kids filed into the van, excited about ice cream, Sabine turned to Ming. She fished out her pink Glock from her crossbody purse. "You need an extra weapon?"

Ming took it. Pink or not, it was still a Glock 36. Besides, Sabine had hardly used it since she bought it seven years ago. Mainly, she used it at the gun range to keep up her skill that she said she never wanted to use. Lately, she had been practicing throwing her *bo shuriken* spikes to prepare for future competitions.

"We'll pray and call 911," Sabine said.

Ming nodded. He had half expected Sabine to tell him not to do this, but to wait for the SPD to take care of it, but Sabine didn't. She let him do whatever he wanted, which sometimes meant learning things the hard way.

"Be safe." Sabine grabbed the front of his T-shirt and planted a smooching kiss on his lips. "More when you come back."

Ming nearly lost his focus. He cleared his throat.

"Go." Sabine waved him off.

CHAPTER 14

Upstairs, the afternoon sunshine streamed across the polished oak floor in a myriad of colors that filtered through a stained glass window. Ming's kids had played here before, racing their toy cars and rolling a plastic bowling ball into some toy pins that Ming set up at the end of the hallway.

Now the mansion was quiet, save for the sound of vehicles outside, peppered with occasional honks. He didn't hear any voices or sirens.

His Sig Sauer in front of him, Ming treaded slowly, praying that the floor wouldn't creak under his tennis shoes. He'd worn a pair of old shoes that were comfortable.

The empty hallway left him exposed, but muffled voices from the study at the other end of the hallway compelled him to press forward.

He glanced back every few seconds to see if anyone approached him from the stairwell. So far, he was alone. And there was nowhere to hide. If he were to retreat to the location he'd come from earlier, he'd have to sprint. He couldn't run faster than a speeding bullet.

The voices from the study in front of him grew louder, and Ming could see that the door was ajar. He inched closer.

"I only have one hardware wallet." Mama Hu's voice.

No reply.

"The pocket watch is not worth a bitcoin even though we offered a reward of half a million dollars," Mama Hu added.

It sounded like someone had responded to the reward money in a dramatic way, showing up at Mama Hu's house in Savannah.

"How do I know that the pocket watch you hold belonged to my husband?" Mama Hu asked.

"Shut up," a man answered.

A chuckle made Ming think that there was a third person in the room. Ming worried a bit because he was outnumbered. Could he take down two intruders and rescue Mama Hu?

Now he felt like a fool for entering the mansion without backup. He should've called 911 and waited outside. Let the police department deal with it.

Then again, it would only take seconds for the intruders to kill Mama Hu. It would take minutes for the Savannah PD to arrive, especially at this time in the afternoon when traffic was picking up in downtown Savannah.

Still, Ming prayed that the SPD would get here soon.

Meanwhile, he had to go forward to rescue Mama Hu.

Or die trying.

Ming hoped that Sabine and their kids were far enough away from here. He had told her and Iris to drive to the nearest police station, wherever that was. They'd know what to do. Iris had friends in the police department because off-duty officers often visited the gun range that she now managed.

"How about you let me see the pocket watch first?" Mama Hu asked.

Her calm voice made Ming think that either she was stalling for time or she wasn't afraid of the intruders. If the latter was the case, then it meant she might know who they were.

"If you don't shut up, I will announce what you did fifteen years ago." The man's voice lowered.

Ming didn't know what he meant, but his statement confirmed that he knew Mama Hu.

"All right. Here's my wallet. Take it all." Mama Hu's voice sounded dejected. "Just give me the pocket watch."

They had something on her. Ming made a note to himself to find out Mama Hu's secrets, just in case they endangered Sabine and the kids.

"Tie her up while I transfer the funds," the man said.

The second intruder in the room was silent.

"Let me go!" Mama Hu fussed.

Ming was mere feet away from the study when he heard a "pfft" behind him. He jerked back, realizing that he had dropped the ball on his situational awareness.

Six or seven feet away from him, a man collapsed to the floor, his gun clattering away. A black baseball cap fell off his head where blood pooled.

Behind him, several SWAT officers in Kevlar vests and facial shields pointed their weapons at him.

"I'm with you," Ming whispered. He lowered his Sig Sauer.

"We know," the officer mouthed. He motioned for Ming to retreat.

Feeling a huge relief, Ming did as he was told. He passed by a couple of officers he recognized from the past.

More SWAT officers poured into the hallway as Ming entered the stairwell to safety. His knees wobbled on the old spiral steps, and the ground floor couldn't come fast enough.

Outside the building, a collection of SPD police vehicles and paramedic vans had gathered. Ming spotted a Crisis Intervention Team vehicle as well.

Were the robbers upstairs aware of this massive show of force?

Out of the crowd, Detective Cosmo O'Dell walked across the courtyard to greet Ming. "Glad you're okay, man. I hurried over here as soon as I heard."

Actually, Ming was surprised to see him. A regular police officer might suffice, but the great detective himself had arrived in person.

"Anything to do with Mama Hu might be related to Edgar's cold case," O'Dell added.

Ming wondered if that was necessarily true. Yes, O'Dell was in charge of investigating Edgar's murder, having taken over the case from a retired officer.

However, O'Dell had jumped from "anything to do with Mama Hu" to "related to Edgar's cold case."

Ming found it odd but brushed it off.

"You'll need to take my Sig Sauer, I gather?" Ming asked.

"Yes, sir, along with any other weapons you might have carried with you upstairs—whether discharged or not." O'Dell nodded to an officer who bagged Ming's weapons.

"A pink Glock?" O'Dell laughed when he saw what Ming pulled out of his cargo shorts pocket.

"It's my wife's."

"I'm sorry she won't see it again for a while."

"I know. Bummer."

O'Dell took his statement about what happened. It was short and sweet, but O'Dell was particularly interested in the conversation that Ming had heard about Edgar's pocket watch. Ming told him all he knew as O'Dell jotted down notes with a fountain pen on a leather notebook.

Wouldn't it be best if O'Dell had recorded Ming's voice on his phone instead? Ming didn't ask. He wasn't going to volunteer any information that O'Dell hadn't asked for.

"So the pocket watch is upstairs?" O'Dell closed his notebook.

"Well, according to the conversation I heard outside the study."

"Good enough." O'Dell lifted his face to look up at the second floor. The curtains were still drawn. "Your family's waiting for you at the station, so scoot."

O'Dell made a waving motion.

Before Ming left, O'Dell called him back. "If you

think of any details you haven't told me just now, call. You have my number."

"Will do." Ming's phone rang and he answered. "Sabine, are you still at the police station?"

"I'm across the street two blocks away." She told him which intersection. "They won't let me get nearer."

"I'll be right there." Ming used his tracking app to find Sabine's phone. "Are you driving Iris's van?"

"No, our own car."

"I thought you left with Iris."

"I put Hannah and Zach in her van, but I drove our own car to the police station," Sabine explained. "After Iris and I made the police report, I asked her to take the kids to her house. Then I came back."

"You've been waiting for me." Ming was moved.

"And praying."

"Thank you, my love. Stay inside the car. I'll be right there." He didn't want her to stand on her feet too much, but he also didn't want her to be anyone's target.

It took him a few minutes to walk there. He tried to breathe normally so that by the time he reached Sabine, he would look calm. He didn't scare Sabine. The last thing he wanted was to give her a difficult time in her third pregnancy.

When he reached their car, he found Sabine in the passenger seat.

"What? You want me to drive?" Sabine laughed.

Ming opened the driver's side door. Before he could buckle in, Sabine showed him her phone.

"Want to see what happened in the study?" Sabine asked.

Ming's eyebrows rose. "A live camera? Your mom is more paranoid than I thought."

"She has live cameras all over her house." Sabine shrugged.

"Since when?" Ming didn't remember it before he went overseas.

"When she found out that Gene Gilroy collected stolen art and timepieces, including Dad's pocket watch." Sabine made a face. "I think six months ago."

"And we didn't know?"

"Mom doesn't tell us everything. Sometimes she looks like she's about to tell me about her life before Helen and I were born, but then she changes her mind almost immediately. Even Helen can't read Mom's mind."

"What are we looking at here?" Ming pointed to the paused video on Sabine's phone.

"I'll rewind." Sabine rewound the video. "Here's what happened after you left and just before the SWAT arrived in the study."

"You saw me leaving the hallway?" Ming asked.

"I told you. Cameras everywhere."

"Then why didn't we look at the cameras when we were outdoors, before I sent you and the kids away?" Ming asked.

"Because only Mom has access to her home security system," Sabine said. "I had to call Helen to ask her if she knew the access code. She didn't, but..."

"Don't tell me that Helen asked her associates to hack into Mom's security system."

"It was faster than calling the security company and wielding her power of attorney. You know how my sister is."

"You meant that she's decisive and orders people around?"

Sabine chuckled and played back the video.

Inside the study, Mama Hu was bashing a man over the head with a laptop. The man writhed in pain as an ornate and gilded dagger stuck out of his leg.

"I told your uncle that you're a loser and I'm right!" Mama Hu screamed at the man on the floor.

Uncle?

The man had a thick beard, so Ming couldn't see his entire face. However, Mama Hu's words told him that he was...

Garvey Gilroy?

Ming continued to watch the video with Sabine.

SWAT officers pulled Mama Hu away from the man and took over. They pinned the man to the floor and handcuffed him.

Mama Hu threw the laptop onto the floor. "Mistake number one, Garvey. You showed up in person."

She was clearly angry, so it was the wrong time to tell her not to destroy the laptop, which could be evidence.

"How dare you!" Mama Hu pointed a finger at Garvey. The bright-red acrylic nail was dangling off her real nail. "I fed you every time you came over to my house, and this is how you pay me back. You're going to jail for armed robbery!"

"You're going to jail too!" Garvey yelled back. "I know what you did fifteen years ago. You can't hide forever."

"You first, buster!" Mama Hu was visibly shaken.

Hog-tied on the floor, Garvey struggled and groaned, and something fell out of his jacket pocket. It was a gold pocket watch.

"Dad's pocket watch." Sabine sniffled. "Finally."

"Yeah. Finally."

"Do you think they'll let us listen to the audio recorded on it?" Sabine asked tearfully.

"If we're helpful, I think they'll let us hear it before the trial. Otherwise, we'll have to wait. Either way, in due time, they'll return the pocket watch to your family."

"More waiting. We've waited thirteen years, so what's another few months?"

Ming didn't have the heart to remind Sabine that sometimes murder trials could take a year or two. In the grand scheme of things, two years weren't very long. However, now that they knew the pocket watch existed, each day of waiting was more pronounced, being at the forefront of Sabine's mind—and that of her family, for that matter.

Silently, Ming prayed that all those things wouldn't affect Sabine's pregnancy. So far, she'd had it easy with mild morning sickness that had all but gone away.

"I can't believe Garvey would carry the pocket watch with him," Ming said. "Don't you think something is odd about that?"

Sabine nodded. "Maybe he was desperate. Maybe he trusted Mom to keep her word and exchange the crypto money for the pocket watch."

"He asked too much."

"It matters not. Mom would give him all her crypto if she could get the pocket watch back. To her, it is the last thing she doesn't have that belonged to Dad."

"I heard her negotiate, though."

"Yeah, she was stalling for time, but you knew that."

Ming nodded. "Are the kids okay?"

"Yeah. I just talked to Iris before I called you. The kids are running around in her fenced backyard, unaware of the trials and tribulations in the world."

"I love you, Sabine." Ming squeezed Sabine's hand.

"I'm glad you came home."

"I'm not leaving you alone with the kids again— not for more than a week at most." Ming felt more determined than ever.

"What if it's two weeks?"

"Then I won't take the job," Ming said. "From now on, I'd rather earn less than be separated from you."

"Oh?"

Ming could see the tears in her eyes.

He felt awful about the three months of separation he'd put her through. He knew that Sabine's love language was quality time with him, and yet he hadn't cared.

Well, now he would care.

"I've decided to work closer to home," Ming

explained. "I don't want to miss out on being with you and the kids in their formative years."

Sabine didn't say a word. She only nodded.

Somehow Ming suspected that everything he had just said to her was an answer to her prayers in the last three months. He felt that sometimes he had to learn things the hard way. He thanked God that it hadn't cost him his family for him to finally come home and stay home.

"Let's go get the kids and go home," Sabine finally said.

"Yes, let's go home." Ming put his hand around Sabine's neck and gently pulled her face close to his. "But first..."

Their lips met, warm and sweet.

Sabine giggled.

And Ming felt at home again.

CHAPTER 15

Not the brightest crayon in the box, Garvey Gilroy had brought Dad's original pocket watch to Mom's house in an attempt to sell it to her for a million dollars in bitcoin. He had brought his own laptop—that Mom had smacked his head with—to the crime scene.

Now the FBI and the SPD were all over his laptop. Unfortunately, Mom had basically dented the laptop and caused untold damage to the hard drive when she used it to bash Garvey and then when she threw it on the floor in rage.

That was why Cayson Yang had flown to Savannah. His company, Binary Systems, would attempt to recover the laptop to collect evidence of the bitcoin transfer from Mom's hardware wallet to Garvey's offshore bitcoin account.

Cayson was sure to succeed.

And Garvey's get-out-of-jail card was gone.

Looking back, Sabine wondered what she'd ever

seen in Garvey. Well, back then, he was clean shaven and said all the right words. He held the door for her, helped carry her groceries, and did all the things that Sabine expected a boyfriend to do.

For about three weeks.

Then the car accident came, and then Garvey changed his tune. He hardly visited her in the hospital and only sent her flowers for her first surgery. Never called her in the burn unit, never asked her how many stitches she had all over her legs, torso, and arms. Suddenly, he didn't care anymore.

It was a good thing that they'd broken up before Sabine was discharged from the hospital. It gave Sabine a clean break and a new beginning.

The next three years were brutal as she went through more reconstructive surgeries and physical therapy. Sabine's modeling career was over, and she had to find new work. She didn't want to go back to Hu Knows because it reminded her too much of Dad. Dad's signature was everywhere in the headquarters in downtown Savannah.

Selling her shares of Hu Knows to her sister, Helen, was a way for Sabine to cope with her grief of losing Dad. However, she couldn't regret it. She made good use of the money, investing it and funding her budget as she took on a new job as a real estate agent, eventually taking over a brokerage firm as a broker.

But then, taking Mom's place in the flintlock competition and winning first place when it was her first time competing reminded Sabine of all the years she'd been Dad's shadow, learning from him. In many ways, she'd been an apprentice. Dad had said before that between Helen and Sabine, Sabine was more like him. Helen was more like Mom, feisty and fiery.

Truly, Helen was better at running Hu Knows, and Sabine wouldn't want to take that away from her. However, Helen had asked her to return to Hu Knows.

It had been a while, and she was married now, so she had to consider Ming when making decisions such as that. To begin with, she felt that she worked well with Ming. Ming could use a buddy so he wasn't alone in his private investigative business. He wouldn't try to replicate Hu Knows, even though he took whatever Hu Knows didn't want to handle.

"What are you thinking about?" Ming's voice cut into Sabine's stream of thoughts.

"Whether to go back to Hu Knows or work with you in SRI," Sabine answered.

Her mind had wandered all over the place, and she almost forgot she was in their SUV heading toward a meeting in Savannah.

Ming was driving, so she didn't pay attention to how they would get there. The April afternoon wasn't too warm outside, but the air conditioner was on. Sabine felt comfortable in her floral blouse and sandals.

"I thought you already decided to team up with me." Ming sounded disappointed.

"I am leaning toward SRI, yes, but I want to make sure I don't leave any stone unturned."

Ming nodded. "There are pros and cons to both. Hu Knows is huge and has offices in Europe and the USA. SRI is a small outfit with just me running the show. If you come on board, then it'll just be you and me. I do subcontract out to other investigators, such as Pilar, but I don't do big projects. Consequently, my revenue is small. So there's that."

"We already discussed getting out of debt, so that will help our net profit across the board—both in business and at home."

"I look forward to the day when we're debt free."

"Me too." Sabine reached over to rub Ming's arm. She didn't know why she did that, but she liked to feel his muscles. She knew he worked out. Maybe they could expand their home gym to save from having to pay for monthly gym dues.

"If you keep doing that, we might have to turn around and go home," Ming said. "The kids are at your mom's, so we could..."

"Could miss the meeting?" Sabine shut it down right away. "I've waited thirteen years to hear Dad's last words."

"I'm sorry. I didn't mean any disrespect."

"No apologies needed. We're married. You can say anything you want to me, including intimate matters. That's our privilege as husband and wife. We're not sneaking around doing premarital whatnot."

"Whatnot?" Ming chuckled as he turned into a strip mall and parked the SUV in an empty spot across from Watchman Watchmakers that was assisting the SPD to open Dad's pocket watch.

"Are we early?" Sabine unbuckled and got out of the passenger side.

"I think we are." Ming also got out.

Sabine looked around and didn't see any vehicle she recognized. She walked with Ming into the shop and saw Detective Cosmo O'Dell sitting on a barstool at a counter.

"You're early." O'Dell shook Ming's hand and fist-bumped Sabine.

Sabine thought it was interesting that O'Dell had remembered that Sabine didn't like shaking hands. Minding little details like that would make O'Dell a better detective.

She had last spoken with him two days after Garvey invaded Mom's house. O'Dell had called Mom when Sabine had brought the kids over to have ice cream with their grandma. Mom put the detective on speakerphone so that Sabine could join the conversation.

Going back thirteen years, O'Dell had been the first police officer at the scene of Dad's burned-out car, back when he was a patrol cop and not yet a detective.

Sabine didn't know him all too well, but her sister worked with him in the ensuing years. As for Ming, he had met O'Dell seven years ago when Sabine was abducted.

Sabine hadn't seen O'Dell for many years prior to the home invasion at Mom's house two days ago. SPD assigned the case to O'Dell, and he took statements from Mom, Sabine, and Ming.

This morning, O'Dell looked the same as he did two days ago, except that he'd gotten a haircut. His gray hair belied the fact that he was only in his fifties.

As he chatted with Ming, he gestured with his hands. He had what looked like black dirt or grime under a couple of his fingernails. More on his right hand than the left. That would make sense because O'Dell was right-handed.

Maybe he worked in the yard, Sabine thought. Potting soil could get under his nails. But then, soil and dirt would wash off. Sabine quickly ruled out gardening.

What about grime or grease? That might remain for at least a day or two under his fingernails, wouldn't it? Where could O'Dell have gotten grime from?

"Let's go to the back. Wolf Larson is waiting for us with Cayson." O'Dell led the way through a gallery of antique clocks to the workshop at the back.

There, they were introduced to the watchmaker, who had already been poring over Dad's pocket watch, but tried as he could, he was unable to open it at all. O'Dell didn't want him to risk breaking it and thus destroying the evidence, so Wolf refrained from exerting pressure on the unique timepiece.

An Asian man was standing behind Wolf, holding a cup of coffee at four o'clock in the afternoon.

"Cayson Yang." O'Dell introduced him to Ming, but Ming already knew him.

Oh, so he was the Cayson whom Helen had often talked about. At least six feet tall, he wasn't too skinny, but if Mom saw him, she'd say that he needed to eat more food.

"This is my wife, Sabine," Ming said to Cayson.

"Hello." Cayson waved but made no attempt to shake Sabine's hand, for which she was grateful. "I'm Leland's cousin, if that helps with familiarity."

"I've heard of you." Sabine waved back. "Just never met you."

"Same. Leland is a very good friend of your sister, Helen. They work together on numerous projects."

Sabine nodded. "Are you here to crack my dad's pocket watch?"

"I'll help a little." It was all Cayson said as he took his seat beside the watchmaker.

Sabine was certain it was more than that. Cayson's company was a defense contractor, and the nature of Binary Systems' work might make them experts in spyware. If there was a recording device inside Dad's pocket watch, Cayson might know how to activate it.

"My work begins as soon as we open this pocket watch, but for now, nothing is working," Cayson said. "Even the clock stopped running a long time ago."

"Time stood still for this pocket watch," Wolf the watchmaker said. "It has secrets thirteen years old."

"Maybe finally we'll hear what my dad has to say about his own murder." Sabine said it casually, but from the corner of her eye, she noticed a slight surprise in O'Dell's eyes. Why would he be surprised? SPD already knew that the pocket watch contained a recording device.

"There might be nothing on it at all." Ming's gaze was on Sabine.

Did he say that to temper her expectations?

"That's possible too."

Sabine wished that Helen was there, looking at the pocket watch together with her, but Helen was called away to Brussels, where she had an office for her European operations. Busy bee, she was.

Mom absolutely didn't want to come. She said

that it would make her grieve Dad all over again if she heard his voice.

"Let's sit down." O'Dell was a gentleman, pulling out a chair for Sabine, the only woman in the room.

Ming had already sat down next to Sabine, and he didn't react to seeing O'Dell pushing the chair in for Sabine.

Truth be told, Sabine didn't need it. She could handle the chair herself, thank you very much. On the one hand, O'Dell might genuinely be old fashioned, since this was the South, after all. On the other hand, the grime or grease under his fingernails made Sabine curious about what he did when he wasn't at work.

Curiosity had been Dad's secret sauce when he solved crimes for his clients. However, it was also his downfall because Dad had been physically injured many times when his curiosity had taken over caution.

Right now, Sabine wasn't sure whether she was cautious enough not to be too curious about the wrong people. O'Dell was the detective assigned to Dad's case. He was one of the good guys. What he did during his off hours to put grime under his nails was none of Sabine's business.

O'Dell sat down adjacent to Sabine. She thought nothing of it, even though there was another empty seat at the other end of the table, adjacent to Ming. O'Dell placed a small leather-covered notebook and a fountain pen on the table.

The fountain pen barrel seemed to be made of resin and had a swirl design all over it in brown, black, and orange. It could be a cheap no-name pen, but Sabine was curious.

She took out her phone—

"No recording allowed." O'Dell put up a hand.

The grime under his fingernails really bothered Sabine now. However, she had taken out her phone to grab a photo of the fountain pen so that she could identify it without having to ask O'Dell because she didn't want him to know that she was curious.

"Oh. Not even to check the time?" Sabine asked nicely.

"Look around you. We're in a watchmaker's shop. Clocks are everywhere." O'Dell's voice had an edge to it.

What happened to the gentleman who had spoken nicely to her and held the chair for her?

"Sorry." Sabine put away her phone.

"Rules, you know. What can I do? I'd be repri-manded if I don't follow the rules and somehow cause this case to be thrown out in court." His voice was suddenly sweet again.

Was she looking at a Dr. Jekyll and Mr. Hyde? Sabine wasn't sure.

Across the table, Cayson was watching her intently with a slight smile at the corner of his lips.

Sabine wondered what that computer expert was thinking. Maybe he was comparing her to Helen. People did that a lot. Even Mom compared Sabine to Helen. Often, Sabine fell short of everyone's expecta-tions—except for Ming. Ming thought the world of her.

A warm hand on her thigh made Sabine turn her head toward Ming. His eyes smiled brightly at her, and no words needed to be said. This was the man God had given to her. To think they had almost divorced over financial burden. Sabine almost had tears in her eyes, but she steeled herself.

She looked up to see that Wolf was staring at her. His gloved hands were on the side of the tray in front of him. On the tray was Dad's pocket watch.

"I've already X-rayed it. There's a fail-safe mechanism that will destroy the watch if we attempt to open it," Wolf said. "I am going to surmise that there is only one way to open this pocket watch, but I don't know how."

A watchmaker who couldn't open a pocket watch.

When Dad had told Sabine that he'd bought it in Italy, she had thought nothing of it. She assumed that the pocket watch was off the shelf. Never once did she think that it was custom-made.

"You need to wear gloves." Wolf pointed to Sabine. "Who else is touching the pocket watch?"

No one else replied.

"Do you have non-latex gloves?" Sabine asked. "Medium?"

Wolf nodded as he got up from his chair.

"Your dad was also allergic to latex," O'Dell said.

"Yes, he was." Sabine wondered how O'Dell knew that.

"I read through everything related to the case," O'Dell explained before Sabine asked. "The detective who worked on it has retired, but he wrote very good reports."

That made sense, but...

Something bothered Sabine, and she didn't know why. To begin with, had it been important for the police report to note that Dad was allergic to latex when the case had been about a murder?

Wolf returned with a pair of nitrile gloves that fit Sabine's fingers perfectly. Slowly, Wolf pushed the tray toward Sabine's side of the table.

Sabine studied the watch on the tray in front of her. Tears welled up in her eyes. This was the last thing Dad owned that they didn't have.

"Does it look like the same pocket watch that your dad gave to you?" Ming asked, as though trying to keep her mind too busy to feel sad.

"No. Dad gave Mom, my sister, and me plain gold pocket watches. I don't even carry mine with me. Looks like he kept the most intricately designed one for himself." She laughed.

"So they're not alike." Cayson seemed to rehash what Sabine just said for whatever reason.

"Not alike at all. Ours don't have any recording system. They're just plain." Sabine left out something: all three of the *plain* pocket watches that Dad had given them had tracking devices. After Dad passed away, Helen upgraded their pocket watches to work with GPS worldwide.

Now she wished she had carried her pocket watch everywhere just to keep Dad's memory alive. However, she found it bulky. It competed with her phone for space in her purse. And she didn't want to lose the last gift her dad had given her.

Dad's pocket watch was even more special. She hoped that they'd be able to get it back soon from the SPD.

Sabine closed her eyes and tried very hard to recall what Dad had shown her about this watch.

Back then, she was working for Dad and had been the first person to see any new gadgets that Dad bought. This was no exception.

Unfortunately, it had been a while, and she recalled not paying great attention to "yet another thing" that Dad dragged into the office.

Sabine kept her eyes closed and prayed for clarity.

Actually, Dad had the pocket watch for a while before he showed it to Sabine. He didn't show her how the watch worked, but she had seen him work on it when she passed by him. Her eye for observational details would have to come in handy now.

Sabine lifted the pocket watch and turned it to the caseback. The intricate engraving was intact. There were many scratches on the gold, including a dent to one side of the rear casing. There were no hinges.

Now she remembered.

She placed her entire palm on it and twisted it. Nothing happened.

"It's dented." Ming pointed out. "That might stop it from twisting."

Sabine handed it to the watchmaker. "Dad would press his entire palm on the back panel and twist it. I can't remember if it's clockwise."

The watchmaker nodded. He tapped it here and there with his tools, and after a while, he managed to remove the back outer shell the way Sabine had shown him.

It was the first breakthrough.

Inside was a flat surface inlaid with diamonds outlining the shape of a cross in the middle.

"Glitters hidden for thirteen years," O'Dell noted. "How much do you think the pocket watch is worth?"

Wolf didn't want to commit to a figure. "I'll have to appraise it, but if these diamonds are real, it could fetch a pretty penny."

"Not under five thousand?" O'Dell asked. "Diamond inlays are on the dial."

"More than that," Wolf said. "Plus 18k gold is everywhere."

"So how much would this fetch at auction?" O'Dell asked. "At least a million?"

"I don't know," Wolf said. It sounded like a genuine answer.

O'Dell didn't ask any more.

But the fact that he had made Sabine wonder. Why would he ask about the price at all?

Sabine studied the indentation. It was about two inches tall and as deep as...

Sabine looked down at the cross necklace around her neck.

What were the odds?

She lifted her necklace off her neck, and removed the cross from the gold chain. Nervously, she pressed the cross into the indentation on the pocket watch.

Click.

"The cross is the key," Ming exclaimed.

Sabine pushed the tray back to the watchmaker, whose eyes lit up like Christmas had arrived.

"Interesting." The watchmaker studied the complications inside via a magnifier. "Hmm... Very interesting."

Finally he looked up. "I need to study this pocket watch some more, but I can tell you that there are at least fifteen complications on it. It would explain why the pocket watch is thicker and heavier than ordinary ones."

"What's there that's not usually in a pocket watch?" O'Dell cut to the chase.

Cayson leaned over. Sabine did too, staring at the gears.

Wolf probed a bit more and found a panel. Behind the gold panel, they found gold.

"Looks like there's a flash card here and a coin-cell battery that may or may not work after thirteen years." Cayson pointed.

"How did they get a flash memory card into a case that small back in those days?" Ming asked.

"Thirteen years ago is not prehistoric," Cayson said. "MicroSD cards were sold two years before Mr. Hu passed away. From the looks of it, this is one of those tiny cards."

"How do you activate it?" Sabine asked.

Cayson donned a pair of gloves. Sabine assumed that he'd had a pair on earlier and had removed them before he went to get coffee.

They all waited for Cayson to inspect the flash card.

"Yep. I was right. Battery's out," Cayson announced. "I think I need to take this back to my lab in Atlanta. I don't want to break anything."

O'Dell agreed. He turned to Sabine. "Sorry we have to wait some more."

Ming squeezed her shoulder.

"I've waited for thirteen years. What's another few days?" Sabine picked up her cross from the table.

"Best to keep that with the pocket watch for now," O'Dell said. "It's the key, after all."

"Right." Sabine nodded.

"If you want, you can fly with me back to Atlanta." Cayson directed his invitation to Sabine. "I know Ming has clearance to enter Binary Systems, so if I can get a special permission for you, will you come?"

"Yes, I want to." Sabine didn't hesitate. She wanted to be there.

Unfortunately, O'Dell stepped in and disallowed it.

"I brought you here because the watchmaker and Cayson were unable to safely open the pocket watch without the risk of breaking it. Turns out you have the key." O'Dell pointed to Sabine. "It's my job to maintain the chain of custody of this pocket watch so that there's no evidence contamination. We don't want anything being inadmissible in your father's murder trial. So no, you can't go to the Binary Systems lab with us."

"Understood," Ming said.

Sabine said nothing, but she thought that O'Dell was rude not to name Wolf. He had simply called him "the watchmaker." Since O'Dell knew his name, why didn't he use it?

Maybe she was thinking too much, but earlier, O'Dell had remembered that Sabine didn't shake hands. He had also recalled that Dad was allergic to latex. But now he apparently couldn't remember Wolf's name. Perhaps he had chosen not to say it for whatever reason. What would the reason be?

"At the right time, the prosecutor might allow

family members to listen to your dad's recording—if there's any at all to begin with," O'Dell assured them. "Then we'll arrange for you to come to SPD. Okay?"

Sabine nodded. "Thank you."

She felt a slight headache. Maybe she was indeed overthinking these details, but she was starting to get an uneasy feeling about O'Dell, and this was only their second meeting.

What was she missing?

While Sabine nursed her developing headache, O'Dell jotted in his leather notebook.

Sabine glanced at the blue ink flowing on the off-white lined pages. "You have neat handwriting."

O'Dell didn't look up. "Thank you."

He seemed to know that Sabine was referring to him.

He finished his notes and then closed the notebook. He placed the cap carefully over the nib of the pen.

"What a nice fountain pen. Is the barrel made of resin?" Sabine pointed to the swirls.

"Yes, indeed."

"What brand is it?"

"It's a Montegrappa Elmo 02 Croda Rossa." O'Dell put both pen and notebook away, as if Sabine would want to touch them. "You like fountain pens?"

"I usually type on my phone or laptop," Sabine said. "Unfortunately."

"Yes, unfortunately." O'Dell sighed. "Handwriting and calligraphy are both becoming lost arts."

Lost arts.

Funny that he should mention that.

CHAPTER 16

Twenty-four hours later, Helen called Sabine and Ming to tell them the bad news. Ming was at home with the kids, but Sabine was driving home from a house showing in Savannah. Usually, she didn't have to, but one of her real estate agents was out sick, and Sabine filled in for her because she had a couple of hours to spare.

"O'Dell lost Dad's pocket watch." Helen had received the news from Cayson Yang on the quiet. It wasn't something that Ming could talk to Camden about at all, even though the FBI special agent could do nothing if the evidence was missing altogether.

"What exactly happened?" Sabine asked.

With Sabine on audio only in the car in the three-way conversation, Ming couldn't see Sabine's reaction to the news. He could only hear her voice and the slight disappointment in it.

"It's bizarre that this happened, not that it's unusual," Helen said. "O'Dell told Cayson that he drove from Savannah to Atlanta last night. He stopped southwest of Atlanta to get gas."

"Southwest?" Ming asked. "That's kinda out of the way, isn't it, if he was going north to Alpharetta on I-75?"

Ming had driven that way before, and it wasn't that bad a drive through Atlanta on Interstate 75, except for the slow traffic.

"Not really. He had already merged onto I-85 just south of I-20, when he realized he was running low on gas. So he didn't take a detour or miss an exit."

"According to him," Sabine said.

"After he filled the tank, he went inside to get a pack of cigarettes and some coffee for the evening," Helen said. "Then he went back to the car and drove away."

"Oh no," Sabine said.

Did Sabine know something more than what she had told Ming the day before on their drive home from the watchmaker's shop? As much as Ming wanted to believe that Sabine had misgivings about O'Dell, he had reminded her not to be too paranoid, but to trust the SPD.

"Then what?" Ming didn't want to guess.

Calmly, Helen continued on the phone. "When O'Dell arrived in Atlanta shortly after midnight, he went straight to Binary Systems in Alpharetta. Cayson was waiting for him, having flown home late afternoon and working at night. However, when O'Dell went to his backseat to get his messenger bag, it was gone. Guess what was in the messenger bag?"

"You tell us," Sabine said.

"I was hoping you'd guess." Helen sighed.

"O'Dell suspected that someone had stolen the bag from his car when he stopped to get gas. Atlanta PD is all over it, but the surveillance video at the gas station was down, and nobody said they saw anything."

Ming thought that it was a plausible story. "Happens all the time in downtown Atlanta, right?"

"He said he left the door unlocked when he went inside the gas station," Helen continued. "That would be the only place he could think of because he hadn't stopped anywhere else between his house in Savannah and Cayson's office in Alpharetta."

"Could he have forgotten and left it at home?" Ming asked.

"What I wondered too. Cayson told me that O'Dell called his girlfriend to check his house to see if he'd left the duffel bag at home," Helen said. "He's divorced and lives alone in a small one-bedroom townhouse that is minimally furnished. His girlfriend FaceTimed him on live video so that he could follow along as she walked around the house. The duffel bag was gone."

Silence.

Then Sabine spoke. "Let me pull over to a parking lot here and catch my breath."

As Ming waited, he prayed for Sabine to drive carefully. Savannah might not have as much traffic as Atlanta, but Savannah had been where Sabine and Helen had that wreck seven years ago.

"Okay. I've parked the car. Go on." Sabine's voice was calm, given the circumstances.

They were very close to finding out the audio recording—if any—that Edgar had left them. If he had, then the case could be solved, and the Hu family could find closure.

And now this.

"For some reason, O'Dell picked one of the most dangerous parts of town to get gas at ten o'clock at night. He said he was looking for food, having skipped dinner." Helen's voice was calm.

"You believe him?" Sabine asked.

"I've known him for many years," Helen replied. "He's always walked the straight and narrow. Even went to church almost every week when he wasn't working on Sundays. He has always been honest with me. I even comforted him after his divorce. Seriously, I can't imagine O'Dell being anything but a sincere man who loves his job."

"It must devastate him to break the chain of custody on the very thing that could potentially solve your dad's murder," Ming said.

"For sure. That's what I think too." Helen sighed. "I can't talk to him to see how he's doing because I'm not supposed to know all these things. The only reason Cayson blurted it all out to me is that we're working on a project together, and he couldn't help talking about it because it's on his mind."

"Did Cayson suspect anything?" Sabine asked.

"No, he has no opinion." Helen sounded like she believed Cayson. "He told me what happened because he wondered if he should have asked to take the pocket watch with him on his own flight out of Savannah yesterday."

"He couldn't have because O'Dell is in charge of the evidence," Ming said.

"And now the last piece of the puzzle could

possibly be lost forever," Sabine added. "What is the SPD going to do about it?"

"Apparently, due to negligence, O'Dell is on administrative leave pending investigation into the matter," Helen replied.

"I see." Sabine sighed. "We haven't heard the recording—if any—on Dad's pocket watch. If it turns out to be nothing at all, then it doesn't affect the case, right? Dad's murderer would still be at large, unless Gene could convince the court that he's really guilty... or the real murderer somehow shows up after thirteen years."

"It's terrible that after all the hard work we did, we're back to square one." Ming wondered what they could do about it.

"The only thing we can do now is pray for God to show us the truth," Sabine concluded.

"I agree," Helen said. "Someone please volunteer to pray because I have to go in a few minutes."

"I'll pray." Ming cleared his throat. "Father God, thank You that Jesus Christ is the way, the truth, and the life. Today we ask You in His name to show us the truth about this situation. Give us peace so that we will not fret over it. Thank You, Jesus. In Your holy name, I pray. Amen."

Ming had prayed out of John 14:6, which was truer than ever when he was at work, searching for truth.

Jesus said to him, "I am the way, the truth, and the life. No one comes to the Father except through Me.

A chorus of "amen" echoed on the phone, and then Helen hung up.

"You okay?" Ming asked Sabine.

"God is teaching us something."

"Always. This time it's more than just patience, right?"

"I think He wants us to trust Him to show us the way through the roadblocks."

"Sometimes it's also over or around the roadblocks."

"I agree."

Silence.

Then: "Something doesn't add up, Ming."

When Sabine called his name, she meant business.

"Do you believe what O'Dell said about how Dad's pocket watch went missing?" Sabine asked.

"I'm not sure." Ming was being honest. Part of him wanted to trust the detective because Helen had spoken highly of him. However, he was still human and could sin just like anybody else on earth.

"Well, I'm not sure either."

Then and there, Ming suspected that Sabine was going to do something about it.

CHAPTER 17

May

"Don't get me wrong." Sabine put a palm on Ming's knee as they sat in their sunroom with the air conditioner and fan at full blast. "There's nothing between Garvey and me. We broke up seven years ago."

Sleeping in his dog bed in a corner of the sunroom, Pickles opened his eyes to look at the couple on the couch.

"You and I have been married for four years. We have three kids—including this one." Sabine pointed to her belly. "If this doesn't tell you that I've moved on, I don't know what will."

When Ming didn't answer, Sabine continued. "Are you insecure?"

"I'm not." Ming was too quick to say it.

Sabine held his hands and looked straight into his dark brown eyes. "Dear husband, I don't have to remind you that I dated Garvey for a very short time. He dumped me as soon as I became a burden after my accident."

"He must think there's still a connection between you two," Ming said. "Why else would he ask to meet you in person? You remember that his lawyer said he has something to tell you and only you."

"Maybe he trusts me because I'm a Christian."

"You think that's it?"

"I'm taking it at face value. In any case, it's a moot option now. All sides said no," Sabine reminded him. "The Chatham County Detention Center said it would violate the no-contact order between the accused and the victim's family. The judge also said no. So did the prosecution side and the defense attorneys."

"Makes sense. Garvey's defense team was afraid that he might say more than he should, and thus strengthen the state's case against him."

"The prosecutors thought that he might influence my family when we testify about our pain and suffering, among other things, and thereby weaken their case."

"I'm glad you're not going to meet with him."

"Aren't you curious about what he wanted to tell me?" Sabine drew a deep breath. "Bobby Kane poured gasoline all over the leather seats of Dad's car before he towed it to a remote street and set it on fire. Considering that Bobby worked in Gene's garage, maybe Garvey saw something and wanted to confess."

Ming rubbed Sabine's shoulders. "If he's involved,

whether as a witness or an accessory to the crime, will you forgive him?"

"As hard as it might be, I have to forgive, but it doesn't mean I will ever see him again or have anything to do with him, you know?" Sabine's voice was clear. "As we have discussed in January, forgiveness is not the same as reconciliation."

Ming nodded. "You and I forgave each other and reconciled under a different set of circumstances."

"As far as the people who murdered my dad and —or—burned his body afterwards, I can forgive them from over here and release them to be judged over there by the perfect God who is just and fair. I don't ever have to be reconciled with them. Our ways have parted. I bear no vendetta against them or their family."

"Aren't the two of the suspects or persons of interest the last of the Gilroys?"

"I think so. It might explain why Gene was insistent about taking the blame for the murder he might not have committed."

The sunroom fell silent.

"Hmm. Is it too quiet?" Sabine asked nervously.

"Zachary is asleep in his crib upstairs." Ming checked the baby monitor app on his phone and showed it to Sabine. "Yep. He's still sleeping like a baby."

Sabine glanced at her phone. "We can go pick up Hannah from preschool in an hour. Meanwhile, I think we need to call Helen and see what she has to say about Garvey's request."

"Good idea. She has connections."

Sabine sipped water from her water bottle, and

then called her sister on video and relayed to her what Garvey's lawyer said, adding that his request to see Sabine had been denied.

"Interesting." Helen was at her office in Savannah.

Sabine could hear other voices in the room.

"Did y'all hear what my sister just said?" Helen asked people who were off camera. She panned the phone around the room so that Sabine and Ming could see who else was there.

"Hey Earl. Whassup?" Ming waved at the phone camera.

The two men greeted each other.

On camera, Helen dismissed the other people in her office.

"Gimme a sec to switch this over to a bigger screen so that you can see both Earl and me at the same time." Helen motioned for Earl to bring a chair around to her side of the desk.

When Helen had finished setting up her video conference screen, Sabine summarized the situation.

"Hmm." Helen looked at Earl.

"Hmm." Earl looked at Helen.

"Are we starting an emo rap band?" Ming asked.

No one answered him.

"I know some people inside the CCDC." Earl tapped the armrest of his chair.

"You mean like correctional officers?" Sabine asked.

"Like inmates," Earl corrected her. "Since Garvey Gilroy is not in solitary confinement, he's probably mixed in with convicted inmates. The same people in the same unit would eat together. I'll dig around to see if inmates in his cell block might be able to befriend him."

"They could find out what he wants to tell me so badly." Sabine felt relieved. That way, she didn't have to see Garvey ever again.

"Wouldn't the SPD have the same idea?" Ming asked. "Detective O'Dell is sharp and astute."

Had Ming just thrown O'Dell a compliment? Sabine decided she'd better be careful about what she said about the detective in front of Ming—his status as her husband notwithstanding.

"Do you think an inmate who has been convicted by the Savannah courts due to the hard work of SPD officers would do work for them?" Sabine asked.

"Yes, many times over. Maybe they'd get their sentences shortened or charges reduced."

"I see." Learning as she went, Sabine thought of how valuable this inside information might be. "However, we're not SPD and cannot reduce charges."

"And we might mess up the case for the prosecutors," Ming said. "If there's a mistrial, Gene and Garvey might go free."

"They're not going free," Helen said. "I'll talk to O'Dell and see what he has to say."

"That makes sense. O'Dell is not only in charge of the case, but he's a good man." Ming sounded like he liked the detective. "Over the years, I've called him many times to ask for his advice on cases and such."

"Me too," Helen said.

Oh dear. Now her sister too?

Sabine wasn't sure what to think about Helen and Ming both having good things to say about O'Dell. Then again, both of them had worked with O'Dell for many years. So it was expected of them to say kind words. Right?

"No." Sabine's voice was firm. "I think we need to ask someone else outside of the SPD."

"Why?" Ming asked.

"For objectivity." Sabine's answer came swiftly. Truth be told, it was the first thing that popped into her head.

"Who do you suggest?" Helen leaned toward the camera. Her face looked like she was almost using a fishbowl filter. Her nose was on the camera.

"Camden." Sabine prayed for the power of persuasion, something she was short of. Slowly, she began. "Camden la Salle."

"Cam?" Ming looked puzzled. "Why?"

He sounded so much like Hannah when Sabine told her she couldn't put her dirty hands all over the cookie jar.

Why, Mommy? Whyyyyyy?

"Cam's Art Crime Team is investigating Gene and Garvey. He would be interested to know what little secrets Garvey wants to tell me without police presence," Sabine said.

Everyone nodded.

"I think we need to consider the fact that Garvey doesn't want to speak to O'Dell. Why? Isn't that a question we should ask?" Sabine rested her case.

Yeah, overcome them with logic.

Sabine wasn't sure if it would work. She prayed that her sister, who was even more paranoid than she, would take the hint. The last thing Sabine wanted was to argue with Ming so soon after they had reconciled.

"I think you're right, Sister," Helen finally said. "I will call Cam first and see what he says."

"What about O'Dell?" Ming stared at Sabine, as though suspecting something.

"If Cam has information from the FBI to share with SPD, then O'Dell would hear about it," Sabine said.

"O'Dell might ask us why we didn't go to him first."

"We've known Cam and Iris since high school," Sabine said. "We even babysit one another's kids. Why would O'Dell be slighted if all Helen is doing is asking Cam for advice on how to proceed?"

"Exactly." Helen seemed to be on board now. "I'm going to start it that way."

Sabine smiled. Her sister is something else. Helen understood her almost right away. However, it didn't mean that Sabine would jump ship from SRI and go work for Helen. Helen could sometimes be too intense for her.

"Keep us posted," Ming said just as the baby monitor crackled.

"Zachary is awake." Sabine was about to get up from the couch.

"I'll go get him. You put your feet up." Ming left the conversation.

"If you think of anything else, let me know," Helen said to Sabine.

Sabine nodded into the camera.

"I'll call you when I have updates."

"Text me," Sabine said.

"Oh?" Helen made a face, as though she was saying, "Something's up."

Sabine wasn't trying to keep secrets from Ming, her one and only husband, the love of her life. It was just that she hadn't worked with him prior to this. Ming at the office might be different from Ming at home.

Sure, they had been married for four years, but Sabine needed time to recover from the last year, including the especially trying three months she had been separated from Ming.

Yes, time. It would take time for her to recover and regain her bearing with Ming.

Who was to say he wouldn't run off to wherever again without first discussing it with her? Even though she was now a business partner, he'd have to rebuild her sense of security with him.

Sabine couldn't believe she was thinking along those lines.

She was more sure now than ever that she needed to discuss with Ming about going for counseling. She had heard that Diego's semi-retired father was a good marital counselor, although he only worked part time at Riverside Chapel.

If only their marriage was smoother than this, they could be spending time with each other and their kids, enjoying the happy moments of life, instead of having to go to counseling to repair cracks in their marriage.

Then again, Sabine was thankful to God that their church had a godly counseling department.

After hanging up the video call, Sabine prayed silently for wisdom. Before she could finish her prayer, she heard Ming come down the stairs with Zachary. The baby was laughing.

"Do you appreciate my useful skill?" Ming asked as he sat down on the couch with the baby on his lap. "I can make our baby laugh."

Sabine smiled. "That, you can."

"I think something's on your mind." Ming said those words so casually that Sabine was taken off guard.

"A lot of things are on my mind," Sabine replied quietly.

"Including?"

"Marital counseling, for example." Sabine waited for Ming to respond.

"I thought we were fine now." Ming cooed and Zachary cooed back. The baby was all smiles.

"Well, we were fine when we went for premarital counseling during our engagement," Sabine reminded Ming.

"True. So this is like another preventive measure?" Ming looked at Sabine intently, as if it was one of the most important questions he'd ever asked her.

"More like maintenance."

Slowly Ming nodded. "How much does it cost?"

"I know that church members get discounts. I want to say thirty percent off, but I'll have to check."

"If we get Pastor Flores—Diego's dad—I think that's best. We'll pay whatever the session fees are."

"Really?" Sabine's eyes brightened.

"Really." Ming reached over to her arm and drew her closer to him. The baby was still cooing on his lap. "Pastor Flores has been married for decades and has counseled many couples. He's got street cred, so to speak."

"If nothing else, he could tell us stories about how he has stayed married for so long." Sabine chuckled.

"Yeah. Call the counseling office now if you want."

"Seriously?" Sabine checked her phone. "Almost time to pick up Hannah from preschool. I'll call after I come home."

"Since Zachary is awake, how about we all go?" Ming said. "We can call the church from the car."

"Okay."

"Maybe after we get the counseling session scheduled, you can tell me what's on your mind," Ming added.

"Why do you say that?"

"I saw the signals you were sending your sister on the video call."

Oops. "What signals?"

"Like you're hiding something from me."

Sabine was surprised that Ming had noticed. "What are you talking about?"

"Still not talking?" Ming put Zachary down on the rug and gave him a chew toy. The baby salivated all over it.

Ming pulled Sabine up, sat down in his favorite spot on the couch, and gently placed her on his lap. He wrapped his arms around her and stared into her eyes. "Speak."

Sabine giggled. "No."

"Speak, my dearest wife, or I will..."

"You will what?"

Saying not another word, Ming kissed her.

And thereby sparing her from spilling all.

CHAPTER 18

On Wednesday, Ming found himself tailing his wife as she drove out of Savannah. He had to guess where Sabine was going, and it was making him upset by the minute as he drove his truck behind her car.

He was also mad at himself for not asking Sabine directly. It wasn't that he didn't trust her, but that he was afraid of what she might tell him.

He felt that he'd lost forty-nine percent of Savannah River Investigations shares to a potential disruptor whom he might not be able to rein in. How was he going to balance his role as a business partner and a husband?

Then again, wasn't he being hypocritical? The three-month rift in their marriage had been largely due to his doing the very thing he was condoning now.

The Dubai project had come about because Ming hadn't wanted to talk it through with Sabine before he took the assignment—because he feared that she'd be the voice of reason he didn't need at that time.

Sabine would have calculated the return on his investment and found it short. She would've run background checks on his prospective client and found her dubious.

But no. He had to just do it and explain later.

Now tasting his own bitter medicine watching Sabine drive off into the sunset without talking to him —or even telling him—all about it, Ming fumed as he drove on Augusta Road, ten minutes behind Sabine.

Wait a minute. If Sabine was heading to Port Wentworth, why hadn't she taken Georgia Highway 25 going north instead of Augusta Road? That small city was just outside Savannah.

Who had told him that Sabine was going to Port Wentworth at all? Well, the Post It note on the kitchen counter had said so. When Ming had seen it, he'd wondered what could possibly be in Port Wentworth that had pricked Sabine's interest.

When Sabine kept driving north on Georgia Highway 21, heading into the state interior, Ming's heart dropped to the floor of the truck. This area was outside the focus of her real estate brokerage.

Where in the world was Sabine going?

Ming resisted picking up the phone and calling. It would put Sabine on alert and potentially on the defensive. Ming found it more nerve-wracking to follow her and discover for himself.

Fifteen minutes later, they drove through the city of Rincon. When Sabine didn't stop, Ming started to panic.

Four months pregnant, Sabine shouldn't be out

and about after the sun went down. Not wanting to confine her to the house, Ming expected her to be reasonable, sensible, and think of their baby.

Ming wanted to call her reckless, but then he himself had done a lot of reckless things in his life.

I'm sorry, Sabine.

He finally had an inkling of what she had felt whenever he'd run off without an explanation, living and working like he was still unmarried.

Then again, now that they were business partners, shouldn't they have stuck together as a team? Kept each other posted, at least?

All Sabine had told him was that Mama Hu wanted to keep the kids on Wednesday night, and she'd take them to the zoo for Hannah's preschool field trip. Mama Hu enjoyed carrying Zachary in a sling. Hannah would be with her fellow preschoolers and their teachers. Ming felt that it would be safe.

That freed up tonight for...what, exactly?

If Sabine hadn't left a Post It note in the kitchen, Ming wouldn't have an address to work with. So he turned on his phone tracker, put on his Mr. Paranoid baseball cap, and here he was at sunset, trailing his wife on the highway to...where exactly?

He wasn't sure if Sabine would be mad at him if she found out he'd been following her car out of town. If she would, then he'd point out that she had left a clue on the kitchen counter and hadn't turned off her cell phone locator—not that either actions were invitations for him to tag along.

If she fussed, he'd remind her of the conversation at the Hiawassee Hospital in January. Within earshot of Sabine, Helen said that she didn't have time to hire a bodyguard for Sabine, to which Ming said that he would protect her himself.

Here he was, exercising his duty.

At Springfield, the next city on Georgia Highway 21, Sabine's phone remained stationary at a gas station. That gave Ming time to catch up with her.

Minutes away now, Ming watched his mounted phone screen as a blip representing Sabine's car pull into an apartment complex.

No.

Ming's heart raced. She wasn't having an affair, was she?

Sabine's signal became stationary again. She must have parked her car. Looking for Sabine's car, Ming cruised the parking lot around four five-story apartment buildings. The GPS brought him to Building C, which overlooked a fence, some bushes, and a four-lane street.

It was too dark for Ming to see what was on the other side of the street. He could hear vehicles coming and going at a steady pace, including what sounded like work trucks and motorcycles without mufflers. Of course, he'd have to verify if he was right, but in the twilight, he could only go with what he heard.

He found Sabine's car.

Ming found a parking spot about five vehicles away. He backed into the spot so that his license plate didn't readily show. He waited to see if anyone came out of Sabine's car. No one did. The parking lot had a few lights, just enough to show Ming that nobody was walking about.

Sabine had probably parked and left the car quickly before Ming arrived.

He unbuckled his safety belt, climbed out of his truck, and locked it. He tried to act normal, but he walked toward Sabine's car cautiously. The evening air was muggy, and he began to sweat.

When he reached Sabine's car, he saw that it was unoccupied. His thoughts immediately went to the building. She had probably entered the building. Which floor? Which apartment?

He walked toward the building, feeling silly now. There was an elevator on the ground floor near a flight of stairs.

How was he going to find Sabine?

His phone locator clearly stated that she was still in the building, but it couldn't tell her which apartment on which floor.

Desperate, he texted Sabine.

MING

Where are you?

No immediate reply.

Was she ignoring him or was she in trouble?

Seconds later, his phone buzzed.

SABINE

#509.

Sabine wasn't even trying to hide.

Ming's phone buzzed again. He looked at the display to find another text message from Sabine.

SABINE

> Could you get my water bottle from
> the car? I forgot it.

As he walked to Sabine's car, Ming felt stupid at first. Then he felt angry that Sabine hadn't even thought of including him in whatever she was doing tonight.

After retrieving Sabine's insulated water bottle from the front passenger side of the car, Ming wondered if Sabine had only made it sound like she wasn't trying to hide because he'd caught her.

This could go so many ways.

Or maybe I'm overthinking this.

Ming walked up five flights of stairs to calm himself down. By the time he reached the top floor, he was drenched in sweat.

He berated himself for being excessively worried. Maybe rightly so.

Was Sabine punishing him for what she'd called "abandonment" when he'd unilaterally taken that assignment in Dubai without considering her thoughts?

Then again, how could the two situations be alike at all? Who knew what went through a woman's mind?

Ming found himself standing in front of Apartment 509, catching his breath and trying to muster up his remaining dignity.

He could've been at home watching TV or doing bookkeeping for SRI. But no, he had to go all paranoid and follow his wife from Savannah to Springfield.

So, now that he was here, he could ask her what she was doing in Springfield.

He wiped sweat off his forehead, and prayed for mercy, wisdom, and thick skin.

He rang the doorbell.

Half expecting drama and half expecting nothing, Ming waited.

The door unlocked, and standing there was...

Helen Hu.

"Since you're here, you might as well come in, but I'm not paying you for this." Helen held the door and stepped aside to let Ming through.

Ming had no words to reply to his sister-in-law.

The apartment was largely empty save for a few chairs and two folding tables in the center of the room. On the tables were laptops, three of them.

A man was sitting in one of those chairs at the table. Facing away from Ming, he couldn't tell who it was until he turned around.

It was Earl Young, also from the Savannah office of Hu Knows, Inc.

"What happened to your hair?" Ming exclaimed.

"Nice to see you too, bro." Earl ran a large palm over his nearly bald head. "This is my summer cut."

"You didn't have this haircut last summer." Ming sat down next to Earl.

"Last summer, I didn't have to go undercover wearing a wig. You know how hot summer is in Atlanta."

Ming nodded. "When did you get here from Atlanta?"

"Last night. I slept on the most uncomfortable cot in the world." Earl pointed to the lone bedroom.

Yes, Ming was still worried about Sabine, but he didn't want to embarrass himself in front of Helen and Earl by looking possessive. He tried to make small talk with Earl, but tried as he might, he couldn't avoid thinking of his wife.

"Where's Sabine?" Ming asked.

"I wondered when you'd start looking for her." Helen chuckled. Dressed in all black, she looked like she was ready to disappear into the night somewhere. She wore socks on her feet. Ming spotted a pair of platform boots on the carpeted floor near a chair. She must've kicked off her boots to be more comfortable.

Helen pointed to the bedroom. "She's in the bathroom over there."

Ming walked into the bedroom. It was empty save for a cot, which Earl had mentioned earlier. A small rolling carry-on bag was up against the wall, and a pair of sneakers neatly lined up next to it. Earl's belongings.

Ming heard the toilet flush and the sink run in the bathroom behind a closed door.

He waited, wondering what he would say to her.

The door unlocked and opened.

"Oh, my bodyguard is here." Sabine chuckled.

Ming wove his arms around Sabine's distended waist.

"I was so worried about you," Ming whispered between kisses.

"I know."

"Is this my punishment?" Ming pressed his forehead against hers and closed his eyes.

"For what?"

"For four years of being too busy to spend time with you." Ming hugged her gently.

"You spent time with me. How else did we have three kids?"

Ming laughed. He didn't know what else to say except to speak his mind. "I wasn't sure where you went."

"You could've texted me."

"It's more fun this way." Ming tightened his arms around her waist.

"Be careful. Baby on board."

Ming loosened his grip slightly. He kissed her forehead.

"Stop making out, you two, and get back in here!" Helen's sharp voice startled Ming.

Sabine held Ming's hand as they walked out of the bedroom and took two seats at the table between Helen and Earl, who was eating a power bar.

"What are we looking at?" Ming sat down beside Sabine so that he could rub her back.

Earl pointed to his laptop screen, which showed an infrared video of a building. "The Garage of All Things. The GOAT. It's across the street."

Nothing was happening there. No movement. No people. Not even a stray cat. The video looked like a still photograph.

"Like The Museum of All Things? The MOOT?" Ming asked. "That one's owned by Gene Gilroy. Does he own this now too?"

"No," Helen said. "Gene has his own garage, which has been closed for a while now."

Earl drank some water. "It's interesting that even

though Garvey didn't get his request to see Sabine, it was still the big break we were looking for."

"Thanks to your connections, Earl." Helen reached over to grab one of his power bars. "And with a bit of help from Cam, though he doesn't know that we know more than he does."

"Which leads us to this place." Earl moved the computer mouse over his screen. "The GOAT is a part of the Springfield-Stillwell Auto Salvage Yard, cannibalizing its junkyard for auto parts."

"The junkyard covers two acres," Helen said. "In the daytime, we could see rusted vehicles everywhere."

"Whose bright idea was it to build an apartment complex across the street from that view?" Ming asked.

"Beats me. Maybe the land was cheap. If it wasn't, it is now." Earl went on to give a virtual tour of the property.

Ming tried to focus, but he was a bit distracted, having felt that he'd come late to the party. In fact, he had to crash it.

He made a mental note to talk with Sabine later about sharing information in a more timely manner.

"We've been here for three days and three nights, and so far, it seems that nobody works there. The junkyard has been chained up. No one has walked around the yard." Earl turned to Helen to say more.

Helen didn't respond.

"Is it possible that the building has enough food for the people inside such that they don't have to come out to do groceries?" Ming asked.

"Or it's just empty." Earl shrugged.

"You mean your drones didn't hear any sound?" Ming pressed.

"I think the walls are soundproof," Helen said.

"Oh, the plot thickens." Sabine chuckled.

"We won't know if anyone's home until we go inside." Ming turned to Earl. "Don't you get cabin fever, cooped up in this apartment for three days?"

Earl didn't reply.

Helen drew a deep breath. "I think we give them until this weekend."

"Sure. I don't have anything else better to do anyway." Earl laughed.

There was something Helen wasn't saying. Ming could feel it. Not one to depend on his own hunches, he'd worked with Helen long enough to know that the professional private investigator wasn't going to waste seven days unless she knew something was going down.

"Have you two eaten dinner?" Sabine asked Helen and Earl. She sipped water from her water bottle.

"Is it dinnertime already?" Helen laughed.

"What about me?" Ming frowned. "Don't you want to know if I've eaten?"

"Didn't I leave you some chicken and rice in the fridge at home?" Sabine asked him.

"Yes, but I was in a hurry and left the house without eating."

"There you go. Don't blame me." Sabine smiled at him.

Ming wanted to pout, but he felt childish about griping. However, he didn't know how to let it go. He was nursing a hurt that no smiles could ameliorate.

Why hadn't Sabine asked him to come to the apartment before he found out about it? Why hadn't Helen said anything?

Ming wondered if Helen might be attempting to poach Sabine from SRI. He wasn't going to let that happen.

"Is this a Hu Knows operation?" Ming asked Helen.

"It is. However, Sabine's not getting paid, and I suppose you're not either."

"Shouldn't we get paid?"

"Didn't you volunteer to be here?" Helen asked.

Sabine turned to Ming. "How about we make this a SRI-HKI joint project? If we pay ourselves instead of drawing a check from Hu Knows, then they can't tell us what to do."

Oh.

Ming understood now. "Maybe next time we could check in with each other before we drive out."

He didn't know how to say it any other way. He wanted Sabine to be transparent with him, and vice versa.

"Got it," Sabine said. "Actually, I was on my way to install a lockbox at a commercial building in Port Wentworth when Helen called me. She and Earl had been here for two nights, and she asked if I wanted to join them here tonight because they were getting bored."

"Is that so?" Ming asked Helen. "Or maybe you're not bored, but you felt guilty. Your CCDC snitch had talked to Cam at the FBI, cutting us all out of the equation."

"The FBI is building their case also, which is why

Cam didn't tell us what they'd found out from Garvey," Helen confessed.

Ming knew Helen well from their years of collaboration. "So you snuck around and discovered The GOAT. Three nights of surveillance, and you felt guilty that you hadn't included Sabine and me in the fun. Shall I go on?"

Helen sighed. "I'm sorry. If I had asked one of you to come join us, the other would have wanted to come too."

"For sure," Sabine said.

"You're pregnant and I worry that you'll be in danger."

Sabine hugged her sister. "Thank you."

"I had to be sure it was safe for her to stay here in this apartment." Helen pointed to a suitcase near the kitchenette that Ming hadn't noticed before. "I brought ammo and such. If I have to protect my sister, I will."

Ammo and such?

Ming started to worry.

In any case, it would explain the address on the sticky note on the kitchen counter.

"You left a note at home," Ming reminded Sabine.

"I wrote the address down, but I also have it bookmarked on Google Maps. You knew I didn't make it to Port Wentworth. I came here instead."

"I was worried about you." Ming had no other explanation. What could he say in front of Earl and Helen that would embarrass himself any less?

"Thank you." Sabine leaned over and was about to kiss him on the cheek when Helen cleared her throat.

"No workplace canoodling!" Helen snapped.

Earl laughed.

Ming and Sabine giggled like school kids.

"Order in the workplace!" Helen added. "If you two weren't married—"

"To each other," Earl interjected.

"If you two weren't married," Helen repeated herself, "and expecting your third child, I wouldn't have tolerated this lovey-dovey PDA."

Ming wasn't bashful about their public display of affection. He wanted the whole world to know that Sabine was his and only his.

Earl laughed again. "No wonder you're still single, Helen."

"Touché, Earl."

CHAPTER 19

"You might be volunteers, but we're at work." Helen's voice rapped the air like she was a school hall monitor.

Ming didn't say that only Earl was working on his laptop. Helen was munching on Earl's snacks. Ming and Sabine were observers at best.

Speaking of Earl, Ming turned to see what he was doing. The man nearly dozed off. On the laptop, the screen was dark.

"Is it a moonless or cloudy night outside?" Ming asked Earl. "I don't see a thing."

Earl sat straight up. "Oh."

"Oh what?" Helen came around to stand behind Earl.

Helen was petite, and Earl was a big and tall man. His arms alone nearly blocked Helen's view of the screen. Ming got up to let Helen sit in his chair.

"What's happening? Where's my drone?" Earl frantically worked on his app to contact his drone.

"Don't you have a joystick or something?" Ming was not familiar with drones, even though he worked with Helen who was.

Earl shook his head. "It's autonomous. We borrowed it from Binary Systems."

"So where did it go?"

"I'm looking for it." Earl scratched his head.

"How long does the battery last?" Ming knew that commercial drones might last an hour, but since this one came from Binary Systems, it might operate at an experimental level.

"It has a lithium-sulfur battery that keeps it airborne for three continuous hours," Helen said.

Earl displayed an infrared satellite image of the junkyard. He pointed to a location on the other side of the junkyard, just outside a brick wall. "I think it fell into one of the two scrap metal bins."

He zoomed in. "X marks the spot."

The scrap metal bins were as large as roll-off dumpsters that Ming had seen at construction sites. They were filled to the top with steel and aluminum in all shapes and sizes.

"Nice of them to think of recycling," Ming remarked.

The bins lined up against the brick wall that closed off the junkyard. On top of the brick wall were coils of razor-edged concertina wire, making the junkyard look like a prison.

"Can you tell how far down into the bin the drone is in?" Sabine asked.

"Not until I go out there," Earl said.

"You're not planning to walk into the property of

a junkyard you're surveilling, are you?" Ming didn't think it was a particularly bright idea.

Earl displayed the coordinates. "The bins are outside the brick wall, remember? No gates. No barriers."

"Still..."

"The drone is a million dollars," Earl said. "I dozed off just now and lost it. Now I have to go dumpster diving to atone for my mistake."

"Send a rescue drone," Ming suggested.

"Ours is loud and only has a thirty-minute battery." Earl pointed to a drone on the floor. It looked like it was being charged up.

"I didn't expect Cayson's drone to fail," Helen said. "We need to have a good talk with him."

Everyone watched Earl try to contact the lost drone again. Earl was getting frustrated by the minute.

"He might be trying to draw us out," Helen said.

"He who?" Ming asked.

"The owner of The GOAT," Helen said as Earl busied himself calling Binary Systems for advice.

"Who is the owner?" Sabine asked Helen.

"We're only speculating, but if we're correct, it's Enzo Landry hiding behind a trust fund untraceable to him."

"Who in the world is Enzo Landry?" Sabine asked.

Ming had heard of him. He didn't want to confess that it had been during one of those slow work days when he'd spend more time surfing the news and reading about old cases.

"He served time for stealing classic cars, but he's been free for a while now," Ming said.

"Right. Fourteen years free." Helen ate another power bar in two bites. "What you might not know is that the year before he went to prison for grand theft auto, he ran over one of his workers while leaving his garage. No charges were ever filed against him, and he got away with murder—or involuntary manslaughter."

"You still had a dead body," Ming pointed out.

"An old mechanic took the blame, went to jail, and died in prison." Helen looked at her colleagues. "Sound familiar?"

"Do you think Gene heard about that story and decided to do the same for his nephew?" Sabine asked. "Or... Does Gene know Enzo?"

"It didn't look like it at first, but Leland and I found out that they're connected by way of an unexpected third party," Helen said.

"Unexpected?" Sabine's eyes darkened. "Let me guess."

"No need to guess. I'll say it for the record," Helen said. "He was in charge of both the grand theft auto and the murder cases because they intersected at one point or another."

Did she mean Detective Cosmo O'Dell?

Say it isn't so.

"That doesn't mean he's the missing dot," Ming said.

Helen swiped her iPad and handed it to Sabine.

"What am I looking at?" Sabine stared at the screen.

Ming leaned over and found that there were pages of screenshots. "A bunch of receipts?"

"Hospital, doctor visits, treatment plans—both in the States and overseas," Helen said.

"Who is Angelica O'Dell?" The last name made Ming's heart drop.

"His ex-wife?" Sabine asked.

"His daughter," Helen said. "She's thirty-seven years old, and currently lives in Missouri. She wants to move her mother back to Savannah, but it's a process."

Ming had no idea that O'Dell had any children. So closely guarded was his private life that it never came up when Ming talked to him about work.

"Did you know O'Dell has a thirty-seven-year-old daughter?" Ming asked Helen.

"No, I hate to say. I only found out after Earl's contacts talked with Garvey in prison. I didn't even know he had an ex-wife. I never asked. All I know is that he has a current girlfriend."

"Secrets." Still, Ming wanted to give O'Dell the benefit of the doubt. "O'Dell is sixty, so he was around twenty-three years old when his daughter was born."

"There's another name on some of these receipts." Sabine scrolled on the tablet. "Chalina O'Dell."

"That's his ex-wife. They divorced when Angelica was sixteen and in high school." Helen seemed to be making a mental calculation. "So it was twenty-one years ago."

"How could it be that neither you nor I knew O'Dell was married?" Ming asked.

"Best kept secret, huh?" Sabine chuckled.

"All I know is that they had been separated for a

while before their divorce." Helen went to the kitchenette to get a glass of water from the tap.

Ming tapped a few receipts here and there, and then pointed out something to Sabine as they both looked at the iPad.

"ER bills from eighteen years ago." It was all he needed to say to prompt Helen to explain why Chalina or Angelica had to go to the emergency room.

"After their divorce, Chalina and her daughter moved to Missouri. There, she worked as a cocktail waitress and met her then boyfriend. He quickly moved into their apartment, and over the next two years, he abused mother and daughter badly."

"So sorry to hear that." Sabine's voice was one of concern.

"Chalina refused to leave him in spite of her many trips to the ER. Angelica was afraid to move out because she didn't want her mom to face the beatings alone."

"She could have called the police," Sabine said.

"She finally did. She called her dad in Savannah," Helen said. "Feeling guilty, O'Dell paid for her to move out and hire a lawyer. Since Chalina had no health insurance, O'Dell also paid for their medical expenses, which escalated when Chalina was seriously injured in a workplace accident some six or seven years ago. She had internal injuries to her organs that required multiple surgeries. She fell into depression and couldn't work."

"Let me guess. O'Dell continued to support them," Ming stated.

Helen nodded. "That, plus he paid for Angelica's

tuition at the community college. She failed to graduate, but she drew closer to her dad."

"Good for them. Things looked up." Ming pointed to the iPad. "Why are we looking at all these?"

"Relevance," Earl said from his seat. He was busy at his laptop, trying to fly his drone out of the scrap metal dumpster. However, he seemed to have also heard their conversation.

"There's more," Helen said. "One year after Angelica dropped out of college, she was diagnosed with Multiple Sclerosis."

Ming waited for the other shoe to drop.

"O'Dell bore the entire cost himself. For the next four years, he took Angelica everywhere to find treatment, including to quack doctors overseas. Things got worse for her."

"There's no current cure for MS," Ming said clinically.

Helen concurred. "Angelica has severe vision loss in both eyes."

"Is she working?" Ming started to add up the numbers in his head.

"No. She and her mom are both entirely supported by O'Dell," Helen answered.

Which included the year Edgar Hu was murdered.

"At first I thought he'd taken up a side job after hours." Helen eyed Earl's power bar. He grabbed it and put it in his shirt pocket. "Maybe as a security guard or a consultant."

"But these expenses look like they were more than he could earn taking on two jobs," Sabine said.

Ming was afraid of that.

"How did you get these receipts?" Sabine asked.

"Dare we ask?" Ming chuckled.

"Why not?" Sabine countered. "If these ended up being inadmissible in court, how is that going to help us convict Dad's murderer?"

"Angelica gave them to me," Helen replied. "When I found out O'Dell had a daughter, I tracked her down and paid her a visit."

"You flew to Missouri?" Sabine asked.

"That, I did. Last week."

"Why did she give you the receipts?" Ming asked.

"She wanted me to know that her dad's a selfless, compassionate man," Helen said. "What she didn't realize is that these medical costs were more than what O'Dell could afford, based on his detective salary at SPD."

The puzzle pieces were fitting together, but Ming didn't like what they showed.

"I'll have to process this for a bit," Ming finally said. "I'm kind of...shocked."

"I knew you would be." Sabine patted his shoulder. "That was another reason I didn't tell you right away."

Ming couldn't believe what he'd just read and heard. He almost wanted to verify all of it. However, blood was thicker than water. He'd rather believe Helen now, especially since Sabine seemed to as well.

"You process whatever." Earl got up from his seat. "I'm going to rescue my drone."

"How?" Helen looked visibly worried about her employee.

"I'll drive around the block, park, and walk to the bins," Earl said.

"Suit up." Helen pointed to a corner of the living room where Ming saw lockable gun cases, range bags, and ammunition boxes.

What on earth had Helen been planning?

"I'll go with you," Ming suddenly said.

Just then thunder crackled.

CHAPTER 20

Five minutes into radio silence, Sabine started feeling a bit worried, as though something could go wrong at any time. The thunderstorm outside had reduced to heavy rain, but Sabine could still hear rumbling thunder in the distance.

Her unease split her mind and heart, and she sat there in her chair, palms on her belly, unable to think of the next step forward. Well, what else could she do but wait for news?

Her mind reminded her that Ming and Earl had said they would reestablish communication once they retrieved the drone from the scrap metal bins.

But Sabine's feelings started taking her mind to places that she normally wouldn't think about. She thought of their updated will, and how she was going to carry on if Ming...

Died.

Helen looked up from Earl's laptop every now and then. No smile, no word. She took a call from

Cayson Yang at Binary Systems in Atlanta, who asked about the drone.

After the call, Helen turned her chair to face Sabine, who hadn't left her seat.

Sabine was glad that her one and only sister was with her today.

"What does Philippians 4:6-7 say?" Helen asked.

"Is this a Bible sword drill?" Sabine remembered how Dad used to test their Bible knowledge on family road trips. Mom would keep score, even though she wasn't a Christian. Dad was a fount of knowledge about Bible trivia.

"You and I have both memorized these two verses, thanks to Dad. Sometimes it's good to say it aloud."

Sabine nodded and recited the verse. Even as she did, she knew that God had used her older sister to remind her to focus on Jesus.

Be anxious for nothing, but in everything by prayer and supplication, with thanksgiving, let your requests be made known to God; and the peace of God, which surpasses all understanding, will guard your hearts and minds through Christ Jesus.

"I don't want to lie to you and say that they will be okay." Helen pointed to Earl's laptop. There was nothing there for Sabine to see. "But God can see through darkness and fog."

Sabine nodded. "You're right. I need to walk by faith and not by sight. Thanks for the reminder."

For we walk by faith, not by sight.

205

Such a simple verse in 2 Corinthians 5:7, and yet so hard to execute.

"Even walking by faith requires faith," Sabine reminded herself.

"Indeed." Helen stood up beside her chair and stretched. "You want some snacks?"

"I actually want dinner, but it's not a good idea to order takeout, is it?" Sabine reached for her water bottle, but it was empty.

"Let's see what frozen dinners we have left." Helen made her way to the kitchenette, and Sabine followed her.

Sabine stood beside her, and they both stared into the freezer.

"Curry, curry everywhere." Helen thumbed through the stacked boxes of TV dinners. "I should've gone to the grocery store instead of Earl."

"I like curry."

"Isn't it too spicy for the baby?" Helen glanced at Sabine's tummy.

"I don't think frozen dinner curry will be too spicy. Besides, I'm only in the second trimester. I'll be fine."

"Okay, then. Let's have curry. Pick anything you like." Helen stepped aside to let Sabine go first.

Sabine picked chicken jalfrezi, and Helen opted for lamb vindaloo, which was spicier.

"Anything to drink?" Helen pointed to the refrigerator shelves. There was a variety of spring and sparkling water in glass bottles. "No micro plastic. No worries."

Sabine chose a bottle of sparkling water.

"Have a seat and dinner will be ready shortly."

Helen stepped toward the microwave. She used a fork to take out the rectangular frozen dinner chunk. Then she placed it into a shallow bowl that was wide enough. After she put a paper towel over the bowl, she put it into the microwave.

Helen returned to the work table and sat down in Earl's chair again. "Now that we have a moment to talk without your husband hovering over you..."

"Well, I suppose he's been clingy since we came home from Hiawassee." Sabine braced herself. "You could still call me though."

"It's about Garvey Gilroy."

"Ah, he's on Ming's blacklist." Sabine chuckled.

"Garvey swore that he didn't kill Dad," Helen began. "He denied killing anyone at all. Didn't know why his uncle confessed thirteen years later, even though we suspect it's because Gene wanted to protect his nephew."

"Tell me something I don't already know." Sabine wondered why Helen would repeat herself.

"Garvey said that he was working late into the night at the garage and drinking alone. He was about to leave when he saw a tow truck driving slowly on the road in front of the garage. It was dark, but he was certain it was a car, not a pickup truck or a van, sitting on the tow truck that night."

Sabine's jaw dropped. "He saw Bobby Kane's tow truck?"

"I'm guessing it was."

"But he didn't say a word to the police. Why?"

"I wondered too. Maybe he thought that his uncle would be implicated."

"That's odd, considering that the tow truck hadn't

originated from Gene's garage. Police reports established that."

Assuming the police reports had been accurate. If they hadn't been, then perhaps Garvey knew more than he was letting on.

Sometimes Sabine wondered how crime families operated. Perhaps they had their own code of vigilante justice. In spite of that, they didn't trust one another. "All this time, Gene didn't believe a word that Garvey said."

"Garvey said that he'd told his uncle many times that he hadn't killed Dad, but they'd lied to each other so much that neither one believed the other."

Sabine had many questions, but what good would it do? There was Garvey in prison, saying whatever was on his mind to an inmate. Was anything he'd said even true? Wouldn't a chronic liar keep lying?

"By the way, Garvey told Earl's inmate contact that his uncle hadn't planned to drown you at the lake in Hiawassee back in January."

"Oh? The snitch said that?"

Helen nodded. "Garvey said that his uncle had knocked him out too to make him a fake victim. Gene thought that would absolve Garvey."

"So we were both not going to be thrown into the lake?"

"You maybe, but not Garvey."

"Thank God Ming and Cam arrived before it was too late." Sabine realized quickly she had forgotten her own sister. "And you too. You called Cam for help, didn't you?"

Helen nodded. "I did what I had to do."

"They arrived just in time. Thank you." Sabine hugged Helen.

"What are sisters for?" Helen patted her shoulders.

"Was that all that Garvey wanted to tell me in person?" Sabine had let Garvey go seven years earlier, so she had no feelings whatsoever for him today.

"I'm just telling you what Earl found out. You handle the information however you want." Helen went back to the kitchenette to take out the frozen dinner from the microwave. She put the bowl on a tray, along with a paper napkin, a spoon, and a fork.

"You came prepared." Sabine watched Helen put her own dinner into the microwave. Then she brought Sabine's tray to her.

"Looks like you're camping with real silverware." Sabine eyed her tray that Helen put at the edge of the table in front of her.

"Let's say grace so you can start eating." Helen sat down again. "I don't want your baby to go hungry."

Sabine let Helen thank God for the dinner. She wondered how many frozen dinners that Helen had to eat. Would she continue to live and work like this for years to come?

"To be sure, we don't always eat frozen dinners." Helen sounded like she had to explain. "This time, I put Earl in charge of food, and this is what he came up with."

"If you were in charge, he'd be eating ramen noodles out of cups." Sabine laughed.

"Well, I'd add some boiled eggs for protein." She sounded serious. "I didn't take after Dad, like you did. He could cook."

"He sure could." Sabine was silent for a while, and so was Helen. The rainstorm outside seemed to have subsided, so the silence was palpable.

"I miss Dad so much." Sabine's voice cracked. She reached for the cross necklace but it wasn't there. "Oh, that's right. SPD confiscated it."

"Your cross. You always wear it." Helen pulled out her own cross necklace. "Mine is identical to yours."

"Except for the initials inscribed on the back. Yours on your cross, and my initials on my cross."

"I know, but you miss Dad more than I do." Helen paused. "Don't get me wrong. I miss him, but you were the baby in the family, so you spent more time with him."

What Helen said was true.

"Still, don't you want to wear your cross?"

"I'll take it back when the SPD returns yours." When Helen had made up her mind, there was no changing it. She removed her cross necklace.

"All right, Big Sister. Just until the murder trial or sooner," Sabine said reluctantly.

"Let me put it on for you." Helen placed the gold chain gently around Sabine's neck and clasped the necklace in place.

Sabine placed a palm on the cross. It was warm. She blinked away tears. "I wish Dad could've seen his grandchildren, you know?"

"And watch us grow old." Helen drew a deep breath. "That's why we revisit the past, talk to people we would otherwise not want to see ever again—all to honor Dad's memory."

"People we dislike?"

"You know, people like Garvey."

"For the record, Dad had never approved of him," Sabine said. "He only dated me after Dad died."

"Exactly." Helen shook her index finger in the air. "For that reason, I had always suspected Garvey of the murder, but I had no evidence. Now that we do, the clues seem to point away from him."

"Both of us also thought that he had something to do with our wreck seven years ago," Sabine reminded her. "However, it has been established that the people in the other vehicle weren't related to the Gilroy family."

"They were just bad drivers who drove too fast on the highway."

"Thankfully, we survived. You walked away with just a scratch, but my legs were pinned."

"I'm not saying I survived because I was—still am —petite with short legs." Helen tried to make light of the situation, and Sabine knew that her sister's protective shields were up again.

"I believe that God allowed you to be unharmed because you had to get help for me," Sabine said. "You think clearly in such situations. I would've panicked and lost my focus."

"You're stronger than you think, Sabine."

Strong? Right now she didn't want to talk about Garvey, blight in her past. Was she not strong enough to handle history?

Sabine could ask Helen to stop talking about Garvey, but she still wanted clues about Dad's murder. Thirteen years later, she had met Garvey again. Was this providential? As painful as it might be, there might be a break in the cold case, even if it was nothing more than another dot to connect in their quest for truth.

"Garvey regrets breaking up with you."

"Regrets are a dime a dozen." Sabine shrugged. "Repentance, however, is harder to come by. Until he's willing to humble himself at the foot of the cross of Christ, he might never understand true regret and repentance."

"He feels remorse," Helen said.

"I wonder if he's trying to get his sentence reduced. Did he regret what he did to Dad's body? Is he trying to elicit sympathy from us, the victim's family?"

"I don't know how that's going to help him with his uncle claiming to be the murderer." Helen shook her head. "Gene's housekeeper told Earl that Gene was at home the entire night. He'd fallen asleep in front of the TV, and the housekeeper left him there in his favorite recliner before she went home to her own family. The living room camera recorded the entire night, and he hadn't left his recliner until dawn, when his dog fussed at him, wanting to go outside."

"All that didn't come from prison, did it?" Sabine asked.

"Not all."

"Are you reading reports you shouldn't have access to?"

"Third-party intel. You know how deep and wide the Hu Knows network is."

Sabine nodded. "If Dad were alive, he'd be so proud of you."

"Prouder if you come back to Hu Knows and work with me."

Sabine smiled. "I've already committed to helping SRI stay afloat. I think it will also help Ming and me to communicate more with each other about his work."

"What about your brokerage?"

"I might sell my shares to my business partners and retire from being a co-owner of the brokerage."

"Aren't you also one of the principal brokers?"

Sabine nodded. "I don't have to be a principal broker either. I can just be an associate broker without the responsibility of running a brokerage."

It would be less burdensome that way.

"Then you can focus on investigations like this one." Helen folded her arms across her chest. She looked slightly disappointed that Sabine had chosen to pair up with Ming at SRI instead of returning to Hu Knows and partnering with Helen.

"It would seem natural for me to go back to Hu Knows," Sabine said. "I tried to wrap my mind around that, but I miss Dad too much. It would be painful for me to be reminded of him every time I go to the office or call myself a Hu Knows investigator."

"Even though I renamed the company after Dad died," Helen reminded her.

"His traces are everywhere."

"His legacy is in us, Sabine. We will always have Dad's teaching in us."

"True." Sabine started to cry.

"I tell you what I'd like to do." Helen straightened up. "I want to return your Hu Knows shares to you and invite you to be my silent partner. You can pray for our business from the comfort of your own home. You can go work with Ming at SRI. But a part of this company, Dad's legacy, his memories, will be borne by both of us instead of me alone."

Sabine had no idea Helen had carried so much burden. "I can't buy back the shares. I've used the money to buy rental properties and make investments to save up for my kids to go to college."

"I hear you. Hu Knows has grown by a hundred times since you sold me the shares. So I'll willingly return them to you."

"Really?"

"Yeah. It was at thirty percent. If you want more..."

"No, no." Sabine put her hands up.

Sabine knew that Mom had also sold her thirty percent to Helen. Mom didn't want to have anything to do with the company because it also reminded her of Dad.

However, seeing Helen going at it alone, Sabine felt bad. If this was what Helen wanted to do, Sabine felt that she could oblige.

"Thirty percent for not doing anything is too much, Helen."

"That's what a silent partner means." Helen laughed. "We'll have our lawyers spell it all out on paper and make it legal. This is my gift to my own baby sister."

Sabine knew her sister was generous, but today Helen took it to the next level.

"Good thing Hu Knows is a private company with sole ownership, so I can do whatever I want with it." Helen wrapped it up with a picture perfect smile.

Yet the lines under Helen's eyes told Sabine that

she was worn out. If Sabine could help, she felt that she should.

She cleared her throat. "Setting aside the Gilroys for a moment, we have this Enzo Landry dude."

Sabine still couldn't see the whole picture. Fog was everywhere. She listed the major players one by one.

- *Edgar Hu (Dad)*
- *Gene Gilroy*
- *Garvey Gilroy*
- *Enzo Landry*
- *Cosmo O'Dell*

She decided to leave out O'Dell's ex-wife and daughter, keeping them in mind for a future addition to the list should the need arise.

The next second, she decided to add their names in, just in case.

- *Chalina O'Dell*
- *Angelica O'Dell*

"You told me the other day that you'd started suspecting O'Dell at the meeting with the watchmaker," Helen said.

"Yeah. After that, my respect for him dropped several more notches after he lost Dad's pocket watch en route to Atlanta. Yet Ming still gave him the benefit of doubt." Sabine shook her head.

"He'll come around."

"Glad I could talk to you about it instead of to Ming. I was afraid that he'd confront O'Dell about it."

Helen shook her head. "I've worked with Ming longer than you've known him. I can tell you that he would've probably investigated O'Dell behind his back instead—especially if you, his beloved wife, are concerned."

"I figured that too, but I had to be cautious. Sometimes Ming makes decisions... I mean he thinks about it and then he decides all by himself. I want him to remember that we're married and that we're on the same team. He can talk to me and brainstorm, particularly since I have enough background to provide assistance. I can give him perspectives he might not have considered."

"Like what I'm doing now." Helen logged into her iPad. She showed Sabine her notes. "See this question? Who is the real Mechanic? So far we have two. Gene Gilroy and Enzo Landry."

"Are they the ones in control or are they marionettes?"

"Good question, Sabine."

"Who else has yet to appear from the fog? Or is one of the people on this list possibly the real Mechanic?"

Just as Helen was about to answer Sabine, her phone buzzed.

"Earl," Helen read the display.

"Is it safe for him to call you on your regular phone?"

"It's encrypted," she told Sabine before answering it. "Whassup?"

"We can't find the drone—"

Bzzzt!

The line went silent.

CHAPTER 21

Earl had taken a Taser zap for the team.

Flashes of lightning showed his unconscious pallid face as Quasimodo dragged him by one foot through the gates of the junkyard. The linebacker of a man was at least six foot six, wearing rain gear, and holding a Taser in his free hand.

Ming followed behind, goaded on by a cattle prod that his own escort hadn't hesitated to use on him. Rain plus electricity were a bad combination, so Ming had complied as soon as he was discovered behind the dumpsters.

Actually, at that moment Mr. Prod carried a handgun, which he'd pointed at Ming's temple. After confiscating Ming's Glock, Mr. Prod switched hardware to a cattle prod.

I guess it's more humane.

The thunderstorm picked up again, and water washed across the red clay ground, creating a hydroplane to buffer Earl's back and head.

Please, Lord, keep us safe.

Ming worried about Sabine not staying put in the apartment across the street. The best thing she could have done was to call 911, but her sister would have most likely opted to call Camden la Salle and his FBI people instead. What could his Art Crime Team do in a moment like this?

Another flash of lighting revealed the maze they were walking through between two parallel walls of compacted vehicle frames stacked at least ten feet into the air. If this was a fortress, there was no way out without aerial view—

My smart glasses...oh.

Ming realized that he had lost his smart glasses. He recalled how Sabine had also lost hers in the woods in North Georgia back in January. They had fallen off her face when she sprinted across the forest outside Gene's compound in Hiawassee.

In an urban setting now, the glasses hadn't stayed on Ming's nose either.

If he were to provide feedback for the Binary Systems wearable team, he would definitely tell them to drop the aesthetics and go back to goggles that stayed put, ugly straps and all.

That is, if I survive this and can write a report.

He nearly chuckled, if not for the gravity of the situation.

The night was dark again, and Ming couldn't hear a thing in the torrential downpour. His raincoat was no match for the heavy rain, but this was an especially severe form of thunderstorm because it was early. It was only May in Georgia.

Thunder and lightning covered the entire junkyard. Large drops of rain pelted metal, but the impact sounded more solid than if the rain had pinged metal roofs such as zinc or tin.

Ahead of him, Quasimodo was dragging Earl toward a building. From the map he'd seen earlier—when his smart glasses were operational—that building was probably The GOAT. The Garage of All Things.

If possible, Ming didn't want to be trapped inside a building. He'd rather be out here in the open space. In fact, he'd rather not be inside this junkyard at all. Maybe he could run the other way and escape.

He glanced behind him, but all he saw was the cattle prod.

Could he take down a man with a cattle prod?

Sure.

Or at least he'd die trying.

His will had been signed. Everything went to Sabine and the kids. He felt sorry to leave Sabine with debt in SRI, but she could sell it to Hu Knows and cash out. She could go work for Hu Knows or keep her broker job.

He felt relieved that he had married an independent businesswoman who could take care of herself—and their three kids—should anything happen to him.

She could remarry and—

No! I have to go home to my wife and kids.

Ming deliberately slowed down his pace as they approached the building, digging his boots into the muddy ground wherever possible, making a show of sloshing on the rapidly flowing water.

Quasimodo dragged Earl under a battered awning and through a door into The GOAT. He didn't bother to wait for his partner. The door seemed to automatically close behind him.

"Hurry up!" Mr. Prod pointed his weapon of choice at Ming.

The building's outdoor lights cast a pale glow on the man's face. Ming couldn't tell how old he was, but his face was wrinkled wherever there was no facial hair.

Now was his chance.

"Is it safe for you to operate that in this thunderstorm?" Ming pointed at his cattle prod. "You're the one holding that thing with thunder and lightning all over the place."

Ming wasn't sure if appealing to reason at such a time as this made sense, but it was all he could think of to delay Mr. Prod.

Engaging the enemy in a conversation might be a form of distraction, but Ming couldn't think of what he could do next to close the transaction besides wrestling the cattle prod from—

Zing!

Mr. Prod's head snapped back as one hand reached for his forehead.

Ming kicked the cattle prod away from him and threw himself sumo-style on top of the man, crushing him underneath on the Georgia clay, its ochre color now gray whenever flashes of lightning revealed it.

Where rainwater had subsided, the clay was sleek and slippery, and Ming could not hold the man down as they wrestled and slid across the ground. The more they writhed like a pair of entwined mongoose and cobra in a fight to the death, the more the clay stuck to their clothes, reducing friction and creating a mess of clay as though they were stuck on a spinning potter's wheel.

Thunder crackled all around the mud wrestlers, sliding and slipping on top of each other. In the struggle, Mr. Prod nearly crushed the wind out of Ming and gained an upper hand.

The rain continued to fall, but thunder was now far away.

Mr. Prod.

He pinned Ming down on the ground and pounded. He raised his fist again—

Zing!

That sound again. What on earth was it?

Mr. Prod retracted his fist and yelped.

Zing!

Mr. Prod fell over, but he was still conscious. It gave Ming a split-second moment to rise up and overpower him. He pounded the daylights out of Mr. Prod until his muscles and knuckles hurt. But he won the battle because it was a knockout.

Taking a second to breathe, Ming glanced back in the direction where he thought the whizzing sound had come from.

A flash of lightning revealed a figure running toward him through the rain. The figure was wearing an anorak of some sort, with rubber boots all the way to the knees.

A sitting duck with nowhere to hide, Ming felt exposed. He dug into Mr. Prod's raincoat for weapons he could defend himself with—

"Ming! Ming! You okay?" The figure wearing an

oversized raincoat came closer. One hand held a gun pointing down.

"Ming, it's me!"

Oh no.

Not my wife!

CHAPTER 22

"What are you doing here?" Ming couldn't keep his voice down. His heart was beating a mile a minute, pounding at the walls of his chest.

There in front of him was his lovely wife, the last person he wanted to see out here in the danger zone tonight, especially with their third baby on board!

"Protecting the father of my children. Why do you ask?" Sabine handed Ming two cable ties.

Rain fell all around them. If it had been other circumstances, it might've been romantic. However, there was nothing romantic about being in constant danger.

Distant peals of thunder hammered down his dread.

"What am I going to do with you?" Ming took the cable ties from his wife.

"You could kiss me, but the timing isn't right."

Sabine's voice was sweet, a sharp contrast to the crackle of thunder that followed her invitation.

Ming wasn't sure whether to laugh or cry or continue to freak out that his pregnant wife had charged through the rain, throwing *hira shuriken* stars at his assailant, and essentially rescued him.

"Tie him up already." Sabine was suddenly all business.

"Yes, ma'am."

Ming tied up Mr. Prod's wrists behind his back and then ankles. The man was out cold, but they couldn't leave him out in the rain. He recovered his Sig Sauer, his backup one since SPD had confiscated his main Sig back at Mama Hu's house the other day. He returned the loaded weapon to his waistband.

Then he searched Mr. Prod's clothes and found a Smith & Wesson .38 and a Colt 1911. Ming was about to empty out the ammo rounds on them when he decided to take them with him.

"You have your Sig?" Sabine asked.

Ming nodded. "You?"

"I borrowed a Glock from Helen." Sabine showed him the piece. She looked at him. "Where are your smart glasses?"

"Lost them."

Sabine laughed. She patted the pocket of her raincoat. "That's why I put mine away. Well, technically, I borrowed them from Helen."

Ming was trying to figure out how to get Sabine and himself out of the compound. He watched Sabine put on the smart glasses and wished he hadn't lost his.

"You were right, Ming."

"Say that again." Ming leaned toward his wife.

"You were right." Sabine sounded serious. "There are people inside this building. They just haven't come out in three days."

"I was really only guessing." It was the truth, and Ming was willing to admit it in front of his wife.

"Good guess. Good instincts." Sabine pointed at the door that Ming would've been escorted through had Ming not fought back. "I saw Landry use his palm print to open that door."

"Oh, so Quasimodo is really Enzo Landry," Ming said.

"Helen told me so." Sabine pointed to the knocked-out man on the ground. "That one is probably just a worker. However, his palm print might open the door."

"We're not going inside." Ming pointed to Sabine's belly. "Too dangerous for our baby."

If I can't protect my own family...

Ming felt hot tears in his eyes. The last five months had changed him. Softened him. Made him choose differently. He felt like he was really into fatherhood now. He had to keep his wife and kids safe.

"Not us." Sabine flashed him a smile. "I need to deploy drones inside The GOAT, and then we leave."

This wasn't the right time to ask Sabine if Helen was paying her for this mission.

"Help me drag him to the door." Sabine was pulling at Mr. Prod's arm.

"Let me do it." Ming didn't want Sabine to hurt the baby inside of her. He mustered up all his remaining strength and dragged Mr. Prod to the door.

Sabine unzipped her raincoat to reveal a Kevlar

vest of some sort, with extra plates covering her baby bump and thighs. She almost looked like a thirteenth century samurai warrior, sans helmet and shoulder plates.

His ninja wife was back, all decked out in kabuki Kevlar.

She tried to remove her backpack, but it got snagged on the Kevlar edges. Ming helped her.

She squatted on the ground, unzipped the backpack, and retrieved a small water bottle which she handed to Ming.

Ming sipped the water, all the time hearing a mental ticking clock that said they'd better get out of there.

Sabine, on the other hand, didn't look nervous. She and that sister of hers were up to something. Ming could feel it.

What could Ming do? Insist that she leave? He worried about the child in her womb, but somewhere at the back of his mind, he knew he had to trust Sabine and her decisions.

Under the dim porch lights—

Ming's head snapped up. His eyes searched the wall around the closed door. "Cameras!"

"I took them out." Sabine pointed to the broken camera lenses.

"When?"

"When you were mud wrestling."

"Oh. Did you throw stars at them?"

"No, because the security cameras looked like they had vandal-proof casings that my *shuriken* spikes or stars can't penetrate. I had to shoot them out and pray that the thunder would mask the noise."

"Yeah, Georgia law doesn't allow a civilian to use a silencer."

"Because we're not Helen's employees. She has an NFA trust."

Ming nodded. Hu Knows operated with a National Firearms Act trust, by which her private investigators could legally use silencers in Georgia. However, Ming and Sabine were outside her organization.

He prayed that it wouldn't be a reason for Sabine to jump ship from SRI back to Hu Knows.

"Oh, I forgot something." Sabine unzipped an outer pocket on her backpack and retrieved a pair of augmented audio earpieces, which she handed to Ming.

While Ming put on his earpieces, Sabine retrieved two small drones from her backpack and turned them on.

"Helen, I just turned them on. Are you connected?" Sabine asked her sister and waited.

"Affirmative." Helen's voice was clear on Ming's earpieces. "Drop them in and leave ASAP. Don't dilly dally."

"Yes, ma'am." Sabine positioned the two drones on the floor directly in front of the closed door.

She turned to Ming. "We need to get his hand up to the biometric palm scanner."

"No problem." No sooner had Ming said it than he realized that he had tied Mr. Prod's wrists together earlier in the rain. Now they'd have to untie him to get his palm to fit on the palm reader, and then tie him up again.

In real life, things didn't always work according to

plan. Sometimes the plan could not be fully fleshed out until they were right there in the mission theater. Ming understood that he had to be flexible, especially when it came to teamwork. Perhaps this was good practice working with Sabine.

At this point, Ming expected that Sabine and Helen knew what they were doing, but it also didn't mean that he would blindly follow along. He had to participate and contribute as well, even though he and Sabine were technically the supporting cast in this excursion into The GOAT.

He didn't care at all if she took center stage. All he wanted to do right now was to get Sabine out of there and drive her safely home.

"We'll need a pair of scissors to cut off his ties," Ming said.

"Did you just ask me for scissors?" Sabine chuckled.

"Don't you carry that in your purse?"

Sabine dug around her backpack and produced a switchblade that looked familiar to Ming. "Will this do? I've kept it sharpened."

Ming smiled. He remembered the knife. On a couple's day out a few years earlier, he and Sabine had driven with Camden and Iris to a gun and knife show out in the countryside. Ming bought Sabine this small palm-sized switchblade with mother-of-pearl inlays on the walnut handle.

Ming made quick work of the cable ties around Mr. Prod's wrists. He hoisted the unconscious man to a halfway standing position, and Sabine pressed his palm on the palm scanner.

The door slid open.

The two drones crawled inside.

"I thought they were drones," Ming whispered. "Don't they fly?"

"They do both, depending on the situation."

So clear was Helen's voice on both of Ming's earpieces—tuned for spatial immersion—that he felt she might as well be standing in front of him.

As soon as the drones disappeared behind the door, Sabine pressed Mr. Prod's palm against the palm scanner again. The door closed.

Ming let Mr. Prod slump back to the ground. "Do you have any more ties?"

"Yeah, a whole bag." Sabine handed Ming two ties, as well as a small roll of duct tape. "So he won't scream for help."

Ming tore off a piece of duct tape wide enough to cover Mr. Prod's mouth. "What else you got there in your Backpack of All Things?"

"Clever you. The BOAT at The GOAT." Sabine hoisted her backpack onto her shoulders, and put on her oversized raincoat.

She zipped it up. "Smarty Pants, show me the best place to hide in the junkyard."

"Smarty who?" Ming asked.

"Helen's smart glasses. She named them." Sabine's eyes were staring somewhere as she turned her face. "Mine is Cicerone, but the FBI confiscated them in Hiawassee."

Ming guessed that she was looking at a map that her smart glasses had projected using augmented reality software.

"Over there." Sabine pointed up. "No cameras on the empty wall."

Ming nodded. Sabine dashed through the rain, leading the way. Ming tried to sprint, but he was bogged down by his clay-covered boots that made the run slippery. A few times, he nearly slipped and fell as his boots lost traction.

He finally caught up with Sabine, who pulled him under a tarp between a pile of tires and partially gutted vehicles in the salvage processing area.

Sabine turned on the flashlight mode on her smart glasses, dimming it just enough to prevent anyone from identifying the light source through the tarp.

There was enough room for two people to stand, but the gravel ground was too wet to sit down on. Behind them were vehicle parts and a box of tools on a utility cart. They could sit on the cart if they moved the tools out of the way.

"How are you doing?" Ming asked. "Tired?"

Sabine shook her head. "I'm okay. You?"

"We can't stay here too long." Ming took a deep breath. "Ask Smarty if there is a way out of this junkyard."

Sabine talked to her smart glasses and then summarized it for Ming. "The gates are locked. Barbed wires on top mean that we can't climb up and over."

"Hey Helen, can Cayson or Leland unlock the gate?" Ming asked through his earpieces' embedded microphone.

"They're working on it as we speak," Helen replied. "They're trying to get the gates opened for you to get out and for Cam et al to drive in. Stand by."

Everyone was waiting for Camden la Salle and his posse of FBI agents.

"When's Cam arriving again?" Ming knew that when it came to matters of life and death, every second counted.

"The FBI's ETA is fifty minutes, give or take," Helen said through their earpieces.

"Fifty? What on earth? Wasn't it fifty earlier?"

"He waited for a search warrant, and he's driving instead of flying a chopper. Budget crisis in his department."

"But why a search warrant? Isn't Earl's capture reason enough for a rescue operation?" Ming asked.

"That would mean calling 911," Helen explained.

"So? Did they want the three—or four with baby —of us here to die?" Ming wasn't happy at Helen's call.

"Springfield only has a police department. If they call this a hostage situation, Effingham County would contact SPD for support since they have a SWAT team."

"I see. They don't want to tip off O'Dell, but right now I'd rather they lose the lead than our lives." Ming's shoulders slacked.

How deep was the detective in this mess? Ming had called him a friend, but that friendship was over.

"We might die waiting for rescue," Ming added.

"I don't mind spending my last hours with you." Sabine handed him a small packet of something.

"What is this?" Ming touched it. The plastic crinkled.

"Smarty, flash light," Sabine said.

The smart glasses showed a dim flashlight at Ming.

It was a packet of almonds. Ming chuckled.

"Lightly salted, just the way you like them." Sabine nudged him.

"I may not share my last meal," Ming teased.

"This isn't our last meal. After this is over, take me out to dinner at a nice restaurant."

"Do you know something I don't?" Ming was too tired to guess. "Are you asking me to trust Helen?"

"Well, even though she's my sister—and she would agree with this—I'd rather trust God." Sabine reminded Ming of Psalm 118:8.

It is better to trust in the Lord
Than to put confidence in man.

"Oh yeah. I totally agree," Helen spoke into their ears. "We have something. Stand by."

Flashes of lightning came and went, but the rain seemed to be dissipating.

Helen's voice came through Ming's earpieces again. "A Ford pickup just rolled up to the front parking lot on the other side of the building."

Outside these walls. It made Ming wonder if they could exit the compound through the main entrance —even though it would mean they'd have to go inside the building and fight their way out.

Then again, it wasn't the time to test Psalm 56:11. Ming couldn't risk it all. What if God wanted them to stay here in this spot and wait for rescue instead of going inside the building and getting in harm's way?

In God I have put my trust;
I will not be afraid.

What can man do to me?

"Who's driving the pickup truck?" Sabine asked Helen.

"Let me see." Helen took a minute. "Can't tell. The person is wearing a hood."

"Oh, the plot thickens." Sabine rubbed her palms together.

She seemed to be enjoying this field trip a little too much, and it worried Ming.

At the same time, he was proud of his wife for being brave and able to hold her own. If she hadn't left Hu Knows, she might be just as formidable as Helen.

Helen's loss was Ming's gain.

But if they don't make it out of here alive, it would be everyone's loss.

"Oh no," Helen suddenly said.

"What?" Ming didn't like his sister-in-law's tone.

"The drones have taken over the security system inside The GOAT, so they can see everything now."

"Must not be too secure if they can do it in two clicks," Ming said.

"I'll send the live feed to Smarty." Helen stopped talking for maybe ten seconds.

Sabine flinched and shut her eyes. "Whoa."

"What?" Ming removed the smart glasses from Sabine's face and put them on his own. "Replay."

Smarty ignored him.

"Smarty, replay the video you just showed me." Sabine leaned against Ming, breathing heavily.

The smart glasses complied.

What Ming saw startled him as well. He couldn't

watch the video of a chained Earl being beaten up with baseball bats for a second time. What got him was that Sabine only flinched. She didn't shrink back.

She only flinched.

Seriously...

Ming wasn't sure whether to be proud of his fearless wife or be afraid for her.

"When did this happen, Helen?" Ming asked.

"Ongoing now. Three men taking turns."

"I have to get him out of there before they beat him to death," Ming said. "Might be too late by the time Cam arrives."

Ming would have to leave Sabine waiting outside alone. He didn't want her to go inside the building with him.

Sabine didn't argue with him. Gently, she took the smart glasses back from Ming and placed them over her own eyes.

"Helen, you said the drones have commandeered the security system, including the cameras," Sabine said.

"Yes. Just waiting for Cam to show up."

"Can you integrate the drone system with my smart glasses, considering they came from the same company?" Sabine's voice was calm.

Ming wasn't sure what Sabine was about to do. What was she up to? Perhaps all she wanted was to have situational awareness as they waited passively for their rescue—

Not!

Ming knew he hadn't married a dainty princess. He'd married one of the two daughters of Edgar Hu, the illustrious private investigator who would've been proud of his offspring had he been alive today.

"Okay, Sabine." Helen gave in. "I will share the controls with you through Smarty."

"Thank you, Sis."

"Stand by," Helen said.

Sabine tugged at Ming's arm. "You ready?"

"For what?"

"Go get Earl. They're going to kill him any minute now."

Ming debated whether to argue with her and make her stay out here as he himself walked through the valley of the shadow of death inside The GOAT.

Of course, they had to save Earl.

But not at the expense of Sabine's life—and that of their baby.

At the same time, Ming didn't want to hold Sabine back. He knew what she was capable of doing. In fact, she had inherited more of her dad's traits and stayed by his side longer than her sister ever had.

As her husband, Ming wanted Sabine to be free to do what she wanted to do and what God had called her to do, but he would be there to protect her and keep her safe.

But but but...

How would allowing her to charge into a building this big—with guns blazing, stars and spikes flying—meet any safety protocols that Ming had placed around his family?

Better not. Ming felt sorry for Earl, but he had to protect his own wife and unborn child. He prayed that God would keep Earl alive until Camden and the

FBI arrived. Right now, his job was to keep Sabine safe.

His hand reached for Sabine, but only touched wet and greasy metal. "Sabine?"

A flash of lightning showed him that she wasn't there beside him. His eyes snapped toward the building where they had come from. A second bolt of lightning showed a silhouette sidling like a crab against a wall of compacted car parts.

She motioned for him to keep up.

"What in the world?" Ming sprinted toward his wife. "Wait for me!"

CHAPTER 23

Guided by her smart glasses, Sabine walked straight into The Garage of All Things, with Ming behind her and their weapons drawn.

If Cayson at Binary Systems hadn't hacked into the building's security systems via the two drones that Sabine had deployed earlier, neither Sabine nor Ming would have entered the building at all.

As it happened, they were now invisible to Landry and his cohorts. Only Cayson and Helen could see the two heat signatures walking through the repair bay, passing by several classic cars at various stages of restoration. A Corvette here, a Thunderbird there, they didn't seem entirely too luxurious.

Still, the value of those vehicles—and maybe more that Sabine hadn't seen—might explain the tall walls outside with barbed wires on top.

Then again, skeptical Sabine leaned toward a more nefarious reason.

Smarty, the smart glasses on loan from Helen, showed Sabine a layout of the garage as they made their way further into the inner sanctum. They passed by a paint booth, its door opened to reveal sanding tools, work benches, and paint cans on shelves.

The welding area had partitions and no door. Sabine could hear men talking, their speech peppered with rapid-fire f-bombs that bothered Sabine to no end. If not for the hacked videos displaying on her smart glasses, she wouldn't be able to tell that the welding area was also Earl's torture chamber.

Sabine used American Sign Language to tell Ming that they had arrived at their target location.

Ming nodded, sidestepped her, and took the lead.

"Stay behind me," he whispered.

Sabine nodded, but Ming didn't have eyes in the back of his head. He just kept moving forward.

Sabine felt safe behind Ming, but she knew that Helen was also monitoring the situation from her command center across the street. Technology hadn't failed them yet tonight.

Above all, Sabine prayed silently that God would keep them safe. At this point, she wasn't sure if entering the main building had been the right choice. Had it been a providential prompting for them to rescue Earl—or die trying? Or had they charged into danger on their own accord?

If it was the latter, would God still protect them?

Ming stopped abruptly as the door opened. Three men, not especially large, staggered out, as though beating up a fellow human being was an intoxicating high for them.

Ming gave them zero warning, his Sig Sauer firing

shots at their arms and legs. Sabine followed suit with her borrowed Glock, hitting the third man a second time when he flailed on the ground.

Once the three men were down on the floor, Ming charged forward and knocked them all unconscious.

"Why didn't you go for a torso or head shot?" Sabine asked, even though she knew the answer. She handed him cable ties from her backpack pocket.

"Because I don't want them dead. I want them incapacitated." Ming made quick work of the cable ties. "Let the police deal with them afterwards. I don't want to end up in court in this day and age."

"Gotcha."

One of the things that Sabine appreciated about Ming was his sparing use of firearms. If he could solve the problem without causing bodily harm, that would be ideal. The same could be said of Helen and her team at Hu Knows, as well as their friends, Camden, Iris, and Pilar, just to name a few.

Ming and Sabine dragged the three men back into the welding area and left them lying on the floor away from the door.

Red paint—no, blood—was all over the floor around Earl, chained to the wall and beaten to a pulp. Sabine flinched, but to her own surprise, she didn't feel like she was going to throw up.

"Earl." Ming shook him awake.

"You finally came." Earl barely lifted his head. His voice was raspy. He spat something out. It was a tooth.

"Thank God you're alive, buddy."

Earl mumbled something unintelligible.

"We're going to get you out of here." Ming checked the chains.

"I'll monitor security while you get those chains off Earl," Sabine said.

"My thoughts exactly." Ming looked around the cluttered welding area filled with welding machines, torches, cutters, cables everywhere, trash cans, and scrap bins in a seemingly messy and disorganized configuration. The walls, where there were no shelves, had burnt marks on them.

Ming found a bolt cutter hanging next to a welding helmet and a hammer on a wall-mounted pegboard.

Sabine checked her smart glasses. "We're still under the radar."

"Good." Ming nearly tripped on a rubber mat on the floor when he returned to Earl with his bolt cutter.

"Whoa. I still want my body parts." Earl chuckled.

"Since you're doing so well, maybe we shouldn't have bothered to come here to get you." Ming didn't look embarrassed.

"Seriously, thank you for not leaving me behind." Earl's voice cracked.

"You owe us dinner for two—Sabine and me, not you and me." Ming easily cut the chains off Earl with the bolt cutter.

"Dinner on me, for sure," Earl said. "Anywhere you want. Transportation not included."

"Negotiating the reward money already, I see." Ming helped Earl to his feet. "I think they didn't hit his brain too hard, Sabine. What do you think?"

"Tell them to hurry up," Helen said through their earpieces.

"Helen says to hurry up," Sabine repeated for Earl's benefit. Ming had probably heard the same words from Helen on his own earpieces.

"Tell Helen she's paying for my dental bills," Earl said. "I'm going to need new front teeth or there goes my dating life."

Earl hissed in pain when Ming tried to put Earl's arm over his shoulder. "I think they broke that arm. Try the other."

Ming went to his other side.

"They also hit my ribs pretty hard." Earl winced. He favored his left leg and yowled every time he put pressure on his right leg. "My ankle might also be broken."

"You must have a very high threshold for pain," Sabine said to Earl.

"Not as much as a woman giving birth, I think."

"Good point."

Still, it would take forever for them to get out of the building. Sabine looked for a rolling bin of some sort that they could use to wheel Earl around. She spotted a cylindrical container with wheels, but it was piled up with scrap metal. Nearby, there was a rectangular rolling cart with a partial car door sitting on top of it.

"Earl can sit on the cart." She pointed to it.

Ming put Earl down on the floor. Between him and Sabine, they removed the car door from the cart. Ming did most of the heavy lifting, but Sabine held one end to prevent it from tipping over the cart.

Ming pushed the cart to Earl. Sabine held the cart

handle to prevent the wheels from moving while Ming loaded Earl onto the cart.

"Let's get out of here." Sabine turned to Earl and Ming. "Keep your voices down. No unnecessary jokes."

Earl pointed to himself with his one working arm, and widened his eyes. "Me? I'm on my best behavior."

"Going back where we came from?" Ming pushed Earl on the cart through the door. "We've been on that route once, so we know where to go."

"I agree." Sabine took the lead. So far, her smart glasses hadn't failed them yet—

"Three figures are coming your way from the hall-way," Helen said through their earpieces. "Armed. The tall man looks to be Landry."

"We might be able to hide among the vehicles." Sabine made a sharp left in between an Impala and a Corvette. There was enough room for Ming to push the heavy cart through.

"Helen, please dim the lights," Sabine spoke into her embedded microphone.

Helen did so.

Ping!

Someone fired the first shot, and it was neither Sabine nor Ming. It was a bad shot because it pinged off metal—probably one of the cars that were blocking the attackers from getting to them.

When is the FBI arriving again?

Sabine prayed. Before she realized it, she was holding Helen's Glock in one hand and a *bo shuriken* spike in her other hand. Both hands shook a little.

She glanced over to see if anyone noticed. Ming

was handing a Glock to Earl, who took it with his working hand.

"Good thing they didn't break my dominant hand," Earl remarked.

Two or three more shots came toward them. Sabine debated whether to fire back and reveal their position or remain quiet and pray that Camden had entered the building.

Just then, Sabine saw someone walking toward them between two vehicles. He was tall and big, and his weapon was pointed in Sabine's direction.

He would be an easy target if Sabine's hand wasn't shaking so much.

Gunfire exploded.

Wait. What? I didn't fire.

She looked over to Ming. He shrugged. They both looked at Earl.

"Wasn't me." Earl looked just as puzzled.

Sabine wondered if it was Camden—

"I did." O'Dell appeared out of nowhere.

Detective Cosmo O'Dell, wearing a hood—just like the person who'd climbed out of the pickup truck outside had.

O'Dell crouched down next to Ming. "There are three of them, and they're heading this way."

Three of them?

Earlier, Sabine's smart glasses—integrated with the security system—had notified her that there were a total of only three people.

If O'Dell also said there were three people apart from himself, it would make him the fourth person.

Smarty hadn't reported four people at all.

Who or what is lying?

"Landry fired at you, so I came around the back here to assist."

O'Dell might have explained too much. It made Sabine suspicious. Firstly, he had placed a thought in everyone's mind that it had been Enzo Landry indeed who'd shot at them.

By accusing someone else, O'Dell had pointed the focus away from himself. By saying he was assisting Ming and Sabine, he tried to lower their guard.

Sabine didn't speak a word. She didn't want to give away the fact that she was wearing a pair of smart glasses. If O'Dell got ahold of them, he might find out about the building security takeover.

Just like that, the gunfire ceased.

Sabine wondered whether to question the timing. Why wouldn't Landry keep firing until he had defeated them?

Slowly, Sabine pocketed her *bo shuriken* spike and the Glock.

"This way." O'Dell motioned for them to follow him.

"To where?" Ming asked.

O'Dell seemed to sense their hesitation.

"No worries. I've already called 911. They're on the way." O'Dell's voice was soothingly calm. Either he had training in psychology or he was genuinely a good guy and Sabine had misunderstood him.

"The break room is down the hall, where we can wait for the Springfield Police to show up," O'Dell added. "There's a first aid kit there for us to treat Earl, plus water and food."

Okay. It sounded benign.

"How did you know where it is?" Ming asked.

"Since I helped you, my cover is blown." O'Dell looked dejected. "But saving lives is more important than remaining undercover, yes?"

Is O'Dell undercover at The GOAT?

Sabine felt baffled. How could he be undercover when he was the lead detective in Dad's revived murder case? Wasn't he in the news, talking to reporters? How could he be undercover now?

Did he think we're stupid?

"Thank you. Please show the way." Ming pushed Earl on the cart.

Sabine followed along, waiting to see if a shoe would drop.

No one stopped them from getting to the break room. That alone was as suspicious as O'Dell's presence in the midst of gunfire.

He was calm and collected, as a law enforcement officer should be, but something didn't feel right to Sabine. Something amiss.

What was Sabine not seeing?

In the break room near the front reception area of the garage, O'Dell took out a first aid kit from a cabinet near the door. He handed it to Ming.

Sabine wondered what good a first aid kit was going to do for Earl if he was bruised and broken everywhere. He needed to be transported to the emergency room, pronto.

"Water, anyone?" O'Dell moved to the refrigerator. "There's water, juice, soda. Sandwiches if you get hungry."

Sabine felt thirsty, but she was afraid to go near O'Dell. She remembered her bottled water in her backpack and decided to try that first before she drank other people's water.

Perhaps sensing her trepidation, O'Dell closed the door and moved away from the refrigerator. He pointed to it as he looked at Sabine. "Help yourself."

"Thank you." It came out automatically.

Dad had always taught his daughters to be polite to everyone, even the people whom he disliked. Helen and Sabine had taken the advice to heart.

One never knew what the other party was going through, so a simple "thank you" and "please" could go a long way.

So what is O'Dell going through?

Sabine wondered why he had lied about being undercover when it was obviously not the case. The fact that he could come and go at The GOAT without being stopped by Landry said volumes about the detective's position in this facility.

Sabine didn't want to speculate who O'Dell really was, but she didn't like the way he was looking at her now.

"Thanks also for your help earlier," she said. "It was scary in the repair bay, being shot at."

"I know. We'll get y'all out of here ASAP, okay?" O'Dell's deep eyes were on her.

Sabine nodded. She didn't know how to pretend to be a damsel in distress. She wanted to tie him up and question him at gunpoint, but that was highly unlikely and oh so unladylike.

O'Dell seemed satisfied with their conversation. He turned to Ming and Earl. "All right. Keep the doors closed. I'm going back to work. I'll come get you as soon as the officers arrive."

"Okay. See you soon." Ming didn't look like he was suspicious of O'Dell at all. At least, that was the impression he'd given Sabine.

"Lock the door." They were O'Dell's parting words.

Ming got up and did what the detective said. "But this door looks flimsy. There's no way it's going to protect us from gunfire."

He locked it anyway.

At a kitchen table, Sabine took off her raincoat, and removed her backpack from her shoulders. She put the backpack on a chair and looked for her water bottle.

She drank up the water. Then she made her way toward the refrigerator. She found a paper towel and used it to touch the refrigerator door handle before she opened it.

On a shelf, the bottled water caps were all sealed, so there didn't seem to be signs of tampering. Still, water could be contaminated in some way. Say, a sleep aid could be pumped into the bottles.

She decided not to touch any of the food or drinks inside the refrigerator.

At the sink, she poured cold water into her own water bottle. While she questioned the quality of water in a junkyard that could leach chemicals into the soil and underground water system, she was confident that she'd be okay drinking the tap water. After all, Springfield was a city, and in general, water in Georgian cities was fine to drink.

Ideally, she'd filter tap water, but for the purpose of her survival today, she stood there at the sink and drank the water.

"You were overthinking, weren't you?" Ming left Earl on the cart and approached her.

He took the water bottle in her hand and drank from it. "Room temperature."

"Not radioactive." Sabine chuckled. "Where's your water bottle? Didn't I give you one when we were outside?"

"Lost it." Ming grinned.

"You didn't even check before you said that."

He refilled Sabine's water bottle and returned it to her. "I prefer to drink from yours."

"Lazy bones," Sabine teased. "Get your own bottle next time."

"But we're married." Ming grabbed her waist.

"Stop it already!" Earl shifted position and then gasped.

Sabine hid her face in Ming's neck.

"Let's pray," Ming said suddenly.

Sabine and Earl quietened.

"Father God, thank You for keeping all three of us alive thus far," Ming began. "I pray that You will get us home safely all the way—not to heaven per se, but to our homes in Savannah, back to our families. Thank You that You see all things. Please show us the truth about this predicament we find ourselves in. I'm praying all these in the sweet name of Jesus. Amen."

"Amen," Sabine said.

"Amen," Helen said into their earpieces. "Cam is five minutes out. Hang in there."

"Did O'Dell really call 911?" Earl asked.

Nobody could reply.

Sabine tore off a paper towel from the wall-mounted dispenser so that she could dry her water bottle before putting it back into her backpack. The paper towel dispenser was between the sink and a microwave.

She hadn't paid attention to the microwave earlier, but now she had time to look around to see what was on the rest of the chipped Formica kitchen counter. Next to the microwave was a rattan tray of plastic spoons and forks as well as styrofoam plates.

And there, peeking out between two stacks of styrofoam plates, was...

A gold pocket watch, sitting on the counter against the backsplash, as though it had been placed there for an easy find.

Sabine's breath caught. "Ming..."

"What?"

"Come here." She stared at the pocket watch.

Something definitely felt off. It seemed too easy. It was as though the pocket watch had been delivered to her on a platter—in this case, a styrofoam plate.

Ming ambled over. "Whoa."

"Don't touch it. Let's not leave any of our finger-prints." Sabine went back to her backpack and retrieved a pair of disposable gloves. Thankfully, they were non-latex.

"Could this be your dad's pocket watch that had been stolen from O'Dell on his way from Savannah to Atlanta?"

"It looks like it, but we'll find out in a minute." Gently, Sabine picked up not only the styrofoam plate under the pocket watch but a few more plates underneath it.

Slowly, she carried them to the kitchen table.

Ming sat down across from her. "I remember

when we were at the watchmaker's in April. The intricate etching on the case looks similar."

Still wearing gloves, Sabine pointed to the pocket watch. "Helen, you see it?"

"Yes, but I can't tell if it's a bomb or if you should touch it at all," Helen said. "Let's wait for Cam, okay?"

Sabine's eyes welled up with tears. "Considering the probability of all the things we have encountered this evening, I'd say that this is product placement."

Sabine wanted to flip the pocket watch over and open the back to see if there was an indentation of a cross on it. That way, she could confirm that it was Dad's watch.

However, if she touched it, she'd contribute to the breaking of the chain of custody. It could get messy in court, and the pocket watch might end up not being admissible. The evidence had been tampered with enough, as it was.

So they stared at the pocket watch on the table.

Sabine clutched her hands to her chest. "I miss you so much, Dad."

She sobbed quietly. "I love you so much, Dad."

Click.

They waited.

"Hello, my daughter."

It was Dad's voice.

Sabine screamed.

CHAPTER 24

Edgar Hu, the best father in the world, had left Sabine a personal message. It broke her heart into a million pieces that he wasn't there to tell it to her himself. That it had taken thirteen years for his voice to rise out of the grave, but better now than never.

Sabine drew a deep breath.

Ming reached his hand out to her from across the table. She didn't take it. So he left his seat and came over to her side and sat down beside her without saying a word. Truly, he knew her best.

Quietly, they listened to the audio recording on the pocket watch.

"If you can hear this message, it means that the main message has been erased," Dad said.

His voice was still clear, but Sabine could hear

some sort of noise in the background. Maybe the air conditioner in the car was running.

"It also means that my pocket watch is finally in your hands, dear daughter—whichever one you are," Dad continued.

"Did you hear that, Helen?" Sabine gasped.

"Yes." Helen's voice was broken, and it showed when Sabine heard it through her earpieces. "Dad loved us both equally."

Sabine could hear gentle sobs over her earpieces. She wanted to rush across the street to hug Helen, but that was impossible at the moment. She prayed that Helen would be strong.

What am I saying?

Helen was the Iron Lady of the family. That had been why Dad had left instructions to make her the President of Hu Knows, and Sabine the Vice President. Helen had the strength and wherewithal to carry on Dad's legacy long after he was gone.

But Helen shed a tear today.

"Leave it to Dad to install a dead man's switch on his pocket watch." Helen's voice echoed in Sabine's ears.

"Except that it has taken thirteen years to activate." Sabine shook her head.

"Only because someone stole the pocket watch and kept it for thirteen years."

The recording in front of Sabine went silent for a few seconds.

Click.

Soft classical music played. Then it cut off.

"All right," Dad said. "I'm now parked closer to The GOAT. Maybe a hundred yards away. I'm preparing myself for a midnight meeting with Enzo Landry about Johannes Vermeer's painting."

"What?" Sabine was taken aback, but there was no way to pause the recording. "Did Dad just say The GOAT? This garage?"

Ming nodded.

Dad went on to describe the night weather. He was really verbose.

"Wait. Did he say Vermeer's painting?" Earl asked. "Might it be *The Concert*, the most expensive lost painting in the world?"

Sabine shrugged. Vermeer's lost painting had been stolen from a Boston museum in 1990. It had never been recovered.

"Word is that the painting has been at The MOOT all this time," Dad continued. "They're moving the painting tonight because they finally found several private collections who want this painting. I don't have details. On a whim, I called Landry to ask for a cut of the pie, but I'm recording everything to hand over to the FBI Art Crime Team."

It seemed that Dad's involvement with the Art Crime Team preceded Camden la Salle's. However, what he was about to do then might have been what had gotten him killed. Sabine had no idea whether Dad had received approval from the FBI to do any of his activities that night. Her guess was *no*.

Dad had been a maverick sometimes. That had

been his downfall. Then again, that had also been how he'd met Mom. She loved living on the edge, maybe even further on the edge than Dad. At least Dad obeyed traffic rules, if not any other laws. Mom, on the other hand...

Well, bless her heart.

It was a miracle that Mom hadn't been arrested for something.

That had been why Dad had allowed Mom to own a share of Hu Knows, but he'd specifically stipulated that she wasn't to do any official work for Hu Knows. There was no reason to let the family business go down in flames with Mom's shenanigans.

"Landry told me they're already splitting the profits three ways, and they cannot add me. Then he told me to come over anyway, in the hope that his business partners might 'take pity' on me." Dad grunted. "I don't like the way he talked down to me, but I have to see this through. I'm recording this so that if anything happens to me, know that it's probably not an accident."

Dad had a soft southern accent from having been born and raised in middle Georgia, but his words were simple, clear, and to the point.

"Before I go, I want to say a few things, just in case I don't make it home tonight. Firstly, tell your mother to take good care of herself. Eleanora, I love you." Dad paused for a long time.

Sabine wiped tears from her eyes. In her earpieces, she could hear Helen sobbing.

"Helen and Sabine, I love you so much," Dad said. "If you're listening to this, it means I couldn't walk you two down the aisle at your weddings. Make sure you marry godly Christian men. Avoid serial killers."

Sabine laughed. So did Helen, her voice ringing in their earpieces.

"The gate just opened. Someone's walking toward my car. I can't see who it is because he's wearing a hood." A pause. Then: "He's waving for me to park inside The GOAT. I'm going to put my pocket watch in my pocket, and hope it will continue recording."

Sabine heard the car's turn signal clicker. "Leave it to Dad to turn that on even when parking."

"There are two gates in the junkyard, and neither one has high traffic. The roads are paved, but only customers drive on them." Helen's words came through loud and clear.

Sabine nodded, even though her sister couldn't see her. "Dad always obeyed traffic laws. On the other hand, Mom often drives recklessly."

"Is Landry in?" Dad asked someone, who seemed to be standing outside his car.

Sabine couldn't make out what the answer was, except it sounded like "get out" or "come out."

The car door opened and closed.

"Where are you taking me?" Dad asked. He still didn't sound distressed.

Muffled voices followed. Undecipherable words that probably would need to be processed by the FBI or GBI.

Pounding and cracking noises interspersed one another.

Ming's eyes widened.

"What am I hearing?" Sabine asked.

"They're beating him up," Earl answered from the cart on which he was still sitting.

"Nooo..." Sabine's hands shook inside the disposable gloves.

Ming wrapped them in his bigger hands.

Heavy breathing came out of the pocket watch.

"You could've told me no." Dad gasped. "I could've stayed home and gotten some sleep. Instead you told me to come here. Are you trying to kill me? Look, my left arm is dangling."

Someone laughed.

Since Dad had talked to that person like it was a follow-up to a previous conversation, Sabine guessed that the person could possibly be Landry. Voice recognition could confirm or refute that.

A third voice joined in.

"So it's you, Cosmo. What a surprise." Dad panted. "By showing your face, you're telling me that this is the end of the road for me."

Cosmo O'Dell?

He didn't speak, so Sabine couldn't confirm who it was at this point in the recording.

Sabine heard high heels clicking on the hard floor. Probably the cement floor of this very same garage. To think that Sabine was here in the same building thirteen years later, listening to Dad's last words on earth.

"Hurry up, you two," the woman said. "The auction is starting in ten minutes."

"How many buyers do you have now?" Dad asked.

"What's it to you?" the woman snapped.

"No need to raise your voice, Chalina," Landry said.

"Chalina O'Dell?" Sabine nearly fell out of her chair.

"Thirteen years ago. If I remember correctly, she had just divorced O'Dell," Ming remarked. "I gather it was also before she met her abusive new boyfriend, before her life spiraled downward."

"The good old days." Sabine listened some more.

"Don't tell me what to do," Chalina snapped. "If not for my daughter's medical expenses, do you think Cosmo and I would be doing business with you?"

"How sweet it is for you divorced couple to

work together for the sake of your daughter." Dad grunted.

Landry laughed. "Don't get me wrong. I think you're good parents, but you should thank me for helping you fund your vacation homes in Puerto Rico and Estonia."

Sabine glanced at Ming. "Sounds like O'Dell's side gig is lucrative."

Ming nodded, but his mind seemed to be on something else. "I think Chalina was the woman in the forest in Hiawassee."

"How nice it is for you to get along with your ex-wife, Cosmo O'Dell." Dad outright repeated his name.

More noises.

"What are you doing? Why are you carrying pipes? Who are you?"

Dad shouted what was happening to him, as though the play-by-play was his way to get evidence recorded on his pocket watch.

"Don't hit me! Don't hit me!"

Then a shot rang out.

Dad groaned.

Sabine clutched her chest. There was pain there she couldn't describe. The pain she'd felt at Dad's funeral had resurfaced all over again.

She could hear faint snoring in the audio recording.

Snoring?

"You heard that?" Ming asked. "Snoring might

indicate skull fracture."

They listened to the recording some more.

"Did he fall asleep?" Enzo Landry said. "He's snoring."

"Try to wake him up," Chalina instructed.

"What for?" O'Dell said.

"If you won't do it, I will." Shortly after that, Chalina said, "He's not responding."

Landry cussed.

"You killed him, Enzo." Chalina was spitting anger. "What for? You want to go to jail?"

"I didn't," Landry protested. "I shot the floor."

"I think it's the pipes. Enzo's men beat his head too hard. See, it's bleeding," O'Dell said.

"Have cows grown wings? I just heard my ex-husband defend my ex-boyfriend." Chalina laughed. "What's going on with you two?"

Neither of the men answered.

"Put him back in the car," O'Dell said.

"Trunk?" Landry asked.

"No. Driver's seat."

"Then what?"

"Then we look for a fall guy," O'Dell replied. "Know anyone who doesn't work in this garage?"

"Bobby Kane. He's an employee at Gene Gilroy's garage."

"Say what?"

"I pay him to keep an eye on Gene. He reports to my people every week."

"Oh. You planted a spy in Gene's garage?"

Landry laughed. "I have no choice. I'm paying Gene a lot of money to store the paintings. How am

I supposed to know if he sells them behind my back?"

"If you get rid of this Bobby fellow, who else would spy for you?"

"I'll find someone who doesn't ask for more money every other month."

"Great. Tell Bobby to come over here with a tow truck."

"That never happened, did it?" Earl asked from where he'd been sitting.

Ming shook his head. "As I recall, Bobby was busy that night. He was not at the scene nor did he show up anywhere near Edgar or his car."

"Essentially, someone mysterious towed Dad's car to a road near Gene's garage and set it on fire," Sabine said. "We don't know who filled in for Bobby Kane, but now we know who instructed him—or her—to do it."

Sabine almost wished it hadn't been O'Dell calling the shots, but those words from him nailed it. Landry had followed his orders instead of the other way around.

Truly, if O'Dell called the police, he'd implicate himself. Even though he hadn't been the one who killed Dad, he had stood by while Enzo's men bashed Dad. His art theft ring would be revealed. He'd go to jail either way.

The next day, after a stranger saw the burned-out vehicle and called 911, SPD launched an investigation, with O'Dell on the team.

What a phony.

O'Dell had pretended to be one of the good guys while all the time, he was a wolf leader in disguise.

He had gotten away with murder.

Now Sabine, Ming, and Earl were listening to a time capsule where the truth was revealed. Dad had indeed identified his three murderers. Was that enough for new convictions in court?

"Close all the windows and bring me a hose that's big enough to fit over the exhaust," O'Dell said.

Sabine grabbed Ming's hand. They were listening to how O'Dell and Landry were going to conceal their deed.

She heard the car engine start. As soon as the car door slammed, the recording continued for less than a minute. Perhaps the pocket watch battery had run out.

"And then what?" Sabine leaned toward the pocket watch.

Silence.

"The audio recording seems to affirm what the forensic pathologists found thirteen years ago," Helen said over their earpieces. "Except for O'Dell. He was the missing piece of the puzzle."

"Right." Ming nodded. "We already knew how Edgar died. Now we know the people involved in his murder. And we know something else."

"That Chalina on the audio recording sounded like the woman who attacked you in Hiawassee." Sabine turned to Ming. "Her voice hasn't changed much in thirteen years."

"We need to tell Cam," Ming said. "He's still holding her, right?"

"As far as I know," Helen spoke into their earpieces.

Sabine sniffled. "After thirteen years, we finally have answers."

Ming placed his hand on Sabine's back, rubbing it gently. "You've suspected O'Dell since we met with the watchmaker."

"How did you know that was the beginning of my suspicions?" Sabine asked.

"Your body language. Plus your secretiveness thereafter, as though I was going to run to O'Dell and tell all."

"I was kinda afraid you would."

"No, I wouldn't. I believe you, dear wife." Ming pushed back a wispy strand of hair from Sabine's face.

A knock on the door startled Sabine.

"It's me," O'Dell said from the other side.

What to do?

Without a word, Ming snatched the pocket watch with his bare hands and dropped it into a zippered pocket on the side of his pants.

Sabine put the styrofoam plates back on the counter and threw the gloves in the trash can.

Before Ming could open the door, they heard loud shouts, like over a megaphone.

"FBI!"

It was followed curtly by, "Hands over your head!"

Scuffles followed.

"What's going on?" O'Dell asked over and over again. "I'm with the SPD."

Another knock on the door.

"Open up, Ming." It was a familiar voice.

FBI Special Agent Camden la Salle.

Ming unlocked the door. "Cam! So glad to see you."

Camden directed paramedics to attend to Earl. Then he turned to Sabine.

"Helen patched me through," Camden said. "We heard everything—including the snoring. I'm sorry about your dad."

Sabine nodded. It was bittersweet, but at least it was over now.

CHAPTER 25

June

Birds tweeted that rainless morning when Ming drove Sabine and Mama Hu to visit Edgar's grave at the historical Bonaventure Cemetery.

Since they decided to park and take a golf cart on unpaved pathways inside the cemetery, Ming opted not to bring the kids. Hannah and Zachary were happily splashing in the community pool on Tybee Island under the supervision of Aunt Heidi and Uncle Diego, who had taken a few hours off from sermon preparation.

Past the grave markers of war veterans, Ming navigated the golf cart to where Mama Hu pointed. Before they even got off the cart, Mama Hu had started to cry.

It had been years, but Mama Hu hadn't remarried since her husband passed away. She had dated a few people in her mature years, but none of the men could compare with her beloved. She remained single the rest of her time, focusing on social activities with other widows and friends in the neighborhood. She kept herself busy, but she lived alone in that big old mansion on Bull Street.

Sabine held her mother's hand as they made their way to Edgar's grave.

There, under a canopy of swaying Spanish moss on sprawling live oak branches, Edgar Hu had been interred in a family plot inherited by his best friend in the US Army. The story went that Edgar had saved Buddy's life in Vietnam, and they became brothers from that day onward. Buddy delivered the eulogy at Edgar's funeral.

As they stood in front of Edgar's grave, Mama Hu rambled about her past sins and her need to pay penance and seek atonement.

"Mom, only Jesus can fully pay for your sins—and He has," Sabine said.

"Then why don't I feel it?" Mama Hu asked.

"Because you never accepted His payment," Sabine reminded her. "You rejected the premise that God could single-handedly wipe out all your sins through Jesus Christ. You believe that what He's done for you isn't nearly enough."

Ming didn't say a word. He prayed quietly for Mama Hu to see the light and for Sabine to have the anointing of the Holy Spirit to speak the right words.

"I don't want handouts," Mama Hu said.

"Far from it, Mom. Dad believed in Jesus, and his soul is saved forever."

"I remember him telling me, but I didn't think it was that easy."

"It wasn't easy for God the Son to leave God the Father, take on the sins of the world and die on the cross for us. However, it's easy for us because we only have to believe in God the Son, Jesus Christ."

Sabine went on to mention Acts 2:21 for Mama Hu's benefit.

> And it shall come to pass
> > That whoever calls on the name of the Lord
> > Shall be saved.

"Edgar used to read me the Bible too." Mama Hu wiped her tears. "I wish he were here."

"I miss him too, Mom." Sabine hugged her mother.

"Can he play golf in heaven?"

"I don't know, but he's with Jesus, for sure."

"Does Jesus play golf?" Mama Hu laughed between her tears.

Mother and daughter wept together.

"This is hard for us because we're still here with our human nature, feeling the pain and grief," Ming finally said. "However, for Edgar, he's in perfect health in heaven, and he wouldn't want to come back here."

"Will I see him again?" Mama Hu asked.

"Dad would want to see you again. The ticket to heaven is Jesus." Sabine didn't miss the opportunity to share Christ with Mama Hu.

To be sure, both Sabine and Ming had tried to explain salvation to Mama Hu many times over the last decade. Each time, Mama Hu refused to even acknowledge God.

Some seven years ago, Mama Hu came close to the truth when she nearly went to church. However, her desire had worn off and hadn't returned since.

"Crazy world we live in." Mama Hu held Sabine's hand. "I wish Edgar had told me what he'd known about Garvey. Even after your dad died, I wouldn't have allowed him to date you."

"I was already an adult, Mom. Besides, we only went out for a few weeks. Nothing happened between us beyond eating out and movies. If you recall, I was traveling a lot as a model, and I was hardly home." Sabine glanced at Ming while her palm stroked her belly.

Ming decided to take the high road and not appear visibly moved. It was all in the past, anyway, so what was there to rehash?

"Mom, why did you bring up Garvey? He didn't kill Dad," Sabine added.

"Because he was at Gene's garage that night. He saw something, but decided not to speak up."

"Wasn't he drunk at that time? He might be seeing things."

"Stop giving excuses for your ex-boyfriend," Mom snapped.

Ming thought that the greater crime lay in Cosmo O'Dell's hands. Not only had he been a law enforcement officer the entire time, but he had hidden evidence from the detective in charge of the case in the first few years after Dad's death. Eventually, O'Dell himself was assigned to the case, which gave him untold opportunities to sweep evidence against himself under the rug.

Many speculations and conjectures about the mastermind had been formed over time. None of them stuck, and for thirteen years, no one had known that O'Dell was half of The Mechanic, the other half being Enzo Landry. Along with O'Dell's ex-wife, they had caused the death of Sabine's dad.

The case breakthrough had come through an unexpected source: Old Man Leung.

Not everything Old Man Leung had told Mama Hu at his deathbed was true, except for one thing: he had seen Dad's pocket watch on Gene in their rare interactions with each other. Other than that, Leung had erroneously believed that Gene was The Mechanic. He'd also falsely accused him of murder, and even implicated Garvey in the mess.

On the other hand, Helen's own research seemed to confirm Leung's veracity, even though they were all now mostly debunked. That showed Ming that even Helen's people could make mistakes. And that would include Leland and Cayson at Binary Systems.

Nonetheless, Mama Hu's conversation with Leung had been the impetus for her to reinvestigate her husband's murder. Since Mama Hu had delegated the bulk of the world to Sabine, she had ended up at Gene Gilroy's flintlock competition, with access to The MOOT, where Sabine met Gene and saw Dad's pocket watch for the first time in thirteen years.

It was true that Gene sold stolen art pieces and collectors' items. But his claim to have murdered Edgar wasn't true. He'd only done that to protect his nephew, whom he had erroneously believed to be the murderer. However, Gene's insistence that he wasn't The Mechanic was true.

The only person who eventually told the truth without being coerced or prompted turned out to be Garvey Gilroy, whom Ming hated to call Sabine's ex-boyfriend, but he was. Then again, one could say that being behind prison bars along with his aging uncle—albeit for stashing and selling stolen art, and not for murder—might be prompting enough for a person who was used to a life of ease and comfort.

Unfortunately, Garvey's truth had no bearing on Edgar's murder. Still, his confession about being involved in his uncle's art crime ring had led to the arrests of multiple players, including Landry, Chalina, and O'Dell—the three people directly involved in Edgar's murder.

Ming was sorely disappointed with the former detective. Considering their long-term association, he should be feeling sorry for O'Dell, but he wasn't. They weren't that close—not on a first-name basis—but they had worked together many times.

To be sure, Ming still respected first responders and people in uniform, but the situation with O'Dell made Ming realize that as a human being, he was limited in his ability to see the whole truth. Only God could see everything, as Hebrews 4:13 reminded Ming.

> And there is no creature hidden from His sight, but all things are naked and open to the eyes of Him to whom we must give account.

"If O'Dell hadn't been so greedy as to keep the

pocket watch for himself, thinking that he could reformat the flash card and resell the pocket watch on the black market, we would've lost the evidence," Ming said.

"Even though he reformatted the flash card, he made a mistake by putting in a new battery," Sabine reminded them. "The battery caused the voice activation to work on the backup flash card that no one but Dad knew about."

"If Garvey hadn't stolen the pocket watch to begin with, we might never have proof of the truth." Ming did not want to give Garvey any credit, but it was true that if the pocket watch hadn't been added to The MOOT, Edgar's murder case would have remained unsolved.

"Gene is a piece of work. He admitted to a crime he didn't commit just because he thought that his nephew had done it." Mama Hu shook her head.

"He did tell me that he wasn't The Mechanic," Sabine said. "He was telling the truth."

"That might be the only truth he told. Gene is a stolen art broker," Mama Hu said.

"When did he become one?" Ming asked.

"I don't know." Mama Hu shrugged. "All I know is that sometimes art makes people do things that they wish they never did."

"Art?" Sabine replied. "Did you mean stolen art or art appreciation in general?"

"I meant criminal activities. We—I mean, they—do things they normally wouldn't."

Ming didn't want to guess what his mother-in-law meant. He wanted to say that the bottomline was not only greed, but also the love of money.

Well, the love of money could lead to greed, he supposed.

"Yeah. I can't believe that Gene actually bought and sold stolen art. That's crazy," Sabine said. "All this time, I thought he just fixed cars and then retired."

Led by Camden, the FBI's Art Crime Team had their work cut out for them, inventorying Gene Gilroy's collection of stolen art and timepieces, and returning them to their rightful owners.

Sabine and Helen received the reward money for the recovery of some of that artwork. Helen gave the money to Mama Hu. After tithing ten percent to Riverside Chapel, her home church, Sabine used her share to pay off Ming's business debts, which earned her a partnership in SRI.

Sabine was still praying and pondering about selling her brokerage and retaining her real estate license. She wanted to do more PI work in memory of her father. She didn't want to be stretched too thin across two different businesses.

Even though Ming didn't want her to make a snap decision, he would be happy if Sabine worked with him because he didn't want to let Sabine out of his sight. Ever since Hiawassee, he had become his wife's bodyguard twenty-four-seven.

Her baby bump was showing now that she was in her fourth month. Ming had forbidden her to throw things like spikes, darts, knives, and any sort of ninja stars. Oh yes, and he had also told her not to go to the firing range until after the baby was born. He thought it might be too noisy for the baby in the womb.

To her credit, Sabine had taken it all in stride.

Sometimes she looked amused, and sometimes she took him seriously. For the most part, she trusted him enough to go along with it.

Ming had assured her that he wasn't only concerned about her well-being because she was pregnant, but that he was convinced that his job as her husband was to protect her. He'd continue to do so long after they stopped having kids.

"Anyway, good thing my daughter married you instead of Garvey." Mama Hu patted Ming's arm.

"God brought us together." Sabine hugged Ming.

"And He keeps us together." Ming kissed Sabine's forehead.

"I'm happy to see you both so loving toward each other." Mama Hu wiped a tear. "Now I want to spend some time here with Edgar. Maybe you two can go walk a bit. I'll text you when I'm done."

Ming didn't want to correct Mama Hu by telling her that Edgar was not still in the grave. His soul had already gone to be with God in heaven. Mama Hu was not a Christian, and such tenets of Christianity might be lost on her.

"After this, I'll take you two to lunch," Mama Hu added. "Let's go to my favorite restaurant."

As Ming walked away from the grave with Sabine, he couldn't help smiling.

"What?" Sabine asked.

"Your mom's favorite restaurant."

"Belford." Sabine put her arm around his and leaned against his shoulder. "I remember."

"Our first date."

"Was it?" Sabine pulled away. "As I recall, I got there first. I was already eating when you showed up."

"You were chaperoning your mom," Ming reminded her. "We had dinner together. Wouldn't that be a date?"

"You crashed my table uninvited."

"We had a good conversation." Ming pointed to Sabine's cross necklace. "That was the first time you told me about the cross that your dad gave you. Little did we know then that it was the key to the pocket watch."

"Thank God that all these years, I haven't lost it." Sabine looked in the distance. "Yeah, we had a good dinner that night and got to know each other. I'm glad for that, whether it was a real date or not."

"You were staring at my good looks." Ming didn't feel embarrassed about reminding Sabine. "If I don't say it, who will?"

"I don't recall." Sabine chuckled. "However, I have to give it to you. You do take good care of yourself."

"You do too." Ming held Sabine's hand under an oak tree. "You're the most beautiful woman in the whole world. But that's not why I married you."

"Oh?"

"God brought you into my life. I fell in love with your heart for Jesus," Ming said. "We're meant for each other. I don't want to be without you ever."

"Same."

"No matter what we go through, may God always keep us together as husband and wife."

Sabine nodded. "'Til death do us part."

EPILOGUE

July

On a warm Saturday morning in July, Sabine arose early to read her Bible by the bedroom window. Ming was still sleeping nearby, turning once while wrapped up in Sabine's favorite cotton bedsheets. The fan was whirring above them, and the air conditioner had kicked on.

After reading a chapter of Ephesians—the same chapter that she and Ming had discussed at the cabin at Still Waters—Sabine got up from the armchair and went outside to the bedroom balcony. It overlooked the quiet pool and well-tended garden below. This house had island colors and vibes—but it was still one whole block away from the ocean. Sabine could feel the ocean but not see it, though they have a private beach access outside their gates.

The air felt humid, and it wasn't even eight o'clock yet.

Two warm arms encircled her waist from behind. Sabine looked down to see Ming's fingers interlocked over her six-month-old belly, as he kissed her neck.

"Good morning, my lovely wife," he whispered into her ear.

"Good morning." Sabine smiled, holding back tears.

"How is Baby Jonathan?" He gently patted her belly.

"He's well, thankfully."

God had reconciled them and repaired their marriage after that one week of near-death experience back in January.

"You were amazing last night." Ming nuzzled her ear and hair. "You're always amazing."

"It's your fault," Sabine teased.

"All my fault." Ming chuckled. "Don't let our baby number three hear it."

Sabine said nothing. Ming had already apologized seven months ago, and she wasn't going to bring it up now that they had reconciled.

He had already apologized multiple times, but Sabine let him talk. Sometimes it was better for him to learn the lessons himself than for Sabine to teach him a thing or two about biblical marriage. That way, God was his teacher and the Holy Spirit was their marriage counselor.

They were closer now more than ever, not only physically but also emotionally and mentally. Funny how a close brush with death could reset and realign their relationship.

"The kids are still asleep. Why don't we..." Ming turned Sabine around. Her pregnant belly came between them. He gently rubbed it. The baby kicked.

"Seven months along. We didn't waste any time, did we?" Face to face, Ming kissed her forehead, then the tip of her nose, then her lips—

"Mommy!"

The scream was shrill and loud, and very near.

Ming closed his eyes and sighed.

Sabine chuckled, sidestepped him and bent over to pat her daughter's bedhead. "Yes, Hannah?"

The three-year-old was clutching a teddy bear in one hand. In her other hand was the cordless house phone. She lifted it in the air. "Gamma's not answering the phone."

"It's only eight o'clock," Ming said. "Call her later."

"No, Daddy. Gamma said she's coming over for breakfast." Hannah turned down her lips, and she looked pretty pathetic.

Sabine waited to see if their firstborn daughter could pressure Ming in any way.

Wait a minute.

"I didn't invite my mom to breakfast." Sabine turned to Ming. "Did you?"

He shook his head. "Nope."

"I did." Hannah waved the phone around. "Gamma and I want to make pancakes together."

"News to me." Ming leaned down and looked his daughter in the eyes. "Generally, you don't invite people over to our house until you have cleared it with your mom and dad.'"

"I'm clear, Daddy."

Sabine stretched her hand toward Hannah. "Let me have the phone, please."

Hannah gave it up.

Sabine called Mom on her cell. No answer. She left a message. "Good morning, Mom. Please call me back."

After Sabine hung up, Hannah gestured with her hands, palms up and out. "See? She's not there."

Now Sabine was concerned. "Mom never goes anywhere without her phone."

"Maybe she's in her roof-top pool," Ming suggested.

"Maybe she drowned." Hannah climbed on top of her parents' king-sized bed and bounced around.

"Let's not assume the worst." Ming reached for Sabine. "Perhaps her phone is simply out of battery."

"She always charges it every night before she goes to bed." Sabine retrieved her cell phone from the side table next to the bed. "Can't call Helen. She's in Germany on an assignment."

She texted her sister anyway to ask her if she had heard from Mom. No reply.

Sabine then called the housekeeper. She knew that Faida had the weekend off, so it was a long shot.

"Mama Hu was fine last night at dinner," the housekeeper said. "We laughed and joked about our dead husbands."

Somehow that sounded wrong, but Sabine didn't correct her. "So that was the last time you saw Mom?"

"Yeah. I have the weekend off, remember? I won't see her again until Monday morning."

"Okay. Thanks." Sabine placed a hand over her chest. She thought her heart skipped a beat.

After what had happened six months ago, Sabine could just imagine the repercussions now that O'Dell, Landry, and Chalina were all sitting in jail awaiting trial for Dad's murder. She feared that they might have thoughts of retaliating against Mom.

Here, Sabine had Ming to protect her family. There, Mom usually stayed alone in the empty house because Helen traveled a lot for work.

Sabine opened an app on her phone and checked the surveillance in Mom's house. "This is bad. The cameras are down."

"Someone turned them off?" Ming asked. "Call the security company."

"Already alerted them from the app." Sabine checked her messages. "They're sending a technician. He'll be at the house in half an hour."

She made a beeline for the closet.

"What are you doing?" Ming asked.

"I'm going to change and go to Mom's house."

Ming stopped her. "I'll go. Zachary is still sleeping. How about you make us breakfast, while I go check on your mom and wait for the security people?"

Sabine was about to protest when Ming held her hands. "Extra pancakes for me. Pecans."

He was calm. So calm.

Sabine wanted to cry.

"It will be okay." Ming hugged her.

"Get dressed." Sabine looked for Ming's phone.

"I'm already dressed." Ming pointed to his T-shirt and shorts. "I just need to find my flip-flops."

"Better wear closed-toe shoes in case you need to run or something."

"Yes, ma'am." He found his phone.

"Is it fully charged?"

"Ninety percent."

"Good enough." Sabine reached for her purse. "I have the spare key to Mom's house here."

Ming picked up his crossbody shoulder bag. Sabine knew his Glock was in it.

"Let's pray," Sabine said.

Ming nodded.

They sat on the edge of the bed, Hannah in their arms.

"We're going to pray for Grandma, okay?" Sabine brushed a strand of hair off Hannah's cute face.

Hannah nodded.

Ming squeezed Sabine's hand. "You're a good mommy."

"You're a good daddy too." Sabine leaned toward him.

"No kissing!" Hannah's hands were up, pushing them away from each other. "Be serious, you two!"

"We're serious." Ming didn't laugh. He squeezed Sabine's shoulder. "You start, I close?"

Sabine bowed her head and closed her eyes. "Father God, please keep Mom safe. We can't get ahold of her. Maybe she just overslept." She paused. "Lord, please keep Ming safe as he goes to check on her. And keep my kids and me safe as we wait for her."

A round of "amen" filled the master bedroom.

They all filed down the stairs. Ming poured a cup of coffee into a travel mug and headed for the kitchen door that led to the garage. "I'll be back, okay?"

"You better." Sabine counted the minutes.

Twenty minutes to get to downtown Savannah.

Five minutes to park in the designated spot and ride the elevator upstairs to the penthouse. Ten minutes to see what was going on.

Before Ming opened the door to the garage, he turned to Hannah. "Hannah, please go upstairs and check on your brother."

"Okay." Hannah skipped off and climbed the stairs.

"Carefully!" Sabine shouted loud enough for her to hear.

"Okay, Mommy!"

Ming turned to Sabine. "Come here."

He grabbed her gently and pulled her close. "It will be okay."

"I guess I'm overthinking." Sabine nodded. "I just got scared after what happened in Hiawassee, is all."

"I know. That's how you felt every time I left town for an assignment or a project." Ming's voice sounded like he finally got it. "So that's why you're my business partner now, and we're going to stay together all the time."

It was a good move for Sabine to invest in Ming's business, Savannah River Investigations, Inc. She had money from her real estate business, as well as cryptocurrency investments she'd made with her inheritance money after Dad had passed away. Ming had rejected all her early offers to help. He changed his mind after she had proven to him in Hiawassee that she was on par with him, if not slightly ahead of the game.

Funding SRI was worth it, even though she was still a minority shareholder at forty-nine percent.

"We think of the worst, don't we?" Ming asked rhetorically.

"Might be our profession." Sabine had left the private investigative business when she mourned the death of her father. She sold her shares to her older sister, Helen. Her modeling job was an escape for her. After the accident, she became a successful real estate agent. However, she hadn't forgotten all the times she'd worked for Dad, tagging along wherever he went.

In fact, Dad had wanted her to work with Helen, even though Sabine decided that it would be best not to ruin their sisterly relationship because she had seen Helen at the office, and Sabine didn't want to work with such an intense boss.

SRI offered her an option she hadn't considered. Well, that was because Ming wanted to handle it on his own. Their time in Hiawassee proved to them that they worked well together as a husband-and-wife PI team.

"Drive safely." Sabine let her husband go.

"Don't forget my pecan pancakes."

"Could be cold when you get home."

"That's what microwaves are for." Ming shut the door.

Sabine heard the garage door open and then shut. Before she could make it to the pantry where the boxes of pancake mix were, she heard crying.

The ten-month-old baby was awake.

She rushed up the stairs, being careful enough not to slide or fall, reminding herself that she was pregnant. "Our next house will be all on one floor. No more stairs."

She picked up Zachary from his crib and changed his diaper.

Hannah watched at the end of the changing table.

"You might not want to be standing there," Sabine said. She didn't explain to Hannah that Zachary could do more than kick her face.

Hannah moved to the other end of the changing table, where she patted Zachary's head. "He was sleeping the entire time."

"Thank you for not waking him up."

Hannah nodded. "I tippy-toed to my room and played with my LEGOs."

"That's fine."

They went downstairs, but Sabine couldn't get Ming and Mom out of her mind. Even though they had prayed, she was still worried.

She put Zachary in his playpen.

This time she did not ask Hannah if she wanted to help Mommy make pancakes. Sabine wanted to make a batch as quickly as possible in case they had to leave or something.

"Lord God, I'm worried." But there she was making pancakes.

Ming understood her well. He'd given her something to do to keep her busy while he drove to Mom's house.

Sabine smiled a little.

While she was chopping up pecans, Ming called on video.

"The house is empty. Nothing seems to be out of place. No signs of struggle. No notes. It's as though Mama Hu just isn't home, like she went to the grocery store or something," he said. "The security guy arrived and within a minute said that someone had tampered with the on-site unit. There was also some attempted remote access. They're investigating and calling it a potential breach of security. "

"Remote?" Sabine turned down the burner heat. "Could it be Mom?"

"No, unless she's using a phone not already registered with the security firm, you know?" Ming explained. "I've called the police."

"Is it related to our case—I mean, the one we just closed?"

"Hmm. I don't know."

"After all, Mom had begun the investigation on her own for months before I came along and took her place in the shooting competition."

Mom had regretted a lot of things, thinking that what she had done a long time ago might have caused Dad's death. She had carried that burden in her heart for many years.

Then it had turned out that Mom was wrong. Dad hadn't been murdered because of her or her past at all.

After his arrest, O'Dell had been held without bail at the Chatham County Detention Center. The grand jury convened a month later and indicted him for the murder of his then girlfriend and the private investigator she had hired, namely Dad. Both of them had stumbled into his activities of aiding money launderers.

At first, O'Dell was determined to fight until the end. However, after his daughter went to visit him at the CCDC, he changed his mind and pled guilty on all counts, thereby forgoing a trial altogether.

In order to avoid the death penalty, O'Dell offered a carrot that the FBI could not resist. He gave up the names of politicians in Congress who received kickbacks via money laundering through various business transactions, including the sale of stolen art that The MOOT and The GOAT facilitated. Many of the transactions were in untraceable cryptocurrency.

The revelation effectively ended the careers of those senators and representatives, with some indicted and awaiting trials themselves.

Sitting in prison with no new income, O'Dell could no longer afford his daughter's MS treatment, but at least his conscience was finally clear. He also forgave her for handing her medical bills to Helen, even though they were eventually inadmissible in court.

For that reason, his daughter respected him once again. She worked hard to raise funds for her own treatment, and even Helen sent a few thousand dollars to her crowdfunding project.

O'Dell's sentencing would commence in another month, but Mom was done with the entire case as soon as she heard his guilty plea. She spent her nights crying herself to sleep, and that made Sabine and her sister concerned. Sabine asked Mom to come stay with them for a few days on Tybee, but Mom refused. She wanted to be alone, and Sabine had to respect that.

"When I talked to her on Thursday, she was mumbling about something but wouldn't elaborate what she was worried about." Sabine tried to recall their conversation, but it had been cut short because Zachary was crying the entire time Mom tried to tell her something over the phone. "But the conversation ended before she could tell me what was on her mind."

So what was Mom so worried about two days ago?

Would Mom have said something to Helen? Sabine stacked the pancakes on a plate and turned off the stove.

She tried to call Helen again. Seven time zones away, it would be midafternoon where Helen was.

This time she picked up on the first ring.

"Whassup?" Helen sounded like she was outside, surrounded by vehicle noises and honks. Maybe she was on a sidewalk somewhere.

Sabine kept her voice calm. "Helen, Mom's missing."

～

DEAR READER:

Thank you for reading *Once Bitten, Twice Shy* (Guardian Sweethearts Book 1), which is the prequel to *Once a Thief* (Protector Sweethearts Book 1). Did you enjoy the novel?

In the epilogue, we learned that Mama Hu went missing. So where is she? As soon as Helen received the call from Sabine saying that their mother was missing, Helen was on the case right away in the next book, *Once a Thief* (Protector Sweethearts Book 1).

Once a Thief (Protector Sweethearts Book 1)
JanThompson.com/thief

As mentioned in the book introduction, *Once Bitten, Twice Shy* is a sequel to *Tell You Soon* (Savannah Sweethearts Book 3), a friends-to-more Christian romance with a side of suspense. Ming and Sabine fell in love and got married in this story. Mama Hu also made an appearance.

Tell You Soon (Savannah Sweethearts Book 3)
JanThompson.com/tell

In *Once Bitten, Twice Shy*, we also met FBI Special Agent Camden la Salle and his wife, Iris. Camden was in *Tell You Soon* (Savannah Sweethearts Book 3) as well as in his own novel, *Love You Always* (Savannah Sweethearts Book 7), in which he had a second chance with Iris.

Love You Always (Savannah Sweethearts Book 7)
JanThompson.com/love

A co-founder of Binary Systems, Inc., Cayson Yang made a cameo appearance in *Once Bitten, Twice Shy*. Cayson tells his own story in *Zero Sum* (Binary Hackers Book 1).

Zero Sum (Binary Hackers Book 1)
JanThompson.com/sum

Earl Young also made an appearance in *Once Bitten, Twice Shy*. Later on, he headlines his own story in *Never a Traitor* (Defender Sweethearts Book 1).

Never a Traitor (Defender Sweethearts Book 1)
JanThompson.com/traitor

Ming mentioned Cade Sumter several times. Cade's story is entwined with Pilar Santiago's in *Never a Hostage* (Defender Sweethearts Book 2).

Never a Hostage (Defender Sweethearts Book 2)
JanThompson.com/hostage

Back to *Once Bitten, Twice Shy* again, if you prefer to read all the books in one series together, there are three more novels in this in-between series.

Guardian Sweethearts
JanThompson.com/guardian

If you like these stories and the story world that I've created, how about signing up for my mailing list? I send frequent newsletters in which I talk about my writing life as well as the characters that populate my story world.

Sign Up for Jan's Newsletters
JanThompson.com/newsletter

And now, continue reading for a sneak peek of Chapter One in *Once a Thief*...

THE NEXT BOOK IS...

PROTECTOR SWEETHEARTS
BOOK 1

She sets a thief to catch a thief.
Will he also steal her heart?

Private investigator Helen Hu must team up with reformed art thief Reuben Costa to rescue her mother, who has vanished while trying to make amends for stealing some bejeweled eggs connected to the Amber Room.

REUBEN'S RECORD...

To protect the woman he loves whom he cannot have because she is another man's wife, Frederico Costa goes to prison and leaves his art theft crime organization to his only son, Reuben.

When his father dies in prison, Reuben vows to never love or marry. He pours the next several years into expanding his father's activities across Europe, all the while sacrificing his own personal happiness.

Some years into Reuben's incarceration, the FBI Art Crime Team and INTERPOL offer him an early release from prison and a second chance for a new life in Greece if he helps them to catch a bigger criminal. Reuben agrees, and is now a free man.

Until they require his services again. This time, he must visit his own family's past in order to help private investigator Helen Hu find her missing mother and twelve Petros eggs, keys to the lost Amber Room.

HELEN'S HAVOC...

Past memories have never been darker for Private Investigator Helen Hu as she deals with a long-lost secret that her mother has hidden from their family for fifteen years. Afraid that it will shame her daughter, Mama Hu tries to fix what she has done and redeem herself. Unfortunately, as Helen fears, she disappears.

The best way for Helen to rescue her mother is to

go underground where thieves and robbers live. Her only ticket into that nefarious world is another art thief. He says he is reformed. Is he, really?

As Helen and Reuben rush to rescue Mama Hu before the matriarch gets herself killed, the unlikely partners end up bargaining for not only life and death but also their own hearts and souls.

Once a Thief is book 1 in *USA Today* bestselling author Jan Thompson's **Protector Sweethearts** Christian romantic suspense series featuring Private Investigator Helen Hu and her associates as they hunt for lost treasures, search for missing people, and defend noble causes.

~

IN THIS STORY WORLD...

The events in *Once a Thief* happen after these stories, where Helen Hu makes several appearances. In fact, *Tell You Soon* is where we first meet Mama Hu.

- Tell You Soon (Savannah Sweethearts Book 2)
- Love You Always (Savannah Sweethearts Book 6)
- Reach for Me (Vacation Sweethearts Book 2)
- Share with Me (Seaside Chapel Book 1)
- Step with Me (Seaside Chapel Book 2)

Once a Thief can be read on its own without your having previously read any of the above books from Jan's contemporary Christian beach romance collections.

Once a Thief (Protector Sweethearts Book 1)
JanThompson.com/thief

Protector Sweethearts
JanThompson.com/protector

Subscribe to Jan Thompson's mailing list:
JanThompson.com/newsletter

ONCE A THIEF
SNEAK PEEK
CHAPTER 1

A plunge away from the Aegean Sea, the town of Oia hugged the Santorini cliffs of the caldera, a haunting reminder of a volcanic past ever present in Helen Hu's mind as she parked the ATV and set off on foot down the pedestrian walkway.

Her company-issued iPhone told her where to go through the mishmash of cliffside buildings and tourist-packed lanes meandering around painted fences, containers of brightly colored flowers, and tiny blue hotel pools. The pastel-colored buildings looked like interlocking Lego blocks glued to the side of the rocky mountain.

Every now and then, Helen spotted blue domes, mushroom caps reaching toward the afternoon Mediterranean sky, portending bright days ahead.

Not!

The signal grew stronger. Helen spotted her mom in the crowd.

Mom was way ahead but slowing down now as she pretended to weave in and out of souvenir shops, stopping to touch a postcard or two, as if to leave fingerprints in case something happened to her.

What, Mom? What?

Swept into a wave of tourists and their multilingual tour guides, Helen quickened her steps across the uneven lanes sandwiched among shops and restaurants, villas and guest houses, private properties and potted bougainvilleas—all the while trying to keep an eye on Mom.

Mom had a distinct walk. Helen could spot her a mile away, always in one of her many identical pairs of five-inch-heeled jacquard boots. Those boots added inches to the diminutive woman and brought Mom to about Helen's height.

And those boots slowed Mom down enough for Helen to catch up to her in the crowded lanes and paths.

Helen suspected Mom wasn't here on Santorini on a quick weekend getaway—without her signature luggage when she had gotten off the ferry from Athens an hour ago.

So what is she here for?

Mom had made no attempt to hide. Her fuchsia blouse was bold and matched some of the flowering plants contrasting the surrounding white and blue architecture.

Every now and then, Mom would glance back, as if searching for something, looking for someone.

Meeting someone?

Helen looked away, just in case Mom spotted her. Even at sixty-eight, Mom's eyesight was way better than Helen's. And she had often said that she could identify either one of her daughters from miles away.

Helen wasn't about to test that now.

Not after all the trouble she had taken to get here. The notification had arrived while she had been in the middle of hunting down a fugitive passing through Frankfurt.

While Helen's Hu Knows, Inc., private investigative firm specialized in recovering lost art and missing persons, the company had grown and expanded into tracking down fugitives—since the day they had successfully helped the FBI apprehend an international terrorist who had abducted Helen's mom and sister.

Her sister had gone on to marry and have kids.

But Mom.

Mom had retreated into her own little world after that episode.

Sometimes Helen wished that Mom would be more forthcoming with her. Since Dad had passed away so many years ago, Mom had tried to carry on with her life in fits and starts. As the years had gone by, she had withdrawn more and more into the recesses of her own thoughts and memories.

And now? Was this a part of Mom's multiyear introspection?

Helen felt a burden to care for her mom. At thirty-four years old and with no prospects of marrying and having children, Helen felt that she had more time than her sister to take care of Mom. In fact, Mom was already living with her back in Savannah.

Helen wouldn't mind if Mom lived with her the rest of her life. She wanted Mom to know that her daughters really wanted the best for her and that it was time for Mom to be transparent.

Yeah, right.

Helen pushed through the crowd toward Mom, as more people swarmed around Helen, down the steps and narrow walkways, looking for balconies to park themselves and set up video cameras and smartphones for their sunset viewing.

Sunset would be in two hours.

When Dad had been alive, they had come here often during summer vacations, only to see the sunset and to cruise on the Aegean Sea. Dad had been quite a yachting enthusiast. Helen and her sister, Sabine, hadn't taken to the water as much as Dad and Mom had. Sometimes their parents would take their own vacation.

The two of them would end up in Santorini—also known as Thira—or they'd sail to Crete, across the water, where they would stay in a villa owned by an old family friend.

Helen stopped.

Her iPhone signal showed that Mom had been inside that souvenir shop for over a minute.

Helen held her breath and ran, her black boots

pounding the cobblestones beneath, the summer sun above her baking her baseball cap and shoulders.

Before Helen reached the souvenir shop, she heard the noise of a motor overhead. A drone in the sky hovered.

Someone taking photos?

She heard a popping sound.

Then another.

And another.

Pop! Pop! Pop!

Someone screamed, and the crowd went berserk.

The racket of screams and shrieks turned into a stampede as the tourists scattered like ants in the narrow lanes, any way they could to get out of the bottleneck, pushing and shoving Helen and everyone else in their paths.

Children and babies crying, people jumping over the low fences into hotel pools, people falling down as they were mowed over by shoes and knees and a mob gone wild.

Helen elbowed her way toward a low iron gate, thinking she could climb over it to safety.

Before she could get there, something whizzed past her ear—

And she went flying to the ground, sacked like a quarterback, sandwiched between the dirty cobble-stone-and-cement lane and someone on top of her.

All around her were hot wafts of stinky shoes from the maddening crowd, the odor of sweat and fear—

And a sudden, distinct, clean smell of fresh soap.

"Get off me!" Helen's elbows and torso twisted this way and that to get the man off her back. She almost hit him with her iPhone, which was still in her grip.

He barely moved.

"Get off me!" she repeated, thinking he couldn't hear her in the concert of loud and chaotic footfalls.

"Shhh. It's still above." His voice was calm. Accented.

And definitely male.

The summer sun continued to beat down on them. The man's weight pushed Helen's backpack against her spine, probably crushing her iPad and magazine inside.

Police sirens blared in the distance, and the drone sounds eased away.

"We have to get out of here," the man said.

"Then get off me!"

As soon as the man eased off her, Helen wiggled out from underneath him as quickly as she could, her right hand reaching into her waistline pistol pouch—

"Helen!"

She heard the familiar sharp tone above the roar of the crowd.

She looked up, squinting in the shifting sunlight and shadows. She realized then that her sunglasses had been knocked off her face. "Mom?"

Mom tapped the ground with her boots. "What in the world are you doing here?"

Instead of giving Helen a hand, Mom leaned toward the man who had rolled off Helen.

He was trying to get up. He clutched his chest. "What sharp objects do you have in that backpack?"

"You okay?" Mom asked.

Helen scooted back against the gate to prevent herself from getting kicked by the rushing crowd.

"I think I'm okay." She brushed dirt and grime off her clothes.

"Not you. I meant him." Mom picked some grass off the man's hair. "I see you two have met—or shall I say, made contact."

Helen's eyes widened. "Please tell me you're not dating a man half your—"

"No, no. He's not my type. In fact, I think he's more your type."

"Mom!" Helen rose to her feet too quickly. The world swirled around her.

But strong arms caught her before she fell.

She smelled a whiff of clean, fresh soap again.

Male cologne.

Once a Thief (Protector Sweethearts Book 1)
JanThompson.com/thief

Protector Sweethearts:
JanThompson.com/protector

Sign up for book news from Jan Thompson:
JanThompson.com/newsletter

ACKNOWLEDGMENTS

Many thanks to my Georgia Press publishing team for keeping up with my writing schedule.

Thank you to editor Kim Kemery for editing and proofreading this novel. And special thanks to two of my early readers, Christie and Zanese, for their feedback.

I want to acknowledge these professionals for their help in my research.

- For postmortem forensics, I thank Dr. Judy Melinek, forensic pathologist and coauthor with T. J. Mitchell of *Working Stiff: Two Years, 262 Bodies, and the Making of a Medical Examiner*.
- For concussion and medical questions, I thank Dr. John Galt Robinson, an emergency medicine physician and author.
- For crime scene procedurals, I thank author and Detective Dony Jay, as well as Patrick J. O'Donnell's *Cops and Writers* discussion group that includes law

enforcement officers, federal agents, and attorneys.

- For information technology fact checking, I thank my husband who is an IT consultant.

As per usual, not all of my extensive research materials make it into my books, but I feel that it is necessary to thank everyone for their time and kindness in answering my many questions. And yes, all mistakes and creative licenses are mine.

I am grateful to God for my husband and son for their support and encouragement. I also thank God for my parents and my three brothers for my happy and memorable childhood. I'll always remember my beloved mother and my late father for having instilled in me the love of reading and writing from a very early age. I miss my father here on earth, but I will see him again in heaven someday.

Most of all, I am eternally thankful to my Lord and Savior, Jesus Christ, who died on the cross to save me from my sins and rose again from the grave to give me eternal life. Without Him, I can write nothing (John 15:5).

Joyfully in Jesus,
Jan Thompson
John 3:16

BOOKS BY JAN THOMPSON

CHRISTIAN BEACH AND ISLAND ROMANCE

Seaside Chapel (7 Books)
JanThompson.com/seaside
Journeys of Love through Life's Ups & Downs

CHRISTIAN COASTAL ROMANCE IN THE SOUTH

Savannah Sweethearts (12 Books)
JanThompson.com/savannah

CHRISTIAN TRAVEL ROMANCE

Vacation Sweethearts (8 Books)
JanThompson.com/vacation

CHRISTIAN CHRISTMAS ROMANCE IN THE CITY

Midtown Christmas (4 Books)
JanThompson.com/christmas

CHRISTIAN CHRISTMAS ROMANCE ON THE COAST

Christmas Sweethearts (3 Books)
JanThompson.com/christmastown

INTERNATIONAL CHRISTIAN ROMANTIC SUSPENSE

Protector Sweethearts (6 Books)
JanThompson.com/protector
Treasures Lost and Found

Defender Sweethearts (6 Books)
JanThompson.com/defender
Defending the Defenseless Worldwide

NEAR-FUTURE TECHNOTHRILLERS WITH CHRISTIAN ROMANCE

Binary Hackers (4 Books)
JanThompson.com/binary
Cyberthrillers

CHRISTIAN SUSPENSE IN BETWEEN SERIES

Guardian Sweethearts (2 Books)
JanThompson.com/guardian

Subscribe to Jan Thompson's mailing list:
JanThompson.com/newsletter

PROTECTOR SWEETHEARTS

Private investigator Helen Hu and her associates specialize in searching for missing persons and hunting for lost treasures. Join them in their adventure suspense around the world in *USA Today* best-selling author Jan Thompson's Protector Sweethearts, a series of Christian Romantic Suspense with a side of mystery.

Protector Sweethearts is a spin-off of Savannah Sweethearts and Vacation Sweethearts.

~

JanThompson.com/protector

- Book 4: *Twice a Fighter*
- Book 5: *Twice a Convict*
- Book 6: *Twice a Soldier*

DEFENDER SWEETHEARTS

Defender Sweethearts is a sister series to the Protector Sweethearts Christian romantic suspense collection. While the heroes in Protector Sweethearts search for lost treasures and lost people, the Defender Sweethearts novels focus on protecting the helpless and hopeless. The main characters in Defender Sweethearts come from the supporting cast in Protector Sweethearts.

∿

JanThompson.com/defender

- Book 1: *Never a Traitor*
- Book 2: *Never a Hostage*
- Book 3: *Never a Fugitive*
- Book 4: *Always a Maverick*
- Book 5: *Always a Champion*
- Book 6: *Always a Guardian*

GUARDIAN SWEETHEARTS

Guardian Sweethearts is a collection of Christian suspense novels in between other books in Jan Thompson's story world. These sandwiched stories feature married couples who met in the books before the present ones. Therefore, the books in this series are both prequels and sequels or preludes and postludes.

JanThompson.com/guardian

- Book 1: Once Bitten, Twice Shy: A Christian suspense novel in between Tell You Soon (Savannah Sweethearts Book 3) and Once a Thief (Protector Sweethearts Book 1)
- Book 2: Check Once, Check Twice: A Christian suspense novel in between

Love You Always (Savannah Sweethearts Book 7) and Never a Traitor (Defender Sweethearts Book 1)

- Book 3: Going Once, Going Twice: A Christian suspense novel that comes after Reach for Me (Vacation Sweethearts Book 2)
- Book 4: Fool Me Once, Fool Me Twice: A Christian suspense novel that comes after Wait for Me (Vacation Sweethearts Book 3)

BINARY HACKERS

Like more suspense with your Christian romance? Like to read suspense thrillers? If you're looking for clean near-future romantic suspense without compromising the Christian faith, these books are for you.

From *USA Today* bestselling author Jan Thompson come these inspirational near-future cyberthrillers combining technothriller and romance, starting with Binary Hackers that feature computer specialists living at the edge of cyberspace, where they have to juggle being law-abiding truth-telling Christians while carrying out their assignments by any and all means possible.

The Binary Hackers series is set in the same story world as Jan's other books, and characters from the other series may make cameo appearances in this series and vice versa.

～

JanThompson.com/binary

- Book 1: *Zero Sum*
- Book 2: *Zero Day*
- Book 3: *Zero Out*
- Book 4: *Zero Trust*

SEASIDE CHAPEL

Welcome to *USA Today* bestselling author Jan Thompson's Seaside Chapel Christian beach romance series. These novels are set on real-life St. Simon's Island, Georgia—a beach town where history is all around and the future is a moment away—and the neighboring fictitious Seaside Island, where the rich and famous live.

Savor the small-town atmosphere and the warm southern beaches of St. Simon's Island and the idyllic Golden Isles along the Atlantic Ocean. Enjoy the music of the orchestra and hymns of the church, and hang out with our Christian friends who attend Seaside Chapel, a little church by the sea known for its beach weddings and fair share of love and life.

As these Christians grow in their knowledge and understanding of God, they are tested in their spiritual maturity, their love lives, and their relationships with others. Share their heartaches and healing, and cheer them on as they celebrate faith, family, and friends.

~

JanThompson.com/seaside

- Book 0 (Prequel): *His Surprise Proposal*
- Book 1: *His Longing Heart*
- Book 2: *His Wake-Up Call*
- Book 3: *His Morning Kiss*
- Book 4: *His Quiet Serenade*
- Book 5: *His Waiting Love*
- Book 6: *His Beach Retreat*

SAVANNAH
SWEETHEARTS

Welcome to the new south! From *USA Today* bestselling author Jan Thompson come these clean and wholesome, sweet and inspirational Christian romances set on the romantic beaches of Tybee Island and in the coastal town of Savannah, Georgia. Meet a group of multiracial and multiethnic churchgoing Christians who love the Lord, work hard in their careers, and seek God's will for their love lives. Against a backdrop of ocean, sand, and sun, these inspirational romances showcase aspects of the human need for God and for one another. Have some tea, settle in a comfortable reading chair, and enjoy these sweet celebrations of faith, hope, and love in Jesus Christ.

JanThompson.com/savannah

- Book 1: *Ask You Later* (Artist Romance)

- Book 2: *Know You More* (Multiracial Romance)
- Book 3: *Tell You Soon* (Asian-American Romance with Suspense)
- Book 4: *Draw You Near* (International Romance)
- Book 5: *Cherish You So* (Wheelchair Billionaire Romance)
- Book 6: *Walk You There* (Old-Meets-New Tour Guide Romance)
- Book 7: *Love You Always* (Romance with Suspense)
- Book 8: *Kiss You Now* (Multiracial Romance)
- Book 9: *Find You Again* (Multiracial Romance)
- Book 10: *Wish You Joy* (Christmas-Themed Romance)
- Book 11: *Call You Home* (Deaf Chef Romance)
- Book 12: *Let You Go* (Asian-American Romance with Suspense)

VACATION
SWEETHEARTS

Travel with our friends from Savannah, Georgia, to the coast and to the mountains. Cheer them on as they celebrate the immeasurable grace and undeserved mercy of God through Jesus Christ.

The Vacation Sweethearts novels are a spin-off of Jan's Savannah Sweethearts series, and fans will recognize familiar faces from Riverside Chapel, a church in the coastal city of Savannah, Georgia. In fact, we might even visit the beach town of Tybee Island from time to time to visit old friends and beloved families...

~

JanThompson.com/vacation

- Book o (Prequel): *Time for Me*
- Book 1: *Smile for Me* (Beach Romance in the Bahamas)

- Book 2: *Reach for Me* (Romance with Suspense in the Smoky Mountains)
- Book 3: *Wait for Me* (Romance with Suspense on a Cruise Ship)
- Book 4: *Look for Me* (Romance with Suspense in a Florida Beach Town)
- Book 5: *Pray for Me* (International Romance in the City of Atlanta)
- Book 6: *Care for Me* (Small Mountain Town Romance)
- Book 7: *Cheer for Me* (International Romance)

∼

Read *Time for Me* (Prequel) for free:
JanThompson.com/time-free

CHRISTMAS SWEETHEARTS

Welcome to Christmastown, that holiday decorating company that is now run by Cyrus Theroux and his lovely wife, Amy Untermeyer-Theroux. Their story is first told in *Wish You Joy* (Savannah Sweethearts Book 10), the prequel to this Christmas Sweethearts series.

When this holiday romance series begins, Amy's Christmas Tree Farm and Christmastown have merged their daily operations at their Savannah headquarters.

∾

JanThompson.com/christmastown

- Book 1: *Wish You Faith*
- Book 2: *Wish You Hope*
- Book 3: *Wish You Peace*

MIDTOWN CHRISTMAS

Big city romance, small town feel. Four Christian couples minister at Midtown Chapel in metro Atlanta, and Midtown Village, the community of tiny homes for needy families. From November to January every year, this place turns into a Christmas Village for a small-town feel right there in the metropolis of Atlanta, Georgia.

JanThompson.com/christmas

- Book 1: *Let Me Hold You* (Levi Theroux and Maggie Jacobs from *Pray for Me*)
- Book 2: *Let Me Adore You* (Erika Song from *Look for Me* and Hiroki Yamada from *Walk You There*)
- Book 3: *Let Me Honor You* (Forsythia

McDevitt from *Call You Home* and
Owen Grayson from *Find You Again*)
- Book 4: *Let Me Love You* (Leila Patel
  from *Find You Again*)

ABOUT JAN THOMPSON

USA Today bestselling author Jan Thompson writes clean and wholesome contemporary Christian romance with elements of women's fiction, Christian romantic suspense with an air of mystery, and inspirational international thrillers with threads of sweet Christian romance. Jan's books are for readers who love inspiring stories of faith, hope, and love in Jesus Christ.

Raised on a tropical island in the eastern hemisphere, Jan now lives and writes in the western hemisphere. Her international background gives her a unique multicultural and multiracial perspective to her novels and books. The island has never left her, and she reminisces about beach life in her beach romance novels.

When Jan is not busy writing small-town stories, she writes big-city romantic suspense and international technothrillers, a nod to her previous career in computer science. She weaves technology with human interests, reflecting the current and future digital world. And romance. There's always romance.

Beyond the printed page, Jan is a wife, mother, family scribe, avid reader, occasional artist, erstwhile pianist, and chief of staff to the family cat.

~

Find out more about Jan Thompson:
JanThompson.com

Subscribe to Jan's book news mailing list:
JanThompson.com/newsletter

 X

For God so loved the world,
that He gave His only begotten Son,
that whosoever believeth in Him should not perish,
but have everlasting life.
—John 3:16

www.ingramcontent.com/pod-product-compliance
Lightning Source LLC
Chambersburg PA
CBHW020214260626
47156CB00002B/374